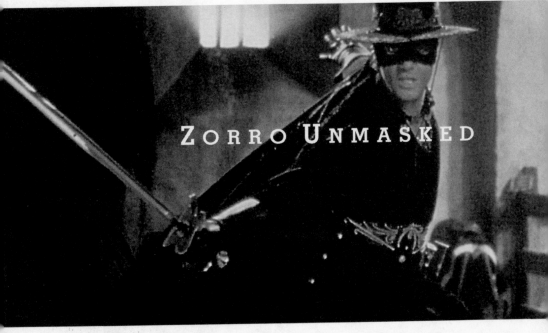

ZORRO UNMASKED

ZORRO UNMASKED

The Official History

S. R. CURTIS

HYPERION

NEW YORK

Library of Congress Cataloging-in-Publication Data

Curtis, Sandra R.
    Zorro unmasked : the official history / Sandra Curtis. — 1st ed.
       p.   cm.
    Filmography: p.
    Includes bibliographical references and index.
    ISBN 0-7868-8285-9
    1. Zorro films.   2. Zorro television programs.   3. Zorro—
(Fictitious character)   4. McCulley, Johnston, 1883–1958. Mark of
Zorro.   I. Title.
PN1995.9.Z67C87   1997
791.43'651—dc21   97–36453
                                                               CIP

Designed by Karolina Harris

FIRST EDITION

10   9   8   7   6   5   4   3   2   1

In memory of
Mitch and Irene

For
John, Nancy, and Mich,
who were born under
the sign of the
Z

CONTENTS

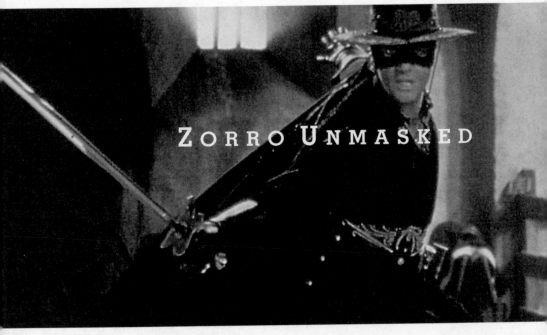

Zorro Unmasked

INTRODUCTION

*L*IKE many baby boomers, I grew up watching the Disney Zorro television series, never anticipating that the character would become intimately entwined with my life. As a seven-year-old, I knew nothing about the character's history, the writer, or the actors who portrayed Zorro. To me, Guy Williams *was* Zorro. I reveled in the excitement generated each week as my family gathered around our black-and-white TV set to watch Zorro's latest adventure unfold. The lightning etched against the sky, forming the letter Z as the theme song echoed, "Zorro, Zorro, Zorro." Sergeant Garcia's look of horror as Zorro carved a Z in his pants is an image ingrained in my memory.

One of the biggest thrills of my childhood was a chance encounter with Guy Williams at Disneyland. Every summer my family visited the Magic Kingdom, eagerly anticipating a full day and night of entertainment. During the hour's drive from our house, my sister, my cousin, and I debated several plans for how to maximize the use of our valuable E tickets. Our favorite activity, however, was boarding the keel boats for the ride to Tom Sawyer's Island. We played hide-and-seek in Injun Joe's caves, bounced on the barrel bridge, explored the tree house, and peered through the telescope in the fort, while my parents, little brother, and grandmother waited in line for the next show at the Golden Horseshoe Review.

At noon, we gathered along the Main Street curb, awaiting the big parade. On that memorable hot day in August 1958, the parade ended and we scurried across Main Street. We headed toward Mark Twain's paddle wheel boat to see Zorro's sword fight. Knowing the park like the back of our hands, we took a little-used shortcut past the old burro ride in the Painted Desert to avoid the crowds. Thunder Mountain roars through that same Painted Desert today.

Our shortcut was the very one Guy Williams took to reach the paddle wheel boat after the parade. He strode past us, his long legs propelling him easily across the distance that my short legs took several steps to cover. As he swept by, cape draped over his arm, I looked up and smiled. I was too surprised to speak but that didn't seem to matter. He'd probably seen the same look of astonishment and awe in the faces of thousands of kids before me. He reached out to tousle the hair on the top of my head, flashed his fabulous smile, and said "Hi!" A simple word and gesture, but they lifted me as if I'd been touched by an angel. Zorro hadn't reached out to anyone else in my family, just me. I felt wondrously special.

Years later, when I met John Gertz, we joked that Williams's gesture had been a sign that I was destined to marry the owner of Zorro. John and his twin sister, Nancy, owned the rights to the character. While completing his doctoral work, John ran the Zorro business part time. I was working with a start-up software company as its research director, but as our life together evolved, I slowly took on responsibilities in the family business.

Through the years, I designed games, worked with licensees, and eventually, with my husband's prodding and support, wrote seven Zorro novels for middle readers. When the opportunity arose to create *Zorro Unmasked*, John was reluctant to ask for my help. While still carrying out my responsibilities as the vice president of creative affairs for Zorro Productions, I was also pursuing an independent writing career, and I would have to put another manuscript on hold in order to do the Zorro book. However, the chance to research many of the questions that neither John nor I knew the answers to was very intriguing.

For instance: Where did John's father, Mitchell Gertz, meet Johnston McCulley, the creator of Zorro? Why did McCulley sell Mitch his rights? Was there really a Californian bandit on whom Zorro was based? What did McCulley really know about California history? Zorro had inspired other writers to create dual-identity heroes, but who had inspired McCulley?

The researcher in me wanted to track down answers to these questions, and our company archives gave me access to materials not available to other writers. As a former academic, I was itching for an excuse to delve into the archives of the Bancroft Library on the UC-Berkeley campus, famous for its early California collection.

I agreed to do the project without any real sense of how much information needed synthesis. Once I began, however, the material seemed overwhelming. The floor of my generally neat office was covered with piles of articles, books, and files.

My family was incredibly supportive, tolerating my unusually long work schedule with amazement and sympathy. "Mommy, are you *still* working?" became my daughters oft-repeated evening refrain. They grew accustomed to my late-night forays between the TV and the computer as I took notes on old Zorro movies.

Slowly, I uncovered the puzzle pieces that had enticed me into the project. Small moments became revelatory. In a conversation I had with John's uncle Irving, he mentioned that his brother Mitch had worked for Nat Levine. As *The Bold Caballero* flashed across the television late one night, my blurry eyes noticed the producer's credit. Nate Levine had produced this first talking Zorro film in 1936, based on a McCulley story. I had found the Mitch/McCulley connection. In that quiet morning hour, the only family member with whom I could share my discovery was our dog, Rinny.

I am most grateful to the people who provided me with research materials. Joel Reizor, of Weller-Grossman Productions, sent me transcripts of the interviews he had done for the Arts & Entertainment Zorro special. I couldn't have known at the time what a wealth of information they contained. My ever-supportive dad, Sid Curtis, helped with the early library research on Rancho Zorro. Mary and Bill Culver, Jean Barnes, Wally Neff, and Fran Johnson shared articles, stories, and pictures of Rancho Zorro. James Nottage graciously provided slides from the summer 1994 Mask of Zorro exhibit at the Gene Autry Western Heritage Museum. Gerry Dooley's research on the Disney series was meticulously detailed and perceptive.

Nancy Larson shared her memories and old letter files, while John continued his dual role as my most ardent supporter and my harshest critic. He spent hours poring over drafts of the manuscript, liberally wielding his red pen with the dexterity of Zorro's sword. Dan Fingerman and Steve Levinson offered insightful critiques of the manuscript out of friendship. Ben Kaplan graciously read the book in his off hours, despite working hard every day as our highly valued licensing manager. Collectively, their insights shaped and refined *Zorro Unmasked*.

My heartfelt thanks to David Cashion at Hyperion, who has been the most considerate, understanding, and delightful editor with whom I have had the pleasure to collaborate.

"Justice for all!" is more than a motto. It is Zorro's sacred trust. And although promoting the fox is our vocation, fostering his ideals is our avocation. We encourage others to join in Zorro's work, furthering the cause of social justice in their communities.

S. R. Curtis
Berkeley, California

THE LEGEND BEGINS

1

"Señor Zorro, eh?" Gonzales cried in a terrible voice. "Is it my fate always to hear that name? Señor Zorro, eh? Mr. Fox, in other words! He imagines, I take it, that he is as cunning as one. By the saints, he raises as much stench!"

Gonzales gulped, turned to face them squarely, and continued his tirade.

"He runs up and down the length of El Camino Real like a goat of the high hills! He wears a mask, and he flashes a pretty blade, they tell me. He uses the point of it to carve his hated letter Z on the cheek of his foe! Ha! The mark of Zorro they are calling it! A pretty blade he has, in truth! But I cannot swear as to the blade—I never have seen it. He will not do me the honor of letting me see it! Señor Zorro's depredations never occur in the vicinity of Sergeant Pedro Gonzales! Perhaps this Señor Zorro can tell us the reason for that? Ha!"

He glared at the men before him, threw up his upper lip, and let the ends of his great black mustache bristle.

"They are calling him the Curse of Capistrano now," the fat land-

Zorro was introduced on August 9, 1919, in Johnston McCulley's *The Curse of Capistrano*.

lord observed, stooping to pick up the wine mug and cards and hoping to filch a coin in the process.

"Curse of the entire highway and the whole mission chain!" Sergeant Gonzales roared. "A cutthroat, he is! A thief! Ha! A common fellow presuming to get him a reputation for bravery because he robs a hacienda or so and frightens a few women and natives! Señor Zorro, eh? Here is one fox it gives me pleasure to hunt! Curse of Capistrano, eh? I know I have led an evil life, but I only ask of the saints one thing now— that they forgive me my sins long enough to grant me the boon of standing face to face with this pretty highwayman!"

With this dramatic introduction, the expectation was set for the appearance of the legendary fox, Señor Zorro, in *The Curse of Capistrano*. Created by Johnston McCulley, the character debuted in the August 9, 1919, edition of the pulp fiction journal *All-Story Weekly* and ran for five installments, through September 6, 1919. Wearing a mask to conceal his true identity and cloaked in a long cape, the mysterious rider of the night, Zorro (*Zorro* is the Spanish word for "fox"), stirred the imaginations of his readers.

As *The Curse of Capistrano* opens, Sergeant Gonzales boasts to the fat tavern owner of his desire to cross blades with Zorro and claim the reward offered by the governor of California. He chastises Zorro's unwillingness to appear wherever the sergeant is, describing the fox as "like a fleeting sunbeam . . . and with about as much real courage!" Gonzales believes that the *frailes* (friars) of the mission are the ones who have hidden and fed the mysterious Zorro. Spurred by the wine he has consumed, and to amuse the soldiers and the tavern owner, Gonzales launches into a humorous battle with shadows.

His blade had leaped from its scabbard. He swept it back and forth through the air, thrust, parried, lunged, advanced, and retreated, shouted his oaths, and roared his laughter as he fought with shadows. . . ." Have at you, dog! Die, hound! One side, poltroon!" He reeled against the wall, gasping, his breath almost gone, the point of this blade resting on the floor, his great face purple with exertion and the wine he had consumed, while the corporal and the soldiers and the fat landlord laughed long and loudly at this bloodless battle from which Sergeant Pedro Gonzales had emerged the unquestioned victor. "Were—were this fine Señor Zorro only before me here and now!" the sergeant gasped.

His wish granted, the door opens suddenly and a man

entered the inn on a gust of the storm . . . The newcomer had his back toward those in the long room. They could see that his sombrero was pulled far down on his head . . . and that his body was enveloped in a long cloak . . . When the landlord was within a few feet of him . . . the stranger whirled around. The landlord gave a little cry of fear . . . Sergeant Pedro Gonzales allowed his lower jaw to drop and let his eyes bulge. For the man who stood straight before them had a black mask over his face that effectively concealed his features, and through the two slits in it his eyes glittered ominously. "Señor Zorro, at your service."

Holding a pistol in his left hand to control the landlord, three soldiers, and a corporal in the inn, Zorro forces Gonzales into a duel as punishment for brutally beating a native four days before. He toys with Gonzales for a time, deflecting his tricks as the sergeant tries to attack again and again. Then Gonzales notes a change in the eyes laughing through the mask.

> We have had enough of playing. It is time for the punishment! Zorro pressed his attack. The tip of his blade seemed to be a serpent's head with a thousand tongues. Zorro had Gonzales backed into a corner but someone began pounding on the tavern door, giving the Sergeant hope. But Zorro's blade took on new life. It darted in and out with a speed that was bewildering. It caught a thousand beams of light from the flickering candles and hurled them back. And suddenly it darted in and hooked itself properly and Sergeant Gonzales felt his sword torn from his grasp and saw it go flying through the air.
>
> Gonzales awaited the stroke. A sob came into his throat that this must be the end . . . but no steel entered his breast. . . . Instead, Señor Zorro . . . slapped Pedro Gonzales once across the cheek.
>
> "That for a man who mistreats helpless natives!" he cried. Gonzales roared in rage and shame.

Somebody is battering on the bolted tavern door, but Zorro gives it little thought.

> He sprang back, and sent his blade into its scabbard like a flash. He swept the pistol before him and thus threatened all in the long room. He darted to a window, sprang upon a bench. "Until a later time, Señor!" he cried. And then he went through the window as a mountain goat jumps from a cliff . . . In rushed the wind and rain, and the candles went out.
>
> "After him!" Gonzales screeched. But there was little use in it. It was so dark a man could not see a distance of a horse's length. The beating rain was enough to obliterate tracks almost instantly. Señor Zorro was gone . . .

With his thirst for justice, audacious flair, superior swordsmanship, and athleticism, the dashing Señor Zorro burst on the scene of popular fiction. At once captivating and romantic, passionate and righteous, the fox was a noble and heroic creation. Zorro, "friend of the oppressed," punished "none except brutes who mistreated natives." He had not "slain any man," preferring to punish and humble his victims.

McCulley cloaked Zorro's alter ego in a personality diametrically opposite that of his heroic fox. Don Diego Vega, son of wealthy widower Don Alejandro Vega, lived in Los Angeles during the "day of the decadence of the missions." The Vega family controlled thousands of acres, countless herds of horses and cattle, plus bountiful fields of grain. Diego personally owned a large hacienda and a house in the *pueblo*, and in addition, stood to inherit three times the property he already owned from his father.

Diego's great wealth positioned him as a man to be respected, yet he was known up and down El Camino Real, the highway that connected the twenty-one Spanish missions in California, for disdaining the pursuits of the full-blooded youth of the time. He wouldn't "ride like a fool, fight every newcomer, or play the guitar under a woman's window like a simpleton." Diego wore his blade as a matter of style. The inhabitants of Reina de Los Angeles doubted whether he could use it, for he was a gentle soul who disliked action. Affecting a tired, bored demeanor, Diego protested against talk of bloodshed and violence, preferring to listen to words of wisdom regarding music or poetry. This character could hardly be construed as Sergeant Gonzales's "terror of the highway." Yet Diego was the perfect foil for the fox.

McCulley had no way to predict that his masked hero would become an enduring legend. Consequently, at the end of the five-part series, he revealed Zorro's true identity not only to Don Diego's love, Señorita Lolita Pulido, but to the entire *pueblo*, including the governor.

"Unmask, man!" cried the governor. "I would see the features of the person who has fooled my troopers, has gained caballeros to his banner, and has forced me to make a compromise."

"I fear that you will be disappointed when you see my poor features," Señor Zorro replied.... He chuckled, glanced down at the Señorita Lolita, and then put up a hand and tore off his mask.

A chorus of gasps answered the motion, an explosive oath or two from the soldiers, cries of delight from the caballeros, and a screech of mingled pride and joy from one old *hidalgo* [gentleman].

"Don Diego, my son—my son!"

And the man before them seemed to droop suddenly in the shoulders, and sighed, and spoke in a languid voice.

"These be turbulent times. Can a man never meditate on music and the poets?"

"Explain! Explain!" they cried.

And so, Diego explained.

"It began ten years ago, when I was but a lad of fifteen. . . . I heard tales of persecution. I saw my friends, the *frailes*, annoyed and robbed. I saw soldiers beat an old native who was my friend. And then I determined to play this game. It would be a difficult game to play, I knew. So I pretended to have small interest in life, so that men never would connect my name with that of the highwayman I expected to become. In secret, I practiced horsemanship and learned how to handle a blade. . . . One half of me was the languid Don Diego you all knew, and the other half was the Curse of Capistrano I hoped one day to be. And then the time came, and my work began. . . . It was difficult to fool you all, but it has been done. . . . Only years of practice allowed me to accomplish it. And now Señor Zorro shall ride no more . . ."

How wrong McCulley was when he wrote those words! Zorro has been riding a wave of popularity that has spanned more than seventy-five years. The masked hero of old California has become an intergenerational, cross-cultural icon. The character has become a vehicle for stars of the silver screen, establishing actors and film genres, as well as for countless dual-identity imitators. Such an illustrious future could hardly have been imagined by the freelance writer who brought Zorro to life.

Zorro's creator, author Johnston McCulley, was born in Ottawa, Illinois, on February 2, 1883. He was educated by private tutors and in local schools. In 1925, he married Louise Munsey Powers.[1] The couple had one daughter, Beatrix Maurine. On the back jacket of the Penguin Signet Books paperback version of McCulley's *The Caballero*, a glimpse into the author's personal life was presented.

Author McCulley confers with actor Guy Williams, the star of Disney's Zorro television series.

A wizard as a history student, he began writing historical and period serials in high school and it was not long before he was turning out "pulp" under a dozen pseudonyms. Finally, tiring of stereotyped backgrounds, he did research on the early mission days in California . . . McCulley has come to love California. He writes that he has simply moved in on his daughter, Maurine, a well-known portrait painter, who had a place on Strawberry Flats, a government reserve high in the Lake Arrowhead resort district of the San Bernardino mountains. Fishing and motoring are his main recreations and he admits something of a reputation as a naturalist. He says he is a sucker for agreeing to make speeches at clubs, swearing off and then doing it all over again. He believes he is most noted, however, for holding in heroically just so long and then blowing his top with a bang.

Wade Austin, in *Twentieth-Century Western Writers*, describes Mc-
Culley as

> a hack writer with no pretensions other than to write adventure stories
> steadily and successfully.... One doesn't look to McCulley for realistic
> writing on the West or for writing in a straight western tradition ... His
> pedestrian craftsmanship turns out adventure stories with an eye al-
> ways on commercial possibility. And, of course, Zorro.

Despite Austin's claim that McCulley contributed "little, if anything
at all, of artistic value to literature in general or to western literature in
particular," many writers would be envious not only of McCulley's output
and general success but of the endearing and enduring legacy of his character, Zorro.

McCulley began as a newspaperman, working as a special correspon-
dent in the United States and abroad, including a stint as a police reporter
for a sensationalist tabloid, the *Police Gazette*. He moved on to become a
playwright, screenwriter, novelist, and prolific author of stories ranging
from crime thrillers to westerns.

McCulley lived and worked primarily in New York City before moving
to Southern California following the publication of his first novel, *The Lord
of Lost Hope*, in 1908. His stories began appearing in 1907 in magazines
such as *Blue Book*, for which he wrote a six-part series titled *Todd, the
Tourist*, and in *Railroad Man's Magazine*, in which six episodes of *The Courage Club* appeared. He penned hundreds of stories that were published in
magazines such as *Woman, Cosmopolitan, Scrap Book, Bohemian Adventure, American Boy*, and *Top Notch*.

His western-genre stories appeared in *Argosy, Adventure, All-Story
Weekly, Western Story, Thrilling Ranch Stories, Texas Rangers, Cavalier Classics, West, Exciting Western*, and *Short Stories for Men*. Also an author of
crime thrillers, McCulley published nearly twenty mystery novels, including *The Black Star* (1921), *The Demon* (1925), *Alias the Thunderbolt* (1927),
The Avenging Twins (1927), and *The Rollicking Rogue* (1939).

During World War I, McCulley served as an army public affairs officer. After the war, when the country was eager for escapist fantasy and the
popular romance of the Old West, McCulley's Spanish fox appeared in the

pulp magazine *All-Story Weekly*. By this time, the author was a thirty-six-year-old seasoned writer. Pulp magazines had become extremely popular for adult readers during the early 1900s, and reached their heyday in the 1930s and 1940s. They blanketed newsstands in almost every popular fiction genre of the time, everything from westerns, science fiction, and police stories to romance and horror tales. Printed on poor-quality wood pulp paper (hence the name "pulp"), these cheap publications were marketed with colorful, enticing covers that often featured lurid portraits of lovely women in distress and handsome men attempting to rescue them.

Stories were serialized over consecutive issues, each of which could be purchased for only a dime. The inexpensive price attracted young working-class adults and teens who would not have been able to buy the more expensive magazines of the day. The pulps allowed readers access to people, places, and action outside their life experience and lured them with strange villains, mysterious heroes, beautiful women, and exotic locales. The action-packed adventures featured in the pulps, along with their unique characters, filled a societal niche of their time that has been virtually supplanted today by television. Frank Munsey's *All-Story Weekly*[2] was the best of its genre. It filled an adventure niche that strove for as much realism as possible. Hence, the quality of writing expected in the stories gave authors who were world travelers or fond of research an edge. McCulley fit the latter description with his interest in history. Munsey, who had popularized *Tarzan of the Apes* when he published Edgar Rice Burroughs's creation, followed up this success with Johnston McCulley's heroic Spanish fox.

Other successful novelists who got their start writing for the pulps included Dashiell Hammett, creator of detective Sam Spade; Carroll John Daly, with his hard-boiled bad guys pitting wits against tough, street-smart detectives such as Race Williams; Ray Bradbury, author of the science fiction classics *Fahrenheit 451* and *The Martian Chronicles*; Max Brand; H. P. Lovecraft; and Raymond Chandler.

The popularity of McCulley's first Zorro story in *All-Story Weekly* set his life on a path in which the author and his creation remained entwined until McCulley's death forty years later. During his subsequent writing career, McCulley published sixty-four Zorro stories for the pulps; four of those stories were featured in four to six installments and one was a two-parter. His last Zorro story, *The Mask of Zorro*, appeared in 1959 in *Short Stories for Men*.

After his fox became such a hit, McCulley tried to create other similar characters. His panoply of early California takeoffs on Zorro included *Captain Fly-By-Night* (1926), *Don Peon* (1936), *Señor Vulture* (1938), *The Black Grandee* (1938), *Don Renegade* (1939), *Señor Devil-May-Care* (1940), and *Devil's Dubloon* (1940). For the mystery pulps, McCulley created Thubway Tham and the Crimson Clown. Although *The Curse of Capistrano* (1919) was a hit, followed by *The Further Adventures of Zorro* (1922), the 1920s were not distinguished as McCulley's Zorro writing period. That was reserved for the 1940s. Rather, the author penned over ninety Thubway Tham stories for *Detective Story Magazine*.

McCulley authored fifty novels over his career, but he also wrote under an assortment of pen names, including a female moniker, Rowena Raley. His other noms de plume included George Drayne, Frederic Phelps, Harrington Strong, and Rayley Brien. Despite his prolific output as a writer, none of his other creations attained the long-lasting life of Señor Zorro.

If *The Curse of Capistrano* had remained imprisoned on the printed page, Zorro's legend might never have developed. However, a year after the story's publication, Douglas Fairbanks Sr. breathed life into Señor Zorro and his alter ego, Don Diego, with his 1920 silent film, *The Mark of Zorro*. Film images have become synonymous with the character from Zorro's beginning. Success in print has walked hand in hand with success on the screen, feeding and embellishing the masked hero's image. The popularity of the Fairbanks film paved the way for more Zorro stories for eager fans.

In 1922, McCulley obliged his fans with *The Further Adventures of Zorro*. The six-part series began publication on May 6 in *Argosy All-Story Weekly*. The cover of the pulp magazine wrote the name of the title of the story as "The Further Adventures of Zoro." The identity of the character was evolving, down to the spelling of his name. Though Zorro had killed Captain Ramon in *The Curse of Capistrano*, McCulley simply ignored the captain's death in the 1922 sequel, enabling Ramon to once again be the primary villain. In the original tale, Ramon forced his affections on Zorro's love, Señorita Lolita, and in turn Zorro engaged him in a duel to defend the lady's honor. In the end, Zorro carved his trademark Z on the captain's forehead before fatally running him through with his sword. In the sequel, the resurrected Ramon bears Zorro's mark. Not only is he consumed with revenge for Zorro and unrequited lust for Lolita, Ramon is also driven by a duplicitous appetite for thievery.

On the night before Lolita's and Diego's wedding, Ramon plans to loot Los Angeles in an alliance with the pirate Bardosa, as well as abduct the bride-to-be and take her to the pirate's ship, where she will be forced to marry him. Meanwhile, Diego is hosting a bachelor dinner with his caballero friends. They toast the sword of Zorro and Don Audre mourns the loss of Diego, his closest friend.

> "This scion of Old Spain, this delicate morsel of caballero blood to be gobbled up by the monster of matrimony! . . . We shouted praises of him because he took us out of our monotony. . . . What has become of the wild blood that coursed your veins," he queries Diego, ". . . those precious, turbulent drops that were Zorro?"
>
> "They linger," Diego replies. "It needs but the cause to churn them into active being."
>
> "Ha! A cause!" Don Audre shouts. "Caballeros, let us find him a cause."

No sooner is this exclaimed than the joyous gathering is attacked by pirates, eager to loot Diego's rich abode. In the exciting tale that follows, Diego once again dons his Zorro costume. He and the caballeros have found their cause. Intrigue, pirate superstitions, shifting alliances, daring escapes, and wild sword fights fill the story as the fox returns to save his lady love. McCulley once again kills Ramon in this story, but this time his death does not come by Zorro's hand. Rather, the evil Ramon meets his fate after double-crossing Bardosa. The pirate grabs a dagger from the belt of one of his guards and throws it at Ramon. It lodges in the captain's back, the point embedded in his wicked heart.

During the 1920s, McCulley worked on novels and in Hollywood generating screenplays and story ideas. His films included *The Kiss* (Universal, 1921), *Captain Fly-By-Night* (Robertson-Cole, 1922), *Ride for Your Life* (Universal, 1924), *The Ice Flood* (Universal, 1926), and *Black Jack* (Fox, 1927).

After publication of *The Further Adventures of Zorro* (1922), *The Curse of Capistrano* was reissued in hardback. Grosset and Dunlap took Fairbanks's film title for its 1924 edition of the story, publishing it as *The Mark of Zorro*. The phrase was taken from a line at the end of the story. Zorro duels with Ramon and marks him with a *Z* just before killing him.

> Like the tongue of a serpeant, Señor Zorro's blade shot in. Thrice it
> darted forward and upon the fair brow of Ramon just between the eyes,
> there flamed suddenly a red, bloody, letter Z. "The Mark of Zorro!" the
> highwayman cried. "You wear it forever now, commandante."

Zorro returned to the pulp pages in 1931, reemerging in *Zorro Rides Again*, a four-part series for *Argosy*. However, the hero was depicted on the cover without a mask. He was dressed in a white shirt with a brown jacket, hat, and pants, not a black outfit with a flowing cape. He was brandishing his whip seated atop a brown horse, rather than his trusty black steed, Tornado. The boastful Sergeant Gonzales, bully of the Presidio, once again holds court in the tavern. He reminisces about Zorro.

> "Three years ago . . . when Señor Zorro rode the highway . . . Ha! What a
> man! Friend of the oppressed!"

Could the sergeant have been expressing admiration for the "terror of the highway"? In *The Curse of Capistrano*, Gonzales wanted to capture Zorro to enhance his reputation and to earn the reward. Had the boastful sergeant changed his colors? In this 1931 story, Gonzales boasted,

> "How we chased him up and down *El Camino Real*—and prayed that
> we'd never catch him! He sought out those who robbed the *frailes* and
> abused the natives. He used his whip and his blade. On his big black
> horse he rode, darting about like a shadow. They called him the Curse
> of Capistrano, yet he was a blessing."

Apparently, the sergeant had become an admirer of the fox.

Though three years have passed, Diego still has not wed Lolita. She was "seized by a sickness" and her father took her to Spain. With her re-

Following the popularity of Douglas Fairbanks's film *The Mark of Zorro*, based on McCulley's *The Curse of Capistrano*, the story was released as a book in 1924 using the movie title.

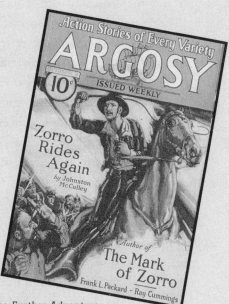

McCulley reintroduced his masked hero in *The Further Adventures of Zoro* (1922) after the success of Fairbanks's silent film. Note the spelling of the hero's name. In another story from McCulley's *Zorro Rides Again* (1931), Zorro cracks his whip but wears no mask.

covery and return, a rich wedding was planned and Zorro was but a faded memory.

> "Zorro has put aside his blade and his wild ways," laments Gonzales. Don Diego Vega is "now . . . but an ordinary man . . . a woman ruined him . . . the fairest feminine flower in the garden of California."

Suddenly, a trader raced into the tavern, shrieking that he'd been marked by Zorro. The new *commandante* of the Presidio, Capitán Valentino Rocha, rushed to Diego's home to accuse him of the vicious deed, for everyone knew that Diego had been Zorro. Rocha further charged Diego with killing his predecessor, Capitán Ramon. Just as McCulley had found it convenient to ignore Ramon's death in *The Further Adventures of Zorro* (1922), in this new story, he now recalled the duel between Zorro and Ramon that had resulted in the captain's death.

Diego dismissed both of Rocha's charges, claiming that the fight with Ramon had been a fair duel in defense of his lady's honor. As to Rocha's current charge, Don Diego pointed out that the *Z* on the trader's face was done in three strokes instead of one, as he would have done it (even though, in the original *Curse of Capistrano,* McCulley described Zorro's blade as it marked Ramon: "Thrice it darted forward"). It is clear to Diego that someone is trying to give Zorro a bad name.

Bardosa has returned to this story, too—as a reformed pirate. He retired some years before, becoming a man of peace, and eats, drinks, and sleeps his days away, often conversing with his friend, Fray Francisco. When the padre and the pirate are lashed on the road by a masked rider who looks like Zorro, and a widow is harassed by the same masked man, the town turns against the fox.

Diego is determined to discover the enemy who is trying to blacken his name and make him "a thing of scorn." The bogus Zorro must be caught in a manner that preserves Diego's honor, the Vega family name, and the reputation of Lolita. Diego informs his father, "Zorro rides again . . . to save himself. Outcast I'll ride—until I can prove the truth."

Zorro Rides Again was filled with examples of Zorro's wit, plus the typical exciting action elements. In one scene, Zorro tied three of Rocha's soldiers outside Lolita's home, gagged them, and then chased off their horses. He then arranged their bodies in the form of the letter Z. A later scene featured Zorro in a "trial of truth" with his blood brother, José of the Cocopah Indians. José's and Zorro's left arms were lashed together, each held a knife in his right hand, and the two men struggled in a battle to the death. Diego emerged victorious. But rather than killing José, he exercised his right to demand that the Indian serve him, and had José organize the Cocopahs to help capture the impostor.

In the exciting climax, the real Zorro dueled with the false Zorro. After Zorro killed the impostor, Zorro unmasked the villain, and to the astonishment of the onlookers, the fake Zorro turned out to be Capitán Rocha, who, with the governor's secretary, Don Esteban Garcia, had plotted to undo the fox. The story closed with Diego and Lolita starry-eyed and kissing in Alejandro's mansion with Sergeant Gonzales looking on, exclaiming, "Goat's milk and meal mush!"

As Zorro evolved in the movies and on the written page, contradictory elements such as Ramon's reappearance after his death were simply ignored. Sometimes people knew that Zorro was Don Diego. At other times, they did not. Often Zorro's identity was reduced to false rumors and suspicions. Throughout the stories written for *West* in the 1940s, Zorro's identity remained secret. In *The Task of Zorro*, the padre, Fray Felipe, enumerated the three people who knew that Diego was Zorro—his father, Don Alejandro; Bernardo, his servant; and himself, Diego's confessor. However, by McCulley's final Zorro story, *The Mask of Zorro* (1959), Fray Felipe had disclosed

> Only two men in the entire world—I, your confessor, and Bernardo, your body-servant—know that you are Zorro. Your father will be proud of you when he learns the truth.

Zorro/Diego's love life has been as elusive as the fox at night. He never married Lolita Pulido, the object of his affection in the first three stories. A romantic interest named Carmelita Ramon appeared in *The Mysterious Don Miguel* (1935), and it is unclear whether Diego married her. However, at the beginning of *The Sign of Zorro* (1941), Diego is mourning for his wife, who "died of a fever before they had been wed a season." At the end of this story, Diego is about to wed Panchita Canchola. But, in the long series of *West* stories that followed, Diego had no consistent love interest.

The minor characters changed, too. In *The Curse of Capistrano* (1919), Bernardo was a servant whom Diego cherished as a gem. McCulley described him as one who "cannot speak or hear, cannot write or read, and [has] not sense enough to make your wants known by the sign language." Bernardo bobbed his head as if he understood when Don Diego's lips ceased to move, but the servant really did nothing more than accompany Diego to his father's hacienda to get away from the tumult caused by Zorro. By McCulley's last Zorro story, Bernardo was described as Diego's personal servant, born a mute but not deaf, who had a sharp ear for what was said around him. In the 1940s *West* stories, though, Bernardo's role expanded to the more familiar one of Zorro's accomplice popularized by the Disney television series of the late 1950s. In *The Task of Zorro* (1947), Bernardo took Zorro's clothing and horse to their hideaway, a small abandoned winery on the Vega rancho.

By *The Mask of Zorro* (1959), Pedro Gonzales was no longer the angry, boastful sergeant of the initial stories but had simply metamorphosed into the tavern owner. Sergeant Garcia replaced Gonzales as second in command of the Los Angeles Presidio and his attitude toward Zorro mirrored the change in Gonzales's view of Zorro, first expressed in McCulley's *Zorro Rides Again* (1931). Garcia was more clearly an ally of Zorro than an adversary. McCulley even used an identical phrase to describe Gonzales and Garcia: Each "blew out the ends of his mustache."

Don Diego's family name changed from merely Vega to the more regal sounding de la Vega. Their living arrangements changed, too. Diego now lived with Don Alejandro and they traveled between Alejandro's mansion in town and his huge rancho near the San Gabriel Mission in *The Mask of Zorro* (1959). Alejandro reminded Diego that some day it would all be his, yet in *The Curse of Capistrano* (1919), Alejandro threatened to give his lands to the padres if Diego didn't marry, even though Diego had his own house off the plaza and was already in possession of his own lands.

McCulley's writing was influenced by Douglas Fairbanks's embellished film portrayal of the Diego character. While Diego was a languid fellow who passed a handkerchief across his nose in *The Curse of Capis-trano*, he added magic tricks to his repertoire on the printed page in the 1922 *Further Adventures of Zorro*. Magic tricks done with his handkerchief were a distinguishing feature in Fairbanks's portrayal of Diego in his silent film adaptation, *The Mark of Zorro* (1920).

Despite much later significant evolution of the characters, the rudi-ments of the Zorro legend were set in McCulley's initial story. His masked hero fought for the oppressed against injustice and humiliated evildoers to teach them a lesson. Zorro was not a common thief who stole for monetary gain or to redistribute wealth, and he only dispensed punishment to the wicked in measure equal to the abuse they themselves dispensed. In *The Curse of Capistrano*, when Capitán Ramon made unwelcome advances to Señorita Lolita, Zorro not only dueled with him, he forced Ramon to kneel and humbly beg her pardon. As retribution for forcing the padre to run miles to the plaza tied between two horses and then endure a public flog-ging, Zorro tracked down the actual swindlers and lashed them in order to teach them to be "honest and fair." Then he proceeded to have the *mag-istrado* tied to a post in the plaza and lashed for ordering the padre's flog-ging.

Over many years the distinguishing features of the Zorro legend have evolved to become the identifiable fox wearing a mask, cloak, and hat. He displays the skills of a masterful swordsman, performs expertly with a whip, and is cleverly athletic. Zorro toys comically with his adversaries, and he even talks to his intelligent black horse. The masked hero retains a deeply romantic, passionate nature—the dark, mysterious lover. His alter ego is the well-dressed dandy Don Diego, who dislikes violence, engages in no exertions, and seeks intellectual pursuits. He remains friendly with the padres at the missions and matches wits with a string of successive *com-mandantes* and villains. A sergeant who is forever pursuing Zorro, and is humiliated in the process, remains a standard character in the saga of the fox. These enduring characteristics have persisted, providing the old Cal-ifornia hero with his lasting legacy.

Zorro not only became a vehicle for stars such as Fairbanks, the char-acter also directly inspired numerous dual-identity imitators, including Batman, the Phantom, the Lone Ranger, the Green Hornet, and Superman.

More recent characters developed along the general Zorro model include the Ninja Turtles. Bob Kane, the creator of Batman, has no reticence about describing how Zorro inspired his creation of Bruce Wayne.

> Zorro had a major influence on me on the creation of Batman in 1939.
> When I was thirteen years old, I saw *The Mark of Zorro* with Douglas
> Fairbanks, Sr. He was the most swashbuckling, derring-do, super hero
> I've ever, ever seen in my life, and he left a lasting impression on me.
> And of course later, when I created the Batman, it gave me the dual
> identity, 'cause Zorro had the dual identity. During the day, he played a
> foppish count, Don Diego . . . a bored playboy, and at night he became
> Zorro. He wore a mask and he strapped his trusty sword around his
> waist. He came out of a cave . . . which I made into a bat cave, and he
> rode a black horse called Tornado, and later on I had the Batmobile. So
> Zorro was a major influence on my creation of Batman.

Kane even tied a significant element of Bruce Wayne's life to Zorro when he had the nascent hero's parents killed in an alley after seeing *The Mark of Zorro*. In addition, while growing up in the Bronx in New York, Kane was a member of a youth gang called "The Zorros." They wore black masks and tried to emulate Fairbanks's swashbuckling acrobatics.

If Zorro inspired Batman and other characters, where might McCulley have found his inspiration?

Though Zorro has often been referred to as the Robin Hood of old California, as Wade Austin pointed out in his review of McCulley in *Twentieth-Century Western Writers*, "a definite similarity exists between Zorro and the Scarlet Pimpernel. The Pimpernel took his name from a flower; Zorro took his from the fox. The Pimpernel protected the French aristocracy; Zorro, more of a democrat, protected the peasants."

Baroness Emmuska Orczy created the dual-identity Pimpernel in her 1905 book. McCulley would have been twenty-one years old at the time, near the beginning of his publishing career. Though the similarities between the characters are convincing, they are merely speculative.

The Baroness's *The Scarlet Pimpernel* was Sir Percy Blakeney, an English nobleman who rescued French nobility during the Reign of Terror in France under Robespierre. She was encouraged to write by the works of

Dickens and Bret Harte, as well as by the newly popular light fiction from America. Like McCulley, she was a prolific author, penning dozens of romantic novels, detective stories, and plays, but like McCulley, she, too, is best remembered for one creation, *The Scarlet Pimpernel*. The idea for the character came to her on a London underground platform. The story took just five weeks to write, and like the first Zorro story, it became a huge success in print, on stage, and on film.

Beyond the obvious similarities—their dual identities and their marks, the primrose and the etched Z—deeper analogies exist between the Pimpernel and Zorro. From the superficial setting in which each is introduced—an inn on a rainy night—to the league of noblemen who follow them, the characteristics that define both Don Diego de la Vega/Zorro and Sir Percy Blakeney/the Scarlet Pimpernel, along with those of their lady loves, are remarkably parallel. Both men are young, wealthy, and good-looking, but possess irritating habits—principally sleepy, yawning behavior. They are described as passive and courteous, with languid demeanors. Each dresses impeccably and owns fine horses, plus great acreage.

Their ladies are the fairest of young women, neither of whom initially knows of her man's secret identity. Both Marguerite St. Just, Sir Percy Blakeney's wife, and Lolita Pulido, Diego de la Vega's love, disdain their men for being either a "laughing stock," according to Lolita, or an "empty-headed nincompoop" from Marguerite. Yet, each praises the secret identity of her hero for the strength, bravery, and loyalty they enjoy from the men who follow them. Each woman's suspicions regarding the true identity of her male companion is aroused after perusing her man's private quarters. Each woman stands by her man in his darkest hour, preferring death to betrayal.

As for the heroes, both the Pimpernel and Zorro are passionate men, committed to a cause that puts them at great personal risk. Their heroic actions, however, come from different motivations. The Pimpernel is motivated by sport, while Zorro's motivation comes from years of planning and training after witnessing persecution of the natives.

McCulley appropriated for his hero a real mask, one that concealed the fox's true identity, much simpler than the creative costumes the Pimpernel employed. Chauvelin, the agent of the French government who was pursuing the Scarlet Pimpernel, called his adversary a "cunning fox."

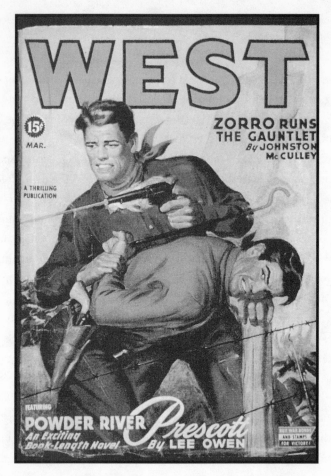

The cover from *West* magazine's edition with McCulley's *Zorro Runs the Gauntlet*.

McCulley gave his hero the image of the fox, whose positive attributes make him the clever spirit of the night.

With his interest in old California, McCulley created a milieu for Zorro that was at once novel and romantic. The author laced his stories with intrigue, action, and villainy, and set them in a time of missions, ranchos, and traders in an era that preceded the more familiar domain of American cowboys and Indians. Other than Helen Jackson's *Ramona* (1884), a tale of love between an Indian and a señorita, little popular fiction had been written with early California as its background.

McCulley's long career spanned not only the writing of novels and pulp fiction, he also contributed story ideas for more than fifty screenplays. He is credited with the stories for the following original western films from the 1930s through the 1950s: *The Outlaw Deputy* (Puritan, 1935); *Rootin' Tootin' Rhythm* (Republic, 1937); the first talking Zorro film, *The Bold Caballero* (Republic, 1937); *Rose of the Rio Grande* (Monogram, 1938); *Overland Mail* (Universal, 1942); *Outlaws of Stampede Pass* (Monogram, 1943); a Cisco Kid film, *South of the Rio Grande* (Monogram, 1945); and *Mark of the Renegade* (Universal, 1951). During the last years of his life, McCulley was fortunate enough to see his creation become a public craze with the success of the Disney television series.

Johnston McCulley was laid to rest at the Forest Lawn Cemetery in Glendale, California, on November 23, 1958, but his legend lives on. Zorro continues to inspire new generations and old fans with the hopes and aspirations of his noble pursuit of justice. It is questionable, however, whether Zorro's legacy would have survived had Douglas Fairbanks Sr. not adapted his remarkable athletic and comic talents to the character for the silent film screen.

DOUGLAS FAIRBANKS
MAKES HIS MARK

*S*EÑOR Zorro came to life on the silver screen through the creative genius of the silent film star Douglas Fairbanks Sr., who wrote, produced, and starred as Zorro in a film he titled *The Mark of Zorro*. The film premiered on November 28, 1920, just a year after publication of *The Curse of Capistrano*, on which it was based. The film was a fortuitous break for Johnston McCulley. Fairbanks's production catapulted Zorro into worldwide recognition, far surpassing the author's limited audience of pulp readers. The silent film transformed McCulley's two-dimensional hero from the printed page into a rollicking, debonair, clever, romantic, athletic, comic creation of flesh and blood. Fairbanks fed the public's appetite for heroic escapades. In developing Zorro, he also launched a new element of his own career as a star of a new film genre—the action/adventure movie.

Fairbanks portrayed Don Diego Vega as an effete young nobleman with a taste for tasseled sombreros and juvenile silk-hanky magic tricks. At the first sign of danger, however, Diego cloaks himself in black, grabs his well-honed sword, and rides the countryside as the mysterious Zorro, slicing his infamous *Z* into the faces of those who promulgate oppression.

He pauses to romance the young woman whom his shy alter ego lacked the courage to address.

Fairbanks's fans were not disappointed with his new screen personas. He brought to the role of Diego/Zorro the agility and charm that made him Hollywood's most adulated movie idol. He transformed these qualities into exciting action sequences that blew with the force of a tornado through theaters across the land.

This role was a deliberate departure from Fairbanks's previous roles as an acrobatic comedian in topical social farces. Fairbanks wasn't certain his fans would accept him in a historical thriller, so he balanced Zorro's dynamism with Diego's whimsical effeteness and by doing so blended deft comedy with action thrills. The result ushered in the actor's legendary cycle of adventure films and established the genre of the American action film. Douglas Fairbanks Sr. had been a successful stage and silent film star by the time he decided to make Zorro a swashbuckling romantic hero of the silver screen. Though his full-moon face and double chin made him a long shot for movie swoondom, and his stage-bred gestures looked like cheer-leader antics in close-ups, he possessed an incredible muscularity and in-fectious brio. His stock in trade was motion—leaping, tumbling, and clammering his way through stories with great exuberance. This energy turned out to be the key to the genre Fairbanks virtually created: the ad-venture comedy.

Born May 23, 1883, the same year as McCulley, Fairbanks was an irrepressible youth with rambunctious high spirits, prone to pranksterism. He turned his world into a gym, making ordinary obstacles such as steps and fences and ordinary heights such as porch roofs occasions for displays of his boyish, graceful motion. His personality revolved around his zeal-ously developed, jealously guarded physical tricks and skills. The screen persona he cultivated was one of perpetual youth with boundless energy and optimism. He expressed his ebullient personality physically and pro-jected amazement and delight at what his body could achieve. His physical skill demanded a commitment to a rigorous discipline of conditioning.

At the height of Fairbanks's career, his days began with a prebreakfast jog on the grounds of Pickfair, the palatial home in Beverly Hills he shared with his wife, Mary Pickford. After arriving at the studio (well-appointed in a suit and tie), he would then change back into exercise attire. Bored while waiting for director D. W. Griffith to find him a role, the thirty-two-year-old actor had created a gym on the lot where he exercised at least once every day, in addition to perfecting the skills and stunts in his films.

Even at age fifty, Fairbanks continued to engage in several hours of rigorous daily exercise. His regimen predated Pritikin's no-fat diet and Jane Fonda's aerobic videos, but was prescient about the health and lifestyle concerns of today. Up at six-thirty every morning six days a week, Fairbanks started his routine with a hard, half-hour bicycle ride, followed by a cold swim and a light breakfast at eight A.M. He would work at the studio from nine until four, and then would take off to play for three hours—any sport: boxing, badminton, tennis, running, or gymnastics. Next came a sauna, a plunge in an ice bath, a short rubdown, and dinner at eight. The simple fare he preferred was made without butter or sugar.

Despite his star status, by 1920 Fairbanks's promoters were concerned about his bookings. Exhibitors were beginning to complain that his films were too much alike. In film after early film, Fairbanks played a sissy or a seriously inhibited youth who found within himself the surprising resources to rise to difficult challenges. This formula was developed by John Emerson and Anita Loos, who had originally worked for Griffith at Triangle Pictures but moved to United Artists with Fairbanks and company. Emerson was an old friend of Doug's from New York, and Loos wrote comedy scenarios.

Their formula for Fairbanks was a simple one, as described by Douglas's biographer, Richard Schickel.

> All the acting took place in the early going when Fairbanks might be discovered, in monocle and spats, idling about some mansion or watering place, good-natured but a figure of fun to everyone but himself. As a variation, he might be seen as a repressed or inhibited dreamer, trapped in some routine job and longing for adventure. The point was simply to set up a situation where the true Fairbanks—resourceful, daring, gallant— could emerge and demonstrate his remarkable heroic gifts. In his first Loos-Emerson film, *His Picture in the Papers*, Doug was seen in a long match with a professional boxer, dove from the deck of an ocean liner into the sea, and took a mighty leap from a speeding train.

Such athletic feats were typical of Fairbanks' films. He often portrayed a poor little rich boy to whom the simple, hearty joys of ordinary life, not to mention the richer pleasure of plain-spoken masculinity, were denied. Which, of course, made his eventual breakthrough to normalcy all the more satisfying.

The qualities Fairbanks nurtured on screen appealed to male viewers, but men didn't go to matinees. Women made up the afternoon audiences. Consequently, whenever his movies were booked, afternoon business did not bring in the expected revenues—but the remedy was simple: Bring in the ladies. The way to attract females was to address a fault in his previous pictures. He hadn't developed sufficient love interest and without that element, women didn't care to see his films. His advisers suggested he carve a new niche in dramas that exploited the skills he could do better than any male star in the business.

This career advice came during a period of heightened business activity and intense emotions for Fairbanks. He had just married America's silent film sweetheart, Mary Pickford, on March 28, 1920. A little more than a year before their marriage, on February 5, 1919, Mary and Doug had formed United Artists to produce and distribute films with their good friends Charlie Chaplin and director D. W. Griffith. The influential Hollywood stars, dubbed the King and Queen of Hollywood, set off on their honeymoon cruise to Europe with Doug contemplating a change in the direction of his film career. Nourished by his own love interest, Fairbanks began searching for a vehicle that would not only showcase his athletic prowess but would present a classically romantic, heroic figure. It was McCulley's good fortune that he found *The Curse of Capistrano*.

Before their honeymoon was over, Doug Senior had cabled orders home to begin building sets and sewing costumes for McCulley's tale. Over the years, there have been numerous versions of the story regarding how McCulley's *Curse* ended up in Fairbanks's hands.

Douglas Fairbanks Jr. recounted that Ruth Allen, a friend of the family who was also a literary agent, read it in a pulp and suggested it might be adapted as a possible vehicle for his father. In his autobiography, Doug Junior offered this description:

Out in California, Mother's best friend, the tweedy agent Ruth Allen, had persuaded Dad to buy a short story about early California called *The Curse of Capistrano* by Johnston McCulley. At first he needed considerable urging to appear in period costume. Dad maintained it was risky to change from his established "ultra-modern" image, but he finally gave in. When the retitled picture was released, it turned out to be by far the most successful movie he had ever made. . . . Indeed, it became a more than minor classic of its kind, widely imitated and remade (without distinction) several times since. It was called *The Mark of Zorro* and was to be his trademark for years to come.

Fairbanks's biographer Booton Herndon gave four possible accounts for the acquisition of McCulley's story:

(1) Doug found . . . a story in a pulp magazine, *All-Story Weekly*. (2) Mary wrote later that she had taken the magazine to Europe, awaiting the propitious moment to give it to him. (3) Robert Fairbanks' (Doug's brother) daughter Letitia said that it was her father who put the magazine in his hand. (4) Richard Talmadege, Doug's stunt man at that time, years later said with a chuckle that the responsible party was really a semi-literate cowboy buddy of Doug's named Charlie Stevens.

"Who else would have read it in the first place?"

Another, though somewhat dubious, version of the acquisition came from biographer Gary Carey:

It was Mary who discovered the property that allowed Doug to set off in this new direction. On their honeymoon she had read a *Saturday Evening Post* story called *The Curse of Capistrano* and passed it along to Doug with the suggestion that he acquire the film rights. Doug shared Mary's enthusiasm and on his return to Hollywood he announced that his next film would be *Capistrano*, later retitled *The Mark of Zorro*.

Given that McCulley's story appeared in *All-Story Weekly*, not the *Saturday Evening Post*, the veracity of Carey's source may be less than accurate.

Whether it was the dainty fingers of America's Sweetheart (Fairbanks's wife, Mary) or the callused paw of a bronco buster that tendered *The Curse of Capistrano*, Fairbanks read it and saw its possibilities. Still, the decision to make a film based on McCulley's story took courage. At the time, conventional wisdom in Hollywood held that period pieces played to empty theaters, and this nineteenth-century tale in which men wore Spanish costumes and women wore lace mantillas was a considerable risk. Fairbanks envisioned *The Curse* as an excellent, yet not overly expensive, way to test himself in a period role. He believed Zorro would continue to attract his male audience, yet appeal to women as well. The settings were readily available in his local surroundings. Dozens of westerns had been made in what amounted to almost his own backyard.

The Mark of Zorro was produced on a comparatively small budget. To cover his losses if *Zorro* failed, Fairbanks shot *The Nut* immediately afterward. A 1921 release that satirized social workers, the film turned out to be the last of his modern comedies and one of his few commercial failures.

Zorro, however, was a huge success and an immediate hit. It opened at the Capital Theater in New York, the world's largest theater, taking in the largest gross ever collected on a single day. The box office recorded 19,547 patrons who paid over $11,708 to see the film. The police, who were in attendance for crowd control, had to close the theater after the nine o'clock show and shoo people away.

Critics found it impossible to place the film in a specific category. It was a comedy-drama with flights into melodrama, along with a liberal dose of pathos. Criticism was leveled at the scenes in which the priest was publically flogged and Zorro carved his trademark *Z* into Ramon's flesh. But the public loved it. In several popularity polls at the end of 1920, Doug was voted the most popular actor, surpassing his good friend Charlie Chaplin and even his wife, Mary.

As Zorro, Fairbanks displayed the superb athleticism of his previous films as he outrode, outran, outdueled, and outfoxed the soldiers. He wielded his sword with panache, having hired Henry J. Uyttenhove, the fencing coach at the Los Angeles Athletic Club, as his fencing adviser. But it was Fairbanks's portrayal of Don Diego that was a clear departure. His wistful, languid demeanor drew rave reviews. Audiences were captivated by his antics as he yawned repeatedly and demonstrated magic tricks with his lacy handkerchief. Most important, he developed a love interest to attract the ladies. As the debonair, poetic lover of Señorita Lolita Pulido, Fairbanks filled the matinee audiences. Biographer Booton Herndon attributed the forceful sexiness of Fairbanks's portrayal of the masked fox to his passionate marriage with Mary Pickford. His real-life fulfillment as a lover came across on the screen.

The success of *The Mark of Zorro* can also be attributed to the historical milieu. Though World War I was over, peace had brought disillusionment. America became isolationist. Fear of communism was rampant. Repression and violence reared their heads. Labor strife raged. People wanted to be transported to faraway times and places, away from their everyday existence, and Zorro hit the mark.

Fairbanks cowrote the film adaptation of McCulley's *The Curse of Capistrano* with Eugene Miller under the pseudonym Elton Thomas (his full name was Douglas Elton Thomas Fairbanks, thus he took his middle names as a nom de plume). Fred Niblo directed the project, with stars Noah Beery as Sergeant Gonzales, Marguerite De La Motte as Lolita Pulido, Robert McKim as Captain Ramon, and George Piolat as Lolita's father, Carlos Pulido. The script generally followed McCulley's storyline but incorporated significant adaptations—some for dramatic effect, others to showcase Fairbanks's skills.

The writers dramatically emphasized the theme of a champion of the oppressed in the opening text.

> In California nearly 100 years ago, with its warmth, its romance, its
> peaceful beauties, this dread disease, oppression, had crept . . . Then out
> of the mystery of the unknown—appeared a masked rider who rode up
> and down the great highway—punishing and protecting and leaving
> upon the vicious oppressor . . . The Mark of Zorro.

The action begins in the pueblo tavern on a rainy night. A soldier has had a Z carved on his cheek for beating a native and maiming him for life. Those gathered in the tavern reel with fear.

Douglas Fairbanks tosses back his head with a roguish laugh in his 1920 silent film hit based on McCulley's *The Curse of Capistrano.*

This Zorro comes upon you like a graveyard ghost and like a ghost he disappears.

The antagonist, the "greedy, licentious, arrogant governor" in the north of the province, orders his troops to accompany him south in pursuit of Zorro, who "poses as a protector of the poor and breeds rebellion."

However, in squalid huts, the oppressed natives acknowledge that Zorro is their "only friend."

While at the home of the fair maiden Lolita Pulido, her father anguishes over the financial ruin the merciless governor has imposed.

The blustery Sergeant Gonzales boasts to Diego of how he will carve up Zorro.

Back in the tavern, the rough Sergeant Gonzales boasts of how he will carve up Zorro when the meek Don Diego Vega enters behind his big, black umbrella requesting a pot of honey.

Diego's character, who abhors violence, declares, "I detest swords and bloodshed." Once Diego has his honey, he leaves.

A reward notice is posted for Zorro: 10,000 pesos, dead or alive. It is signed by Ramon, the commandant, by order of the governor.

Gonzales wants the reward.

Our hero enters smoking nonchalantly, guarding his identity with his cape. He closes windows, reads the reward poster, and slices a Z over it. The crowd charges him but he waves his gun to frighten them into a corner and he proceeds to fight Gonzales.

Irreverently, Zorro toys with the sergeant, getting him to look at his boot, then slices a water bag overhead. It discharges its contents, drenching Gonzales and causing Zorro to toss his head back with delighted laughter. The masked man bounds over the table, then sits cross-legged on it, toying with the sergeant. He takes a bean from a bowl and flicks it in Gonzales's eye, wonderfully amused with himself. He carves a Z in the seat of the soldier's pants, flings the sergeant's sword into the ceiling, leaps on the mantle while drinking wine, and declares, "Justice for all! Punishment for the oppressors of the helpless—from the governor down."

When Gonzales calls to the guards outside, Zorro leaps to the window. But the fox doesn't exit. He crouches in the window opening, then comes back into the tavern, amused. Zorro sneaks out behind Gonzales, playfully delivering his final coup de grace. He hits the sergeant in the rear end, making Gonzales believe that the soldier beside him did it, just before disappearing into the rainy night.

Once Zorro has escaped, he leads his black horse into a cellar camouflaged by flowers, goes through a fake panel in the wall, climbs up dowels in the wall, and comes through the floor of an upstairs room. Zorro looks through a peephole behind a picture to see his father, Don Alejandro, enter the main salon. Zorro sends Bernardo, his Indian servant, to detain his father, then comes through the fake grandfather clock as Diego, where, yawning with his handkerchief in hand, he greets his father.

Alejandro chastises Diego for staying shut up in the house since his return from Spain three months earlier. He demands that his son perpetuate the family name and "get a wife," and to that end, he writes a formal letter of introduction for Diego to the Pulidos, a respected local family with a fair daughter of marrying age. Diego responds with the first of several magic handkerchief tricks to divert attention during an awkward moment.

The next day, Diego arrives at the Pulidos' and engages in a humorous sequence of give-and-take with his hat before being introduced to Lolita.

As they sit uncomfortably at a table, Diego yawns, telling the girl that his father insists that he get married. He proceeds to tell her that he has a servant who is wonderful on the guitar and offers to send him to serenade her, but with biting sarcasm, Lolita replies that she has a maid who is passionately fond of music.

Diego then invites the Pulidos to stay at his town house while he is at his hacienda so Lolita can see how richly his home is furnished. If he can't get her by charm, there's always the money angle!

Later, Lolita sits in the garden, pensive and beautiful. The setting is perfect for a romantic rendezvous. Zorro rides up, jumps off his horse, and leaps over the wall, but her father sees him and decides to inform Captain Ramon to win the governor's favor. Our heroine, who is surprised by the masked lover kissing her hand, attempts to rebuff him with numerous slaps but he merely laughs and recites poetry to her.

> The high Sierras I would level to your feet—
> The wild waves on Capistrano's shore should pay you homage—
>
> I'd make the desert a million roses yield—to die in shame before
> your beauty—if this could be!

Lolita's smitten, but Ramon is in pursuit. Zorro sends his horse off alone to confound Ramon's men, while the commandant ardently pressures Lolita with his love. Zorro tosses Lolita a rose through the window.

The Pulidos accept Diego's invitation to stay at his town home. Lolita's parents then go off to plead their case to Ramon since the governor has shown them no mercy. They have been wiped out except for their house. Meanwhile, the lascivious commandant hides outside Diego's house. Once the Pulidos leave, he demands to be alone with Lolita. Dismissing the protesting servant, Ramon assaults Lolita. Zorro watches their struggle from an upstairs window and drops between them to defend Lolita. As the men duel, Zorro's sword strokes Ramon's neck once. The vigorous fight continues up and over tables and couches, and Zorro nicks Ramon again, then finally delivers the third stroke. Fighting with his back on the floor, Zorro inventively uses his feet to trip Ramon. The commandant loses his blade. Victorious, Zorro presses his sword against Ramon's neck to show him the blood imprint of the Z carved in his neck. He forces Ramon to apologize to Lolita on his knees.

Lolita offers her hero "freely—the kiss he would have taken."

Ah! Sighs from the matinee seats still echo in the imagination.

When Diego returns the next morning, Don Carlos wants his daughter's insult avenged with blood, but Diego wears no sword. He tries to entertain his guests with a magic trick, but the Pulidos leave in disgust.

The governor arrives in the *pueblo* just as the mission padre Fray Felipe is falsely accused of swindling hides and is sentenced to a public lashing. He protests, "Were I a follower of a licentious governor instead of a robed Franciscan, the hides would have been good." For his treasonous words, the friar, stripped to the waist, hands roped above his head, is given extra lashes.

Zorro uses the padre's unjust sentence as a rallying cry for the caballeros and has the *magistrado* publically lashed. The Pulidos are arrested for being Zorro's accomplices. Meanwhile, Diego amuses himself by making hand shadows on a wall as he waits for his father.

The caballeros, who have been out searching for Zorro on behalf of the *magistrado*, arrive at Alejandro's, where they accept an invitation to enjoy his wine cellar. Diego, fatigued from the ride, excuses himself and reappears as the masked hero exhorting the caballeros for being

idlers, wasters and fashion-plates who sip wine while the naked back of an unprotesting soldier of Christ is lashed. The heaven-kissed hills of your native California swarm with the sentinels of oppression! Are your pulses dead? Thank God mine is not and I pledge you my blood's as noble as the best. No force that tyranny could bring would dare oppose us— once united. Our country's out of joint. It is for us, caballeros, and us alone to set it right.

The rallying cry has been issued.

The caballeros pledge themselves to the cause. They raise their swords, united. "Justice for all!" they shout.

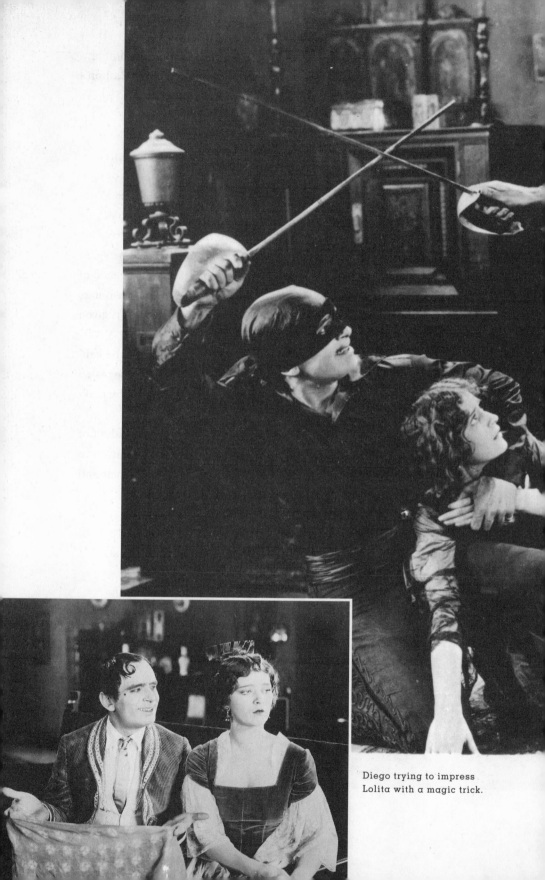

Diego trying to impress
Lolita with a magic trick.

Zorro defends Lolita's honor against the lascivious Capitán Ramon.

Meanwhile, the Pulidos are locked up, accused of treason. The caballeros meet Zorro at the jail, where their horses pull down the door and the Pulidos are helped to escape. The soldiers pursue the escaped prisoners. A wild horse chase ensues in which Ramon, disguised as a caballero, pulls Lolita aside.

Meanwhile, Zorro is leading the soldiers on a wild-goose chase, daring them to catch up with him. He uses a rope to swing onto a windowsill to avoid the pursuing soldiers, enters the window, and swings back out, Tarzan style, after they pass. At the bottom of the rope's arc, he swipes the sword from a soldier standing on the ground, swinging up onto another window balcony. An audacious and hilarious romp follows in which the masked hero displays his athleticism and relentlessly outfoxes his pursuers.

Zorro scales the church bell tower, leaps across a roof, jumps into a haystack, burrows down, leaves the friar's robe showing, and crawls out, having left the robe for the soldiers to tear apart. He stops to eat, telling a surprised *señora*, "Never do anything on an empty stomach—but eat!"

From a window, Zorro spots Lolita with Ramon, and he jumps the commandant, knocking him off his horse. He sweeps the fair maiden into his secret hideout. With soldiers swarming over Diego's town house, Zorro changes his disguise, sneaks through the clock, and comes down the stairs as Diego, yawning, in a dressing gown. Unfortunately, Lolita sneaks through the clock, too, but leaves the door ajar. Her mistake is discovered by a soldier, who grabs her. Ramon arrives, accusing Diego of making his home a rendezvous for Lolita and her bandit lover because he couldn't win her for himself. Diego slugs Ramon and jumps him, challenging the commandant to a duel. As they thrust and parry, Ramon recognizes "that blade." Diego marks a Z on Ramon's forehead to the shocked exclamations of the gathered crowd.

"Here your abuse of power ends," Diego tells the governor. "Everyone of noble blood stand with me." He orders the governor to abdicate and take Ramon with him. "Justice for all," Diego exclaims in a final hurrah.

Sergeant Gonzales sees the score and slaps Diego on the back. "I'm with you and I'll cut the ears off any soldier of mine who isn't!" he exclaims.

In a gesture of finality, Diego kisses his sword and tosses it high onto the wall, declaring, "Till I need you again!"

In a humorous escape scene, the fox leads the soldiers on a wild-goose chase.

With a lift from the caballeros, he is boosted over the balcony where Lolita is standing.

The hero has won his lady. She declares, "You talk—you fight—you look like Zorro."

"And I love like Zorro," he proclaims.

Diego pulls out his handkerchief as if to do another magic trick, humorously holding it in front of himself and Lolita. An insistent, brisk breeze refuses to let them kiss behind its shield.

Fade to black.

COMPARING MCCULLEY'S ZORRO TO FAIRBANKS'S ZORRO

The Mark of Zorro condensed, dramatized, and embellished McCulley's *Curse of Capistrano* to showcase Fairbanks's remarkable athletic prowess, but also to delight fans with his comic sensibilities as Diego. The recurring magic tricks, the rope on the hat, plus his humorous touches as Zorro—drenching Gonzales, booting Gonzales in the tavern from behind so he thought it was his own soldier, helping the soldier who was stuck on the fence, pausing to eat and giving advice to the *señora* in the midst of the climactic pursuit of the soldiers—combined to give a swashbuckling panache only hinted at in McCulley's story.

Fairbanks's casting decisions, along with his rearrangement of the characters' actions, visually dramatized McCulley's story. A tiny wisp of an actor was hired as the tavern owner who could easily be bullied by the big, boastful Sergeant Gonzales.

In the film, when Zorro finds Lolita in the garden, their exchange of kisses and slaps is pure Fairbanks: playful, self-confident, persistent.

Zorro duels with Ramon at Diego's town home over Lolita's honor, but in McCulley's original story, Ramon did not carry a blade to Diego's house because of the wound Zorro had inflicted in his shoulder at the Pulidos'. Consequently, there was no duel at this point in *The Curse of Capistrano*. Yet the duel is one of Fairbanks's most dramatic moments in the film. Zorro carves a Z in Ramon's neck, then he hurls Ramon's sword and hat out the door.

In both versions, after Zorro and Ramon spar over Lolita, the heroine utters McCulley's line to her masked hero: "I offer you freely the kiss he would have taken." For the matinee ladies, Fairbanks has the two kiss. McCulley's hero declined Lolita's offer. Zorro would not lift his mask for fear of being identified, but he pledged his love, as Lolita did in return. Fairbanks's film never informs viewers how or why Diego became Zorro.

Fairbanks created his climax with a comedic, athletic display of skill as he outsmarted the soldiers and rescued Lolita from Ramon, but the written story maintained more intense dramatic tension. The image of the lovers ready to die together while beseiged from the outside would have made a visually powerful and richly romantic final scene in the film. Financial considerations might have dictated Fairbanks's ending. The cost of the extras needed for soldiers and caballeros, their horses, and the battering sequence might have been too high for a film considered risky in the first place. And although the original story pursued a more noble, global theme of eliminating persecution by forcing out the corrupt governor and his administration, the film version focused on the more limited theme of avenging Lolita's honor.

DON Q, SON OF ZORRO—FAIRBANKS'S SEQUEL

Fairbanks revisited the fox in 1925, starring in *Don Q, Son of Zorro*. The script, however, was not based on a McCulley story, but rather on a novel titled *Don Q's Love Story* by K. and Kesketh Prichard. Fairbanks plays Don Cesar, the son of Zorro, who is in Spain for a period of travel and study. He is falsely accused of the murder of the visiting archduke. Cesar hides in the ruins of the Vega ancestral home until he can clear his name. His father, Diego, played by none other than Fairbanks himself, comes to Spain to support him. In the final scene, father and son duel together against Cesar's accusers to gain the proof of his innocence.

As the son of Zorro, Fairbanks displays the same bravado, athleticism, humor, and romantic passion that he did as the young Diego. He leaps onto balconies, cleverly evades his pursuers, and romantically reads the fair Dolores's palm, promising to risk all for her. He naughtily drenches the young woman's sleeping *dueña* and lightly harasses the sculptor for whom Dolores is modeling. Fairbanks's leading lady, Mary Astor, was a teenager of seventeen when she played opposite Fairbanks.

For *Don Q*, Fairbanks hired Fred Cavens, a graduate of the Belgian Military Institute. While Henry Uyttenhove, Fairbanks's fencing adviser for *The Mark of Zorro*, began the expert technical staging of screen duels, Cavens brought them style and flair. He magnified movements, giving an impression of strength, skill, and manly grace. The result was enthralling and memorable duels on film.

In *Don Q*, the actor showcased two new skills: his mastery of the Australian stock whip and his ability to dance the Spanish fandango. He spent three months of intensive training for stunts for the picture, including learning how to handle a cape like a professional bullfighter. Using the bullwhip, he sliced off the bottom of a bottle, shredded a piece of paper into several parts, clipped the feather off a soldier's hat with an unintentional flick of his wrist, and wrapped the whip around another soldier to knock him off his feet. Cesar also uses the whip, in characteristically athletic fashion, to swing himself up on a wall. Like a lion tamer, he whips a

After the success of *The Mark of Zorro*, Douglas Fairbanks Sr. starred in *Don Q, Son of Zorro* (1925).

soldier off his feet over and over again. The original exhibitor's campaign book for *Don Q* describes a stunt that never made it into the film—Fairbanks's using the whip to mark a *Q* on one cheek of the villain.

In an ingenious crowd-pleasing scene, Fairbanks used the whip to capture an escaped bull. After wrapping the whip around a post and making a loop in it, he waves a cloak at the bull precisely in front of the loop. The bull charges and gets his horns caught in the hidden trap.

Fairbanks learned to use the bullwhip for *Don Q* from the famous Australian athlete and bullwhip expert Snowy Baker. The skill took six weeks of constant work, the kind of challenge in which Fairbanks reveled.

Douglas Fairbanks Jr. explained, "It didn't take long before Dad was able to whirl the long black snake, make it crack like a pistol shot, and then snap a cigarette out of a brave and steady mouth fifteen or more feet away."

Unfortunately, Doug Junior learned how painful it could be to whirl the whip without the benefit of training. While visiting his father on the

Fairbanks worked with Fred Cavens on his stylish dueling technique, shown here in *Don Q.*

set, Doug Junior picked up the whip and tried to exact the crack his father so skillfully managed. He succeeded only in giving himself a deep cut near his right eye. Doug Junior wore a black patch over his eye for two weeks— one week on doctor's orders and another because it made him feel dashing.

In addition to familial visits, the set proved a popular tourist site, according to leading lady Mary Astor. The film's production was interrupted frequently by a succession of celebrated visitors, including royalty.

At the beginning of *Don Q*, harkening back to the end of *The Mark of Zorro*, Fairbanks has Diego, now gray-haired, read a letter in California from his son. The sword is still in the wall where Zorro tossed it some thirty years before. A clip from the sword fight scene with Ramon in *The Mark of Zorro* is inserted with the screen placard "Till I need you again."

The elderly Diego pulls out the sword, saying, "I need you again." He and Bernardo, his mute servant (who was played by the same actor in both films), leave for Spain.

In another wonderful bit linking the two films, Zorro reveals himself to his old friend, General Muro, the father of the heroine, Dolores. Muro has come to arrest Cesar for the murder of the archduke. Muro is grieved that he must arrest Zorro's son. Fairbanks, in a classic gesture, tosses his head back, laughing, then jabs Muro in the ribs with his elbow. He yawns, does a magic trick, and, yawning again, reveals the card on which the archduke had scrawled the name of his murderer. Cesar's name is cleared, and like Lolita in the first film, Dolores joins her love on the balcony.

Audiences and critics loved *Don Q*. The *New York Times* noted, "This is a photoplay which creates no end of mirth." Iris Barry of the London *Spectator* wrote:

> The patterns which the slender black figure of Fairbanks makes in the unbounded scene of the cinema are as rhythmical as the . . . movements of the Diaghilev dancers . . . he is no longer the purely-athletic film star he once was, any more than ballet-dancers are pure athletes. His movements are almost poetically graceful and what is more they are infused with a light spirit of comedy.

Zorro became more than a film vehicle for Douglas Fairbanks. The character became a part of Doug's and Mary's lives—as a trademark, an

Don Q outfoxes the colonel to foil the plot to kill him.

icon, and a dream. Mary named her wirehaired terrier Zorro, and he left
his mark with a style all his own. Biographer Booton Herndon noted,

> She paid out a fortune over the years in claims, for Zorro bit anything
> that moved—servants, hotel maids and bellboys, delivery men, people
> on the street, and even policemen. The dog bit two Parisian gendarmes
> in one day. He bit other dogs. One day the hotel doorman in New York

brought him back after a walk and explained Zorro's limp as the result of being kicked by a horse. Why had the horse kicked him? Zorro had bitten the horse. Why had Zorro bitten the horse? There wasn't anything else to bite. Mary often took Zorro to the studio, where he not only bit people but left his mark everywhere. No one dared kick the beast for fear that Mary might hear about it. The happiest day in the studio was when Zorro went up to a spider, an electrical receptacle into which a dozen lights were plugged, lifted his leg, and sprinkled it. The shock knocked him across the room.

Enamored of a dream of re-creating an early California rancho, Doug and Mary purchased 3,000 acres twenty-five miles north of downtown San Diego in 1926. They planned to develop a working hacienda in the early California tradition, naming their dream retreat Rancho Zorro. This parcel was part of the original San Dieguito land grant made by the king of Spain to Don Juan Maria Osuna in 1790. The rancho itself was located in the southeast corner of the original land grant, east of the San Dieguito River.

Journalist Caroline King interviewed Mary Pickford about Rancho Zorro for *The Country Gentleman* in May of 1928.

It's such a wonderful place . . . we were camping in a canyon we love, down along the coast, a little more than a year ago, and as we roamed about one day we came suddenly upon a most beautiful spot, with mountain peaks to the north and south of it, the sea on one side—and rolling hilly country, green and brown and purple, between. We fairly held our breaths with the beauty of it all. Then Douglas cried: "I want that" and of course I knew that he was going to have it . . . after we had investigated, made sure that it could be developed, we bought it—three thousand acres of it . . . before so very long, when we have our crops in and doing well and have built our house, then we are going to make our permanent home there. We don't intend to make our ranch a mere amusement for idle hours; it is going to be an actual business with us. Our place must be self-supporting, and our fruit raised as carefully and marketed as exactly as that of every other ranch . . . it may be two years before we are ready to take up our residence there. We've made a good

Orange groves at Rancho Zorro, the citrus and cattle ranch owned by Douglas Fairbanks and his wife, actress Mary Pickford, in San Diego County. (Courtesy of the William Smart family.)

start already, we think, building roads, planting trees, putting in our irrigation lake and planning our improvements. Every time Douglas and I can steal away from Hollywood we run down there to encourage ourselves with a peep at it and to see what progress has been made.

King described motoring down to the Fairbanks ranch:

> Suddenly, we came stealing up to a blue lake, the very heart of the
> ranch, for it supplies water for the entire place. The pumping station, a
> droll little building of Spanish type, shaded by banana and palm trees,
> stands close by. On the wall at the edge of the lake are the names
> "Mary and Douglas" inscribed in a joyful moment by their owners while
> the concrete was wet. Near this site they are planning to build a group
> of small houses in true Spanish style, with patios, gardens and palms.
> Here their ranch workers will live and here, too, will be erected the
> school, church, motion-picture theater and other public buildings neces-
> sary in a model village. From the lake the water is pumped to the young
> orange trees on the sunny hillsides. Eighty acres of these are watered
> by an overhead sprinkler system, the largest acreage in California irri-
> gated by this method; 125 acres of Valencias are watered by the contour-
> furrow system. . . .
>
> The spot which Mary and Douglas have chosen for the house is
> on a high bench, overlooking the broad valleys, the orchards, the lake
> and the site of the Spanish village. It affords a view of Mt. Jacinto, of Mt.
> Palomar, of Mt. Ramona and of San Clemente; through the gaps in the
> hills one catches more than a glimpse of the deep blue ocean, and far in
> the distance when the atmosphere is very clear, one may even sight
> Coronado Islands. . . . "And what name shall you give this charming ro-
> mantic place of yours?" I asked Mary Pickford. When she replied
> "Zorro," it seemed to me that no other name in the world could be so
> apt. "Douglas rather hesitated about it at first. He thought Zorro rather—
> well, sentimental or affected, but it is so very Spanish and fits so well
> with our ideas; and then, too, the picture was, after all, one of his big
> successes. Besides, how well our oranges will look branded with a
> big Z."

Initially, Mary and Doug camped, fished, and rode on the property,
but later stayed at the Inn at Rancho Santa Fe. Occasionally Doug came
down alone to check on the ranch, arriving in an early version of a trailer
hauled by a chauffeured limousine. At times, he and his brother, Robert,
would send down Doug's new movies, shown on an outdoor screen set up

near the Zorro reservoir. The man-made lake was built by Fairbanks, along with a pump house and a caretaker's home. Several biographers have noted that the couple inscribed either their initials, handprints, or the phrase "Doug loves Mary" in the wet cement of their new dam.

Plans for their home, Casa Zorro, were drawn up by the famous architect Wallace Neff. One day Doug and Wally were swimming in the lake when Neff pointed to a knoll and said it would be the ideal place for a home. Fairbanks agreed so enthusiastically that Neff sketched the front elevation that very day.

William Smart was hired to manage the ranch, under the direction of Doug's brother and business manager, Robert. Under Smart's tutelage, Rancho Zorro became a working citrus and cattle ranch. Three hundred acres of citrus groves were planted, scientifically laid out with overhead sprinklers and every tree numbered. In 1938, they produced a record orange crop.

Jean Barnes, daughter of manager Bill Smart, grew up on Rancho Zorro in the manager's house. The 2,000-square-foot house was built during a remodeling of Pickfair, the Fairbanks/Pickford mansion in Beverly Hills. Many of the building materials, including doors and windows, were trucked down from Pickfair. According to Jean, the couple wrote "Mary and Doug" with a stick on the dam—but before bringing down Lady Ashley, his third wife, Douglas had the inscription cemented over. One of the subsequent owners of the manager's home was President Nixon's chief of staff, H. R. Haldeman.

The dream rancho was never completed, stymied by Doug's and Mary's estrangement. In June 1933, Fairbanks returned to England alone to indulge his new passion of golf, in which he scored competitively in the seventies. This wasn't the first separation between the stars. Mary gave gossip columnist Louella Parsons the scoop that she and Doug were parting after fourteen years. However, when Doug finally spoke to the press, he didn't talk about his broken marriage but rather, he announced plans to form a major production company in England with his son, Douglas Fairbanks Jr., and Alexander Korda. Subsequently, he notified the press that father and son would co-star in a film titled either *Zorro Rides Again* or *Zorro and Son*.

Neither the production company nor the film project ever came to fruition. Likewise, the Fairbanks's house at Rancho Zorro wasn't built. Columnist Jody Jacobs of the *Los Angeles Times* offered further details of the reason why.

> ... in true Hollywood drama style Pickford discovered that Fairbanks had been spending time at the ranch with a glamorous blonde, a former London showgirl who had married a title and was now Lady Sylvia Ashley. Poof went the marriage. And poof went the ranch house.

The couple divorced in 1936. Mary kept Pickfair, their home in Beverly Hills, and Doug got the ranch. When Fairbanks died (on December 12, 1939) at the age of fifty-six of a massive coronary, his wife, Lady Ashley, became heir to 50 percent of the Zorro estate. The remainder of Rancho Zorro went to Douglas's nieces, the daughters of his brother, Robert. Family friends reported that Robert wanted Lady Ashley's share bought out, but Sylvia refused to sell her half interest to her husband's friend and attorney, Alex Drisel. Neither Robert nor Doug's son, Doug Junior, liked Sylvia; both men considered her a golddigger.

After the war, the value of the ranch slumped severely. Subsequently, Sylvia, after another failed marriage (to Clark Gable), offered the estate $365,000 for the ranch. Bank of America, acting as trustee, was eager to be rid of its responsibility and accepted this extremely low bid for the entire property, including the mineral rights.

The land changed hands a number of times after it was sold by the Fairbanks heirs until it was purchased by Ray A. Watt, chairman of Watt Industries. In 1978, Watt began development of an exclusive, custom home estate that became known as the Fairbanks Ranch. Watt recovered Wallace Neff's plans for Casa Zorro from Neff's son, Wally Neff. He turned Fairbanks's dream home into a reality, completing the house in 1981. It was purchased by Mr. and Mrs. Don I. McMillian for $2.25 million. The McMillians reportedly had not forgotten that their new home was the dream of Douglas Fairbanks. According to *San Diego Union* journalist Frank Macomber, all their linens were white and were emblazoned with a black *Z* for "Zorro."

Casa Zorro, a one-story home with 7,800 square feet, has six bedrooms and baths, including a maid's quarters. Down a wooden stairway, a hundred feet below the house, is a tennis court beside a small park where Fairbanks used to show outdoor movies to his friends. When an old friend of Douglas Fairbanks Sr., Frenchy Mendez, toured Casa Zorro at age eighty-two, he observed, "This house is exactly the way we had pictured it would be. If only Doug could have seen it. I've walked over this very place with him so many times. It was his dream, his unfulfilled dream."

Fairbanks's legacy became entwined with the masked hero, Zorro. It served as his trademark for years to come. His gamble on Zorro made possible the success of his other action adventures, pioneering a new genre of film that included *The Three Musketeers*, *Robin Hood*, and *The Thief of Baghdad*.

Fairbanks gave a life to Zorro that in turn imbued his own life with a dream. McCulley's fox was in large part the beneficiary of Fairbanks's genius as a performer and a visionary. Many men have played Zorro, but no actor has imbued the California defender of justice with such panache or given Diego such a contrasting, humorous persona. These were Fairbanks's unique gifts and his contribution to McCulley's creation.

FAIRBANKS'S fascination with early California was not embodied only in his dream of Rancho Zorro, it extended into his Beverly Hills life as well. He would rout Pickfair guests out of bed for predawn rides through the nearby hills and canyons in darkness. Breakfast would be trucked to a predetermined campsite where steak, Florida grapefruit, and croissants would be laid out. Then Fairbanks would entertain his friends with the tale of a legendary bandit, Tiburcio Vasquez, whose hideout, he claimed, had been in the very canyon where they were dining.

Doug Junior claimed that Zorro was based on a true story.

Zorro was interesting in so far as it was actually based on a true story. It had originally been written up as a fictional story. But that fiction story was based on a family that is still quite prominent in California circles. I forget their actual name in real life. But they are quite prominent and the character was known to exist in real life.

Was there really a historical Zorro? Could he have been the *bandido* Tiburcio Vasquez? What was the true nature of early California, that period that so fascinated both author Johnston McCulley and Hollywood mogul Douglas Fairbanks Sr.? Was McCulley's setting historically accurate, fictitious, or fantasy seasoned with a sprinkling of history? Who were the real villains and the real heroes of California's history? Were there ever real masked avengers on the scene? What role did the missions and the ranchos play in the state's early history? How did McCulley incorporate these venerable institutions into his Zorro stories?

SETTING

Johnston McCulley set *The Curse of Capistrano* (1919) during the "day of the decadence of the missions." Historically, this description would correspond to California under the Mexican Republic, between 1822 and 1848. In 1822, Mexico gained her independence from Spain, and California became part of the Mexican Republic. The decline of the California missions occurred after 1834, when the ruling government ordered them secularized. Despite these historical facts, as McCulley's Zorro stories progressed over forty years his vague reference to a setting in the "decadence of the missions" moved to firm placement in the Los Angeles of Spanish California.

Part two of *The Further Adventures of Zorro* (1922) began by summarizing the first installment, ". . . with the interests of the common people at heart that had interfered with the crooked politics of Spanish California of more than a hundred years ago," which would place the story before 1822. *Zorro Rides Again* (1931) began with "Once more night descended upon the friendly little pueblo of Reina de Los Angeles in the land of California, in the year 17———." For some unknown reason, the author left the year blank. Since the Los Angeles pueblo was founded on September 4, 1781, that year had to be after 1781. In *The Sign of Zorro* (1941), Bardosa, a reformed pirate, sat in front of his hut, "On this evening in mid September about the year 1800." Finally, in *The Mask of Zorro* (1959), McCulley's last published Zorro story, Don Alejandro claims to be a close friend of the viceroy who ruled on Spain's behalf in the city of Mexico.

McCulley has been criticized by historians for confusing California under Spanish rule with California under Mexican rule. His Zorro stories actually combined elements from each of these two distinct historical periods. The former period was characterized as the days of the missions under Spanish colonial rule, 1769 to 1821. The latter period was characterized as the days of the ranchos, which occurred from 1822 to 1848 under Mexican rule. Historically, missions dominated California's economy from 1769 until secularization in 1834. After secularization, the ranchos came into domination. In McCulley's world, the two coexisted, equally powerful and important.

Historian Abraham Hoffman raised concerns about the historical basis for McCulley's writing, for not only did McCulley place the rancho and mission periods together, he invented a Presidio in Los Angeles. Four Presidios (essentially, fortified settlements) were built in Spanish California: San Diego, 1769; Monterey, 1770; San Francisco, 1776; and Santa Barbara, 1782. Los Angeles was created as one of three civilian *pueblos*, along with San Jose and Branciforte (an extinct town near Santa Cruz).

Hoffman argued that the Zorro legend's greatest shortcoming was

... its existence in a historical vacuum, one that neglected entirely the dramatic events in which California was involved that would profoundly affect California's future—Mexican independence from Spain, contact with Yankees through the hide and tallow trade, the arrival of American fur trappers, secularization of the missions, the Russians at Fort Ross, Sutter's personal empire, the events leading to the Mexican-American War and the acquisition of California by the United States. McCulley mentioned not one of these; his story might as well have taken place on Mars.

Hoffman also found McCulley's title poetic but inappropriate to the story. The phrase "Curse of Capistrano" referred to the mission in San Juan Capistrano, some sixty miles south along the coast between Los Angeles and San Diego. Sergeant Gonzales called Zorro the "curse of the entire highway and the whole mission chain!" which gave a sense of breadth and scope to Zorro's operating range and provided him with an image that was larger than life.

California's missions, Presidios, and *pueblos* with an insert of the founding padre of the mission system, Father Junípero Serra.

CALIFORNIA AS A SPANISH COLONY, 1769–1810

More than a hundred years before the first English colonists landed at Jamestown, Virginia, Spanish soldiers and priests arrived in "New Spain" to spread their civilization northward. Having successfully colonized South and Central America, they moved north through Mexico seeking treasure for the king and converts for the church—although Spain's purported reason for opening the missions was to save the souls of the natives from savagery and paganism, her more pragmatic goal was to win their allegiance. The Spanish government astutely realized the value of using missionaries to conquer native people. Such a policy limited expenses and bloodshed, thereby assuring the riches that would come from colonization.

Spanish colonization rested on three institutions: the Presidio, the *pueblo*, and the mission. In Alta California the relationship among these three was symbiotic. The Presidio was dominant, with its military commander holding the title of governor. The *pueblos* were civic communities whose primary purpose was to support the Presidios with their surplus agricultural products and be prepared for military service in any emergency.

The governor had complete authority over the *pueblo* settlers and was responsible for safeguarding the missions. He could also determine when and where new missions should be established. Of the triad, the missions became the most vibrant institution.

Twenty-one missions, running the length of California from San Diego to Sonoma along El Camino Real ("the King's Highway"), were established between 1769 and 1823. The southernmost missions and the highway that linked them provide the historical context for Sergeant Gonzales's description of Zorro as "the curse of Capistrano."

The Spanish monarch Charles III, appointed José de Gálvez as *vistador-general* of New Spain in 1765. Galvez planned an expedition to occupy and settle the ports of San Diego and Monterey. Colonization, Spanish-style, had always consisted of the sword and the cross. Don Gaspar de Portola led the military branch of the expedition, while the Franciscan friar Junípero Serra headed the religious branch. Along with church ornaments and sacred vessels, Father Serra took the seeds of flowers and vegetables that would create the fecund mission gardens. In addition, two hundred cattle were driven north and their descendants soon roamed California, providing great wealth for subsequent generations.

Each mission along El Camino Real was about a day's ride apart, roughly thirty miles on horseback. Despite its regal name, the King's Highway was merely a dusty path. In choosing mission sites, Father Serra—and Father Lasuen after him—looked for three requirements: a convenient water supply, good soil for crops, and a large Indian population. Due to their foresight, the missions possessed the choicest land in Alta California. Along with their work of converting the Indians, the industrious missions created self-sufficient agricultural communities that raised crops and cattle, manufactured blankets, tanned hides, and made shoes and parts of saddles—as well as pottery, flour, and wine. Labor was provided by the *neophytes*, baptized Indians who lived and worked at the missions.

The price for living and working at the missions was baptism, which may have erased their sins—but it also took away their freedom. The friars exercised complete control over the lives of their *neophytes*, administering floggings and other corporal punishments for a variety of offenses,* to prevent the Indians from leaving the mission and to keep them from leaving and returning to their old ways.

The *Pueblo* of Los Angeles

The *pueblo* that captured McCulley's imagination was founded along the Rio de Porciúncula, between the San Diego and Santa Barbara Presidios. Inaugurated as La Reina de Los Angeles ("The Queen of the Angels"), a name McCulley used repeatedly in his Zorro stories, the settlement was some ten miles from Mission San Gabriel Archangel, another familiar landmark in McCulley's tales.

The San Gabriel Mission, fourth in California's chain, was founded

---

*Tension existed between California's Governor de Neve and Father Serra. The former wanted to train the Indians for self-government by electing officers at each mission, an idea that Father Serra opposed. He sabotaged de Neve's plan by having the padres select rather than elect the Indian leaders. In turn, de Neve refused to enforce a mission policy that the padre demanded—forcibly returning runaway *neophytes* plus further expansion of the missions. These two powerful men hated one another. De Neve called Father Serra "arrogant," "obstinate," "willfully decitful," and an "artful contriver," while the padre wrote to Lasuen that he could scarcely bear de Neve's presence. (M. Margolin, *The Journals of Jean Francois de La Perouse*, Heyday Books, Berkeley 1989) on September 8, 1771, near the Rio de Nombre de Jesus de los Temblores, or Earthquake River. Captain Portola named the river in 1769, inspired by four severe earthquakes that hit when he was present.

The settlement became so prosperous it was known as "the Queen of the Missions." Situated in a fertile valley with adequate timber, fine pasturage, and plentiful water for irrigation, the mission produced abundant crops of corn and beans, and it built up great herds of cattle. It also became famous for its fine wines. Soap making, tallow rendering, weaving, and leather work were also mastered by the Indians.

Ten years after the founding of the San Gabriel Mission, eleven families recruited from Sinoloa and Sonora, Mexico, under the leadership of Captain Rivera, founded the *pueblo* of Los Angeles. They totaled forty-six people of mixed ethnicity, including Indians, blacks, mestizos, and Spanish. The settlement's full name was El Pueblo de Nuestra Señora La Reina de Los Angeles de Porciúncula ("the Town of Our Lady, the Queen of the Angels of the Porciúncula"). It came under the jurisdiction of the Santa Barbara Presidio.

The settlers, or *pobladores*, had agreed to stay for ten years. Each family received generous inducements—a clothing and supply allowance, livestock, and tools for cultivating the land. Taxes were not collected for the first five years, and the *pobladores*'s initial supplies were repaid from crops grown at the new settlement.

They were expected to build their own houses; dig irrigation ditches; cultivate the land; construct roads, canals, a church, and other town buildings, plus be ready for military duty. After five years, they received permanent title to their land. By 1800, Los Angeles was second only to the San Gabriel Mission in agricultural production.

The *pueblo* was a square, six miles on each side, with a central plaza. Three sides of the plaza were designated for home lots, measuring 20 by 40 *varas* (55 by 110 feet), with outlying fields of 200 *varas* (550 square feet). The east side of the plaza had four small lots for the jail, the church, the guardhouse, and the public granary. Between the plaza and the river to the east lay the fields for farming. The land that belonged to the king was located on the east side of the Porciúncula River.

McCulley's *pueblo* did not accurately reflect early Los Angeles. Rather, the author created a *pueblo* to suit his stories and augmented it with historical elements. In *The Curse of Capistrano*, as Lolita's family rode into town in their mule-drawn *carreta*, they could

> ... see the pueblo in the distance—the plaza and the church with its high cross on one side of it and the inn and storehouses and a few residences of the more pretentious sort, like Don Diego's, and the scattered huts of native and poor folk.

The queen of the mission system, *Mission de San Gabriel Archangel de los Temblores*, the closest mission to the Los Angeles *pueblo*. (Courtesy of the Santa Barbara Mission Archives.)

Although a tavern was featured prominently in both McCulley's opening chapter and the story's climax, there was none in the actual *pueblo*, nor were there any pretentious homes gracing the plaza, only single-story adobe houses with flat, tar-covered roofs built by the *pobladores*.

Large land grants deeded to private persons are characteristic of the rancho period, but some large land grants were given prior to secularization by direct authority of the king of Spain. In *Zorro Races with Death* (1947), Don Alejandro Vega protested the intrusion of the new commandant at his rancho: "I hold this property under a grant from the King of Spain himself . . ." McCulley, therefore, knew of the practice, which mitigates criticism that he intertwined the rancho and mission periods.

Less than thirty such land grants were awarded by the crown. They were of considerable size, approximately twelve square miles each. These grants were located beyond the limits of the existing *pueblos* and could not conflict with the property of the missions or the Indian villages. Grantees had to build a storehouse and stock their holdings with at least 2,000 head of cattle.

Five private ranchos were granted near Los Angeles by 1798. The largest of these land grants was awarded from Governor Fages to Manuel Nietos by authority of the king of Spain in 1784. It extended from the Santa Ana River to the San Gabriel River, from the ocean to the mountains, and contained about sixty-eight square miles, over 300,000 acres. The Nietos land grant might have been McCulley's model for the Vega rancho.

The pueblo was not ruled by the commander of the Presidio, as McCulley declared, for there was no Presidio in Los Angeles. A town council, or *ayuntamiento*, headed by the *alcalde*, or mayor, ran the pueblo. He settled all disputes and was assisted by six *regidores*, or councilmen, a second *alcalde*, and a *comisado*, or legal adviser representing the Spanish governor. The *alcalde*'s position was an honor and carried great authority. He acted as mayor, president of the council, and judge. The *ayuntamiento* met every Tuesday and Thursday, deciding all *pueblo* business from quarrels over the sale of horses to domestic disputes.

Life During California's Romantic Period, 1782–1810

Historians have referred to the years between 1782 and 1810 as California's romantic period. C. Chapman described life as

> . . . one continuous round of hospitality and social amenities, tempered with vigorous outdoor sport. There were no hotels in California. Every door was open, and food, lodging, a fresh horse, and money, even, were free to the guest, whether friend or stranger. No white man had to concern himself greatly with work, and even school books were a thing apart. Music, games, dancing, and sprightly conversation—these were the occupations of the time—these constituted education. Also, men and women were much in the open; all were expert horsemen, could throw a lasso, and shoot unerringly, even the women, accomplishments which fitted their type of life, and made hunting a general pastime. When foreign ships came, there were balls and the gayest of festivals, nor were these visits the only occasion for that type of entertainment.

McCulley drew on this period to evoke images of early California, giving a comical interpretation to the custom of serenading. When Diego offered to send his servant to serenade Lolita in *The Curse of Capistrano*, the *señorita* and her mother were aghast at such a suggestion. Though serenading did occur, permission had to be granted by the *alcalde*, and fines were collected if it was unauthorized. J. Guinn extracted the following ordinance from the *Old Pueblo Archives*:

> Ordinance 5. All individuals serenading promiscuously around the street of the city at night without first having obtained permission from the Alcalde will be fined $1.50 for the first offense, $3 for the second offense, and for the third punished according to law.

As historical tradition indicated, McCulley described Lolita as an excellent horsewoman. In a climactic scene near the end of *The Curse of Capistrano* (1919), Zorro believed he was being pursued by soldiers. He

The fandango was a romantic part of the Spanish California lifestyle. Engraving by Casimiro Castro and J. Campillo. (Courtesy of the Latin American Library, Tulane University.)

discovered that Lolita was pursuing him and she was the prey for the encroaching soldiers. Zorro

> ... glanced back over his shoulder—and gasped his surprise. For it was Señorita Lolita Pulido who rode that horse and was pursued by the half-dozen troopers, and he had thought her safe at the hacienda of Fray Felipe. Her long black hair was down and streaming out behind her. Her tiny heels were holding the reins low down, and Señor Zorro, even in that instant, marveled at her skill with a mount.

The *matanza,* or annual slaughter, followed by a fiesta, were two other authentic local customs that McCulley included in his stories. In *A Task for Zorro* (1947), an American wrangler named Barney Burke questioned Diego about the sinful waste of meat either burned or left to rot after the *matanza*. His challenge was a portent of the culture clash to come between American and Hispanic societal mores. While Americans raised cattle for beef, the Californios used their abundant cattle for currency, curing the hides and rendering the fat into tallow to be used as trade items.

Despite the colorful, romantic life of early California, a dark side existed. Californio society was never democratic. A distinct Spanish-Californian aristocracy prevailed. Social class distinctions were based on rank (usually military) and blood. McCulley incorporated the social snobbery of the "blue bloods" into his Zorro stories. His characters were preoccupied with bloodlines, reflecting the cultural attitude of the time.

McCulley first describes Diego as "a fair youth of excellent blood." And when his fictional hero visits the Pulidos to pursue Lolita in marriage, he tells Don Carlos, Lolita's father,

> ... you are of excellent blood, Señor, of the best blood in the land ... Everybody knows it, Señor. And a Vega, naturally, when he takes a mate, must seek out a woman of excellent blood.

Captain Ramon bristled at Diego, "Do you mean to insinuate, Señor, that I am not of good blood?"

Among Californios, parental authority ran so deep that the father, or patron, could legally flog his married children. According to historian L. Pitt, "... no son, even one in his sixties, dared smoke, sit or wear his hat in his father's presence without asking permission." The fact that McCulley had Diego court Lolita at his father's insistence was consistent with Californio culture.

The patron's powerful authoritarianism extended to the operation of the ranchos. Each had its overlord, or *mayordomo*, and its large band of retainers, which historian N. Sanchez likened to slave plantations:

> ... for the Indians of California were hardly less enslaved than were the blacks of the South. On the plantation there was the "Negro quarter" in the rear of the "big house" where the white folks lived; in California there was the "Indiada," as the horde of natives gathered about the mansions of the Dons were called.

The year 1810 was pivotal in California's Spanish colonial history, for that is when the independence movement began in South America. The seeds of the autonomy movement lay in the defeat of the Spanish by the French between 1808 and 1809. In the Spanish provinces in America, the colonists set up their own provisional governments since there was no longer a legitimate national Spanish one.

Though the Californios did not directly participate in the colonial rebellion, they were adversely affected by the insurrection. From 1810 on, the Spanish ships that had previously visited the California coast on a regular basis ceased venturing north from San Blas, Mexico. Without the goods and soldiers' salaries they brought, the missions, *pueblos*, and Presidios were on their own. The hide and tallow trade became the principal means of economic support for the province. Trade was centered at the missions with their prosperous flocks and their experienced Indian workforce who could ride, herd cattle, slaughter the animals, skin them, and render their fat into tallow. This arrangement sustained the province until Mexico became independent from Spain in 1822 and California became part of Mexico.

Since cured hides were the currency of trade, proper curing was critical. After cattle were stripped of their hides and butchered for jerky or salt beef, they were then cured by soaking in saltwater for several days to soften the leather. Subsequently, the hides were stretched and staked on the ground where they were scraped clean. Finally, they were salted and placed on racks to dry in a hot, sunny locale.

Poorly cured hides served as a recurrent accusation leveled against traders in McCulley's Zorro stories. Fray Felipe was lashed for allegedly swindling a dealer in hides in *The Curse of Capistrano*. A trader in hides and tallow was marked with a *Z* by the false Zorro in *Zorro Rides Again*. The character described his business as follows:

"I buy hides from the native scum and pay them what I please. The neophytes are too holy to complain and the gentiles, ah, the gentiles! Many a hide and tub of tallow, cask of olives and jar of honey, do they steal from the *frailes* and bring to me."

CALIFORNIA AFTER MEXICAN INDEPENDENCE, 1822–1834

General Iturbide declared Mexican independence on February 24, 1821, but news of the insurgents' success failed to reach Monterey until January 1822. Isolated Alta California was the last of Spain's northernmost provinces to swear loyalty to the new Mexican Republic, waiting nine months to accept the authority of the government. On April 11, 1822, the commandants of the four California Presidios convened in Monterey to publicly take the oath of allegiance, a ceremony subsequently repeated at each Presidio, *pueblo*, and mission along the coast.

A volatile period in California history was ushered in with Mexican rule. The Californios chaffed under their new Mexican governors, who were perceived as overbearing. Resentment built. Rivalries raged between the north and the south of the state. The *abajeños* (southerners) wanted greater independence, while the *arribeños* (northerners) wanted stronger ties to Mexico. San Francisco and Monterey vied with Los Angeles and San Diego to be declared the seat of government. The greed and petty rivalries that characterized the period could have provided McCulley with examples of unscrupulous rulers—had Zorro been placed in the Mexican, rather than the Spanish, period.

Governor Victoria, who served as governor for one turbulent year from 1831 to 1832, would have made an excellent model for one of McCulley's ruthless commandants. Upon settling in Monterey, Victoria annulled the Secularization Decree of his predecessor, Governor Echeandia. Victoria's act infuriated the Californios, who expected to lay claim to some of the mission lands.

Victoria punished crime with a shortcut to justice. He ordered the death penalty for stealing small sums and other minor offenses. The shocked residents viewed the new governor as a bloodthirsty monster. He arbitrarily issued decrees, jailing and exiling people without trials. A character like Zorro would most likely have been hailed eagerly at the time.

A rebel force, led by men who were exiled or under threat of hanging, arose against Victoria. They took possession of the San Diego Presidio, then marched toward Los Angeles. A minor skirmish with Victoria's troops at Cahuenga Pass sent both sides fleeing. Victoria was forced to give the governorship back to Echeandia until another governor was chosen. Victoria returned to Mexico.

SECULARIZATION

The Spanish government originally planned for the mission lands to be turned into civilian towns after a ten-year period. During that decade, the natives would be converted to Christianity and civilized, working the land as part of the Spanish empire. Sixty-five years passed, however, before the California missions were secularized.

McCulley alluded to the friars' discontent with this eventual development in *The Curse of Capistrano*. After taking an unjust lashing, Fray Felipe complained to Diego:

> It is but another instance of injustice. For twenty years we of the missions have been subjected to it, and it grows. The sainted Junipero Serra invaded this land when other men feared, and at San Diego de Alcala he built the first mission of what became a chain, thus giving an empire to the world. Our mistake was that we prospered. We did the work, and others reap the advantages . . . They began taking our mission lands from us, lands we had cultivated, which had formed a wilderness and which my brothers had turned into gardens and orchards. They robbed us of worldly goods. And not content with that they now are persecuting us. The mission empire is doomed, caballero. The time is not far distant when mission roofs will fall in and the walls crumble away.

The padre was not referring to the Indians as those who reaped the advantages, but rather to the soldiers and settlers who coveted the valuable mission property.

The rank-and-file soldiers were eager for secularization. They envied the padres, and even their Indian converts, who lived in relative affluence compared to the soldiers' own poverty. The soldiers resented being beholden to the missions for all their needs, and having gone without pay since the Spanish-American revolt in 1810, they saw their just compensation in terms of choice mission lands.

A gradual secularization plan was implemented in 1834 by Governor Figueroa. Initially, half of the mission properties were distributed among the Indians and the rest were put in charge of secular administrators who often enriched both themselves and their friends with the spoils of the missions. Although a few were honest, others were merely incompetent.

Property was distributed to the Indians as each administrator saw fit. Without the disciplinary control of the mission system, the natives refused to work. Since the Indians did not understand the concept of private property, nor had they been trained to manage their own affairs, they were unable to hold on to their lands. Despite the provisions of the law, which prohibited them from selling their property or chattel, they sold their properties for anything it would bring.

The soldiers were eager buyers, and although some acquired land grants legitimately, others amassed huge tracts by tricking the natives. When their supplies were gone, many Indians hired themselves out or joined nonmission Indians in horse stealing. Their lives descended into degradation. By 1844, with pressure on the Mexican government to provide defense for a possible war with the United States, the final mission lands were sold into private hands.

The non-Indian mission lands, doled out as political spoils, made up over eight hundred land grants awarded during the Mexican period. Grants were given to any Mexican of good character or to any foreigner willing to become a naturalized citizen of Mexico and accept the Catholic faith. Petitioners could request up to eleven square leagues of land (thirty-eight square miles). All land was awarded free of taxes for five years.

Boundaries for the ranchos were loosely defined by well-known landmarks, such as a clump of cacti or the center of a stream. The quantity of land was guessed at and was described as *poco más o menos* ("a little more or less"). Such vague descriptions caused challenges to ownership when the territory became part of the United States, resulting in huge losses of land by Californios and deep resentment against the Yankees for usurping their inheritance.

On May 23, 1835, the north/south conflict was fanned when orders
came from Mexico that Los Angeles was to become the capital of the territory. Monterey had been the capital for over seventy years. This news
ignited a series of conflicts lasting more than a dozen years, and resulted
in a constant turnover of governors—including five from 1835 to 1836.

When a new governor, Manuel Micheltorena, a former soldier with
Santa Anna in the Texas campaign, arrived in 1842, he brought a company
of three hundred *cholos*, convicts recruited from the Mexican prisons.
These men made life miserable for the Californios by brawling drunkenly
in the public streets, stealing, and murdering, prompting yet another revolt.

By 1845, Juan Batista Alvarado and José Castro challenged Micheltorena's supporters. After a two-day artillery duel, a diplomatic resolution
was brokered that made Castro the major general and Pio Pico, a prominent Californio, the governor. Micheltorena was marched to San Pedro
Harbor and packed off to sea. With his departure, Mexico's direct rule over
California came to an end.

The governing situation, however, was untenable. Pico controlled the
legislature as civil governor in Los Angeles, but José Castro, as military
commandant in Monterey, had possession of the treasury. The northern
and southern factions were soon at odds and ready to battle for control of
the province when sequential developments occurred that altered the
status of Alta California by cataclysmic proportions.

On June 14, 1846, the town of Sonoma, site of the northernmost mission, was captured by a group of Americans who raised a red-and-white
flag in the plaza. The flag showed a grizzly bear facing a red star and read,
"A bear stands his ground always, and as long as the stars shine, we stand
for the cause." This incident became known as the Bear Flag Rebellion.

The Californians lost their fight for independence once the American
military entered the conflict. Commodore John D. Sloat, head of the U.S.
Naval forces in the Pacific, seized the town of Monterey on July 7, 1846,
subsequently ordering that the Bear Flag in the Sonoma plaza be replaced
with the Stars and Stripes. A week later, Commodore Robert F. Stockton
replaced Sloat and ordered his American naval forces to march on Los

During the turbulent 1840s, José Castro (*bottom right*) led a rebellion against California's Mexican governor with Juan Alvarado (*bottom left*), which resulted in an untenable ruling arrangement. Castro became the military commandant in Monterey, sharing power with Pio Pico (*top left*), the civil governor in Los Angeles. They put aside their differences to fight against the Americans in 1846 after Commodore Sloat (*top right*) seized Monterey.

Angeles. On August 13, 1846, Stockton's troops raised the U.S. flag without opposition. For the next month, the Californios under José Castro successfully attacked Stockton's troops, forcing the Americans to retreat.

U.S. General Kearny's 200 First U.S. Dragoons were ordered to support Stockton, moving west from Kansas. They engaged the Californios

The Battle of San Pascual was the largest on California soil. It signaled the end of the Californios' fight for independence. Artist's rendition by William Meyers. (Courtesy of the Franklin Delano Roosevelt Library.)

east of San Diego in the largest armed conflict ever to take place on California soil, the Battle of San Pascual. American losses forced Kearny to request help from Stockton, but once their troops of six hundred men combined, the Californios were no match for them. These troops moved toward Los Angeles from the south, while four hundred men under Lieutenant Colonel John C. Fremont converged on Los Angeles from the north. The Californios were quickly subdued and the Stars and Stripes were raised in the old *pueblo* plaza on January 10, 1847. The Treaty of Cahuenga Pass was signed three days later, making California a protectorate of the United States. Residents became U.S. citizens with their property rights protected.

On February 7, 1848, hostilities between Mexico and the United States over Texas ended with the signing of the Treaty of Guadalupe Hidalgo. Mexico ceded Alta California and her other lands north of the Rio Grande to the United States. The U.S. government paid $15 million to Mexico for California. Though the Californios' struggle to become autonomous within the Mexican republic had ended, their troubles had just begun.

With annexation to the United States, the Californios became an alien culture in their own land, and a culture clash of eminent proportions developed. Californians were forced to adapt to a new way of life, defending their property and reacting to a flagrant rejection of their customs and values. The predominant Protestant ethos of the American Yankees looked down on the Catholicism of the Californians. The Yankees believed that Manifest Destiny, a policy that decimated native populations, was their God-given right. God had given them this land, and the Californios had no business there. In addition, Americans had a general fear of racial mixture. They were judgmental and Hispanophobic.

Some Californios responded to their sudden change in status by becoming *bandidos*. *Bandidos* had established a life on the fringe of society long before, preying on the caravans of settlers who made their way between Mexico City and San Francisco. They were Spaniards who had lost their fortunes, or illegitimate sons of aristocrats who had Indian mothers, or Indians who resented the white man's intrusion on their land, or soldiers and sailors who had deserted, or runaway slaves from the West Indies— along with criminals, misfits, degenerates, and ne'er-do-wells. According to J. A. Burciago,

> By 1856, much of the land had changed to Yankee ownership through armed confrontation, legislation and swindles, as well as legitimate purchase. Lynchings of Mexicans became so common during the 1840s and 1850s that newspapers didn't even bother reporting them. Those Californios who resisted the invading Yankee immigrants became outlaws.

The Californio *bandidos* may have been models for Zorro. One of the most notorious *bandidos* harassing travelers along El Camino Real between Ventura and Monterey in the late 1820s and early 1930s was Domingo Hernandez. He is reported to have collected human ears on a thong of human hide. He skinned some of his victims and made their tanned hides into a formfitting jacket.

The *bandido* Tiburcio Vasquez, whose stories Douglas Fairbanks Sr.

shared with his guests, was an outlaw in the 1840s and 1850s. His people, however, revered him as an avenger who refused to submit to the Anglo conquest. Vasquez came from a family with long-standing roots in California, and his great-grandfather had helped found and settle the Presidio and mission of San Francisco. His grandfather had helped found the *pueblo* of San Jose and became its first *alcalde*.

Born in 1831 in Monterey, Tiburcio began his *bandido* life after a dance in Monterey around 1852 at which an Anglo sailor insulted the locals by not following a dance custom. A fight ensued, and the constable who had been called to quell the disturbance was killed. Vasquez was implicated along with two other youths, both of whom were captured and lynched.

Tiburcio became a hunted robber and served time in San Quentin. Upon his release, he resumed his *bandido* life, elusively avoiding capture and leaving his imprint of resistance against U.S. colonization. He was intelligent, resourceful, and commanding. One of his favorite tactics was to ride with his men in single file so they would appear to be one horseman to the drivers of a stagecoach. At the last moment, his gang would spread out and surprise their prey. Tales of Vasquez's romantic escapades abounded. He was eventually captured, and was hung after a lengthy, well-publicized trial.

California's greatest legendary badman was Joaquin Murieta. He terrorized Calaveras County for three years in the early 1850s. Captain Harry S. Love was assigned the task of finding the *bandido* and he formed a contingent of twenty men modeled after the Texas Rangers who chased the phantom bandit for three months. Finally, at Panoche Pass, a lavish gunfight ensued in which two men were killed. Convinced that the dead pair were Joaquin and his lieutenant, Three-Fingered Jack (otherwise known as Manuel Garcia), the rangers hacked off the head of one and the hand of the other and bottled their trophies in whiskey. The pickled head became a prized trophy in San Francisco and remained a popular attraction at a museum of frontier relics until it vanished in the city's 1906 earthquake. The identities of the two men were never confirmed.

Some question Joaquin's very existence, while others argue that the character seems likely. The legend might have been an amalgam, created by a hundred anonymous storytellers around a hundred campfires. In his heyday, Joaquin possessed an uncanny ability to strike everywhere at once;

The legendary California bandido
Tiburcio Vasquez.

to operate under many names and guises; and to agitate, organize, and unite all Spanish speakers in their antigringo crusade. The Murieta legend did have one profound effect in that it changed the image of the Californio. Prior to 1854, the Californio evoked comforting images of ranchos or *pueblos*, but after the spread of the Murieta legend, that image became one of terror.

An aspiring journalist, John Rollin Ridge, popularized Joaquin's life in 1857. Ridge made Murieta into a brigand of aristocratic bearing and romantic prowess, and most important, he offered revenge as a motive for Murieta's crimes. For Rollins nothing was "so dangerous in its consequences as injustice to individuals—whether it derives from prejudice of color or any other source, that a wrong done to one man is a wrong done to society and the world."

The Murieta legend may well have fueled McCulley's imagination in creating Zorro. Murieta's romantic prowess and aristocratic background, along with his concern for injustice to individuals, are certainly part of the Zorro legend.

Jack Powers, another California *bandido*, possessed skills that Zorro displayed and might also have influenced McCulley's character development. Powers was a roving robber baron like Robin Hood who stole from

JOAQUIN MURIETA

by YELLOW BIRD (John Rollin Ridge)

Yellow Bird, John Rollin Ridge, popularized the story of Joaquin Murieta, who became a character in episodes of Disney's Zorro series, as well as the 1998 film, *The Mask of Zorro*.

Captain Harry Love claimed to have killed Joaquin Murieta, cut off his head, and pickled it in whiskey for exhibit.

CAPTAIN HARRY LOVE

WILL BE EXHIBITED
FOR ONE DAY ONLY!
AT THE STOCKTON HOUSE!
THIS DAY, AUG. 12, FROM 9 A. M., UNTIL 6, P. M.
THE HEAD
Of the renowned Bandit!
JOAQUIN!
AND THE
HAND OF THREE FINGERED JACK!
THE NOTORIOUS ROBBER AND MURDERER.

"JOAQUIN" and "THREE-FINGERED JACK" were captured by the *State Rangers*, under the command of Capt. Harry Love, at the Arroyo Cantua, July 24th. No reasonable doubt can be entertained in regard to the identification of the head now on exhibition, as being that of the notorious robber, *Joaquin Murietta*, as it has been recognized by hundreds of persons who have formerly seen him.

The original of this 1853 broadside was 24 x 32½ inches in size and printed on yellow paper.

the wealthy while befriending the native, the underdog, and the poor. Powers rode with Salomon Pico and took over when Pico retired. For at least four years, he terrorized the coast counties from San Jose to San Diego, much as McCulley's Zorro was accused of terrorizing El Camino Real. Powers began as a soldier who maintained a reputation as a gentleman and was credited by H. Forsyth with being

> ...the best rider in the State...That was no mean compliment considering the fact that all Californians learned to ride almost before they learned to walk...

Powers was also reputed to be a

> ...gay spirit with an appreciation of human values, a love of adventure and a nostalgia for the chivalric Spanish days which were too fast passing....His prowess at riding helped to maintain his alibis and ubiquitous as he was, he seldom appeared in an area in which violence had been done. His operations were so shrewdly conducted that for years many people believed he was a persecuted and slandered man.

Once, Powers purchased a new suit for a confessed murderer's hanging because the man wanted to exit life with the dignity of a Castillian. On another occasion, Powers forwarded a petition to the governor requesting clemency for an Indian about to be hung for murder, but the ship with the governor's reply had not returned by the execution day so Powers persuaded the authorities to wait for the vessel's arrival. The Indian's sentence was commuted to life imprisonment.

McCulley could have been inspired in his creation of Zorro by Powers's riding ability, his shrewd operations, and his ubiquitous disappearances, along with his generosity and his sensitivity to the plight of individuals. A less likely historical figure to have inspired McCulley's Zorro was Salomon Pico, the leader of the gang Powers took over; however, there is no verification for this claim.

Born in 1821 near Salinas, the son of a soldier of the king of Spain, Salomon Pico received a land grant in 1844 near the foothills of the Sierras. When gold was discovered, Pico saw his cattle slaughtered and his pastures burned, but the final insult was the rape and beating of his wife. She died from her injuries, and Pico vowed revenge against every gringo he could get his hands on. Pico reportedly shared the gold he stole with family and friends. And he shared Domingo Hernandez's fondness for stringing his victims' ears on a leather thong that dangled from his saddle horn.

Throughout his long writing career, Johnston McCulley was a creator of fiction. He undoubtedly drew inspiration from many sources, both literary and historical, but just as one cannot pinpoint the historical period in which his stories take place, one can find no historical figure on whom Zorro is based. McCulley took elements of both the Spanish period and the Mexican period of early California and wove them into his Zorro stories, not for the purpose of creating a historically accurate depiction of old California but to energize, excite, and give local color to his audience. He did not evolve his stories from exact events that led to the creation of the state of California, but he did incorporate more actual cultural history than he has previously been credited for.

McCulley sprinkled his text with Spanish words. He placed swindles in tallow and hides at the center of his stories. Trading ships came into San Diego and later San Pedro. Admirers serenaded their ladies. An annual cattle slaughter occurred. Filial devotion to one's father was honored. Even the expert riding ability of women was depicted. These elements, among others, reflected real life in old California, though McCulley strove only to create a milieu, not to provide a history lesson.

Although the author did fabricate a Presidio that didn't exist in Los Angeles and mixed elements of two historical periods, it mattered little to his readers, for he succeeded in his goal of creating a colorful character who has become an intriguing legend in his own right. McCulley played with historical facts as easily as Zorro wielded his sword. The author toyed liberally with his setting and time period to make them suit his plots, developing a rich environment within which he wove adventurous tales for Señor Zorro's pursuit of justice.

While McCulley may have integrated authentic elements into his fiction, he didn't use his writing for social criticism. He accepted the established power structures of history, both social and political. He never confronted the repressive, paternalistic role of the church, and though

McCulley had the *neophytes* mistreated, it was by outsiders, not by the church padres themselves. Church doctrine prevailed without challenge. Likewise, the attitudes expressed by his characters with regard to bloodlines might have been authentic, but that does not excuse them or make them tolerable. Purity of blood creates ethnic divisions that are antithetical to democratic, pluralistic societies.

Despite his shortcomings, McCulley created a folk hero so familiar one doesn't even have to know his name. Inscribing the air with three rapid strokes identifies the fox.

ZORRO BY INSTALLMENT $\mathscr{4}$

$\mathcal{T}$HE transition from silence to sound in movie theaters around the country brought an opportunity to revive McCulley's masked fox. In 1936, eleven years after Douglas Fairbanks Sr. cracked his whip as the heroic son of Zorro in *Don Q*, Republic Pictures presented the first talking Zorro on screen in the crackling action adventure *The Bold Caballero*. Wells Root wrote and directed the film, which was based on a story idea by Zorro's creator, Johnston McCulley. The script, however, was a departure from McCulley's Zorro formula.

The story takes place in Santa Cruz rather than Reina de Los Angeles. Don Diego describes himself as a man from Mexico who offers himself in service to the newly appointed governor. The film opens with the declaration that Zorro, jailed and ready for hanging, has made one mistake—he got caught. The peons plead for Zorro's release from captivity. A message announcing the arrival of the new governor disrupts the proceeding. In the confusion, the Indians help Zorro escape. One peon snaps a whip, sending the horses racing off, pulling behind them the cart that holds Zorro. He wears an ominous mask that covers his entire head. Chased by soldiers, the cart crashes and Zorro escapes. He overcomes one soldier, leaving him dead with a Z carved in his chest.

In Root's adaptation, Diego sets in motion a plan to expose the evil commandant of Santa Cruz with the aid of a local padre and the peons. When the governor arrives to take over the province on orders from the king of Spain, the commandant kills him, leaving Zorro's mark, a Z, etched on the side of the governor's head. The governor's beautiful daughter, Isabella, is determined to rule in her father's place and to catch her father's presumed killer—Zorro. Diego charms his way into the confidence of the commandant of Santa Cruz, offering to arrange a marriage between the commandant and Isabella that would enable the soldier to gain legal control of the province.

With the bumbling grace of a Cyrano de Bergerac imposter, the commandant serenades Isabella, who gazes down on him from her balcony. He mouths the words and seems to strum his guitar while Diego does the actual singing and playing under the balcony. Convinced of Isabella's kind heart, Diego is determined to make her see the commandant's cruelty to the peons. The commandant has jailed the sons of the peons, threatening to send them to work in the mines unless they each pay one piece of gold. Zorro steals the reward money for his capture that has been hung in the town square. He then passes the money to the boys' mothers so they can redeem their sons. Diego cleverly steers Isabella to the plaza against the commandant's orders and she is able to witness his cruelty. In a wild climax, Diego and the peons battle the commandant's soldiers to victory.[3]

Robert Livingstone wore the mantle of Don Diego Vega and Zorro. The rising western box office star was most well-known for his role as Stony Brooke, the lead cowboy in *The Three Mesquiteers*. He played in twenty-nine of their pictures between 1936 and 1941, except for a stretch in 1938 and 1939 when he was temporarily promoted to romantic melodramas. During his absence, a young unknown actor named John Wayne took over the part. Wayne eventually moved from the Stony Brooke role to his career-making portrayal of Ringo Kid in *Stagecoach*, but Livingstone met with little success in nonwestern parts and returned to the Mesquiteers' range.

For the role of Zorro, Livingstone had the benefit of learning to fence from Hollywood's master sword specialist, Fred Cavens. Livingstone told writer B. Price:

Yes, Fred knew his business all right. He taught us all. In addition to myself, screen Zorros Fairbanks, Tyrone Power and Guy Williams all benefitted by his tutelage. Fred passed away in 1962 and has been sorely missed around the studios. As a swordsman, he had no peer.

Though Republic's first Zorro entry in the marketplace was *The Bold Caballero*, a sixty-seven-minute feature film, the studio's forte was action serials. Known in the industry as charterplays, these serial stories featured continuing characters and story lines, with each episode ending in a dangerous, unresolved situation. Common gimmicks often left the hero or the heroine hanging from a ledge or a cliff, which prompted the phrase "cliffhanger" ending. Audiences grew more sophisticated during the Roaring Twenties and adult interest in the melodramatic dramas of the silent-era films waned. The target market for the matinee set shifted to a younger audience. As the Great Depression spread, cliffhangers offered inexpensive escapist fantasies to a broad segment of the population.

When the Republic Studio organization was taken over by Herbert Yates in 1935, the chapterplay was poised to enter its golden age, the period from 1938 to 1944. Nicknamed the Thrill Factory, Republic evolved from the consolidation of a number of minor companies, including Monogram Pictures and Mascot Films. Mascot had been run by Nat Levine and financed by Yates's Consolidated Film Industries. Monogram had a good distribution network, and Consolidated had the best technical facilities in Hollywood. Republic's ranch locations, laboratory facilities, mobile gear, skilled crews, and talented composers gave the studio's thrillers a look unmatched by any productions from smaller companies.

Republic's trademark was fast-paced action with unmistakable sound effects, excellent miniature and mechanical effects, spectacular stunt gags, thrilling musical scores, slick photography, fine performances by its stock company, and exciting story lines. Even though the productions were aimed at a young audience, they were polished, slick, and impressive. The Republic chapterplays set the standard for "B" pictures. No studio ever equaled the Thrill Factory's special effects and stunt work, nor did anyone else generate higher sceen quality on such low budgets.

Yates ran Republic with an iron hand. Known as the Old Man (and other less pleasant nicknames), he counted every penny. Theater bookings went for $5 per episode; consequently, no one got rich working at the Thrill Factory, but they prided themselves on the films they produced. Total production budgets for twelve-part serials averaged between $140,000 and $180,000.

Republic owned the Trucolor process, developed at Consolidated Film Industries, a type of tinted coloring that replaced black-and-white processing. Although primitive by today's standards, and not particularly natural or good-looking, Trucolor was better than what other studios were using, and it gave a tremendous boost to "B" western stars such as Roy Rogers, Gene Autry, and John Wayne.

Republic productions were organized in units controlled by the line producer. The producer had a team of writers with whom the screenplays were developed. Once a chapterplay was approved by Yates and his board of directors, it was budgeted by the production department and overseen by the unit manager. Republic assigned a full-time personal manager to each serial shooting unit and usually two assistant directors per film. The art department head assigned the unit art director; the sound department head assigned the production mixer, boom operator, and recordist; the camera department assigned the director of photography; and so on. The casting department selected the players and chose a stunt crew from its six full-time stuntmen. The location staff made all off–studio lot arrangements, and wardrobes came from the studio warehouse or were leased or purchased from Western Costume.

With the script complete; the budget allocated; the cast and crew assigned; locations arranged; and sets, props, and wardrobe ready, the directors were brought into the project. They had at least one, but never more than two, weeks to prepare for the beginning of principal photography. During those few days of getting familiar with the script and going over other preproduction planning, directors could make minor suggestions and requests, perhaps for a specific cinematographer or sound mixer, but these were never the directors' final decisions. They were treated as requests. Only the various department heads could make the requested changes in personnel, which then had to be approved by the studio production manager and cleared through the line producer who oversaw the entire unit.

Directors were given scripts with not only dialogue but also with every camera angle, which they were required to follow. They did have some leeway in staging fistfights and other action segments, but even these were usually scripted out beforehand. The line producers and writers, in conjunction with studio management, created the style, look, and sound of Republic serials. Directors did not function as creative geniuses but were more accurately described as "on-set traffic cops keeping the shows moving." On completion of the project, directors did not make editing decisions.

Stunt coordinator Enos "Yakima" Canutt developed the fistfighting style seen in all Republic films. Canutt worked out the technique over a number of films with John Wayne. It became an art form among the stuntmen at the Thrill Factory. The young director William Witney adapted a technique used by well-known director Busby Berkeley. After rehearsing a fight, he shot the scene from one camera angle, then put the camera at a different angle, rehearsed and shot that angle, creating more exciting and better staged fight sequences.

Zorro Rides Again began its run on December 3, 1937, as the first chapterplay based on the character of Zorro. Each of the twelve chapters in the Republic series ran nineteen minutes—with the exception of the first chapter, which commanded thirty minutes of screen time. The team of writers included Morgan Cox, Ronald Davidson, John Rathmell, Barry Shipman, Franklyn Adreon, and Sherman Lowe.

The serial featured John Carroll as James Vega, the great-grandson of the original Zorro, and the setting was far removed from McCulley's original *pueblo*. The writers put the fox in a modern western, incorporating trains, trucks, phones, and planes into the plot. This Zorro was equally adept with a gun or his whip but lacked his identifiable cape and sword.

The plot followed the attempts by El Lobo and his crew of evil henchmen to gain control of the California-Yucatan Railroad Company. El Lobo was really an unscrupulous investment broker named Marsden. The railroad was being built by Phillip Andrews and his sister Joyce with the firm's largest stockholder being Don Manuel Vega. Vega sends an urgent letter to his nephew, James, hoping that with the blood of Zorro in his veins, James will be able to help fight off Marsden's men. Unfortunately, the young man appears to be a weak and spineless fop. Of course, the audience knows that James is only pretending to be cowardly. He dons an outfit

Zorro *Rides Again* (1937) was the first of the Republic Zorro serials.

Zorro wraps up one of El Lobo's men with his whip in Zorro *Rides Again*.

ZORRO IN A
GHTY MOTION PICTURE
F THE VIOLENT WEST!!

Beware
the
dreaded
Z

starring
JOHN CARROLL and
DUI

with HE
an

Directors
Written
RANKLYN A

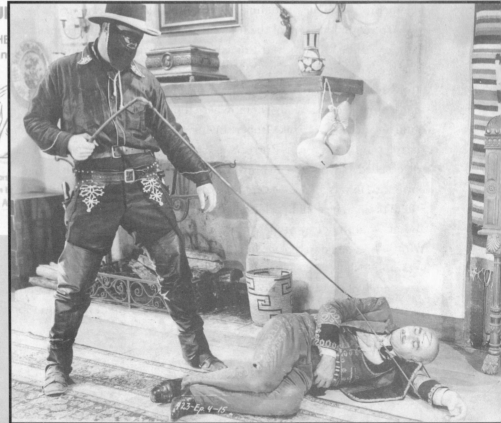

similar to his famous ancestor and begins a one-man war against Marsden's cutthroats. When Don Manuel is killed in a raid, James vows to avenge his uncle's death. His efforts continually put him in harm's way.

True to the genre, each chapter ends with a cliffhanger. At the conclusion of one episode, Zorro's foot is caught in the track as a train barrels toward him. In another, Zorro is trapped in a conflagration, and other episodes leave Zorro inside a runaway railroad car, trapped in a dynamited tunnel, or leaping from railcar to railcar before losing his balance and plunging toward the tracks. In the finale, Zorro uses his wireless to locate the bad guys and bring them to justice.

The twelve chapter titles were typical for serials: *Death From the Sky, The Fatal Minute, Juggernaut, Unmasked, Sky Pirates, The Fatal Shot, Burning Embers, Plunge of Peril, Tunnel of Terror, Trapped, Right of Way*, and *Retribution*.

William Witney and John English teamed to direct the serial *Zorro Rides Again*, which was the first joint effort of what became a peerless serial partnership. Chapterplays customarily used two directors. One directed shooting while the other prepared the next day's work, or one filmed the interior sequences while the other was on location. English and Witney shared assignments so well that they piloted seventeen consecutive serials together for Republic, including *The Lone Ranger* and *Dick Tracy*.

To remind viewers of the first Zorro adventure film, Fairbanks's *The Mark of Zorro*, Witney's and English's Zorro chapterplay featured a full-length portrait of Don Diego. The beaming figure in the painting bore a strong resemblance to Fairbanks. It swung away to reveal a secret passage that led into Zorro's ready room, where a pinto horse and a black riding outfit awaited Carroll. Like Robert Livingstone in *The Bold Caballero*, John Carroll sang in his role as Zorro. Singing cowboys were in vogue, and Carroll excelled, having worked his way around the world crooning in a ringing baritone. He was also an exceptional all-around athlete and found it difficult to pretend he couldn't ride a horse. The relationship between the actor and his youthful director was initially rocky. Carroll was new to film, and Witney threatened to replace him unless he got down to serious work. The actor did his job.

Much of the success of *Zorro Rides Again* came from the superb stunt work of Yakima Canutt, who doubled as Zorro. He might have had more actual screen time than Carroll, having previously stunt-doubled as Zorro for Livingstone in *The Bold Caballero*. His impressive abilities stemmed from his rodeo riding. Canutt had started young, riding his first bucking horse at age eleven. He won a riding and roping contest at sixteen, tied for the world championship at twenty, and then won it at twenty-one. On a rodeo tour in South America, he learned to handle the Argentine whip. He earned tropies as the world champion bronco buster in 1917 and 1920, and retired undefeated as All-Around Cowboy Champion of the World in 1917, 1919, 1920, 1921, and 1923. In addition, Canutt won the Theodore Roosevelt Trophy at both the Cheyenne and Pendleton roundups, was an expert rifle and pistol shot, and could transfer from the back of a running horse to anything that moved.

Noah Beery, the brother of actor Wallace Beery, had played the boastful Sergeant Gonzales in Fairbanks's silent Zorro film. He was cast in *Zorro Rides Again* as the evil Marsden. Beery was known as "Public Badman Number One" in film. Beery's scenes were all shot in one day.

Although *Zorro Rides Again* was Republic's first serial based on or inspired by the Zorro character, it was not the last, nor was it Republic's best Zorro chapterplay. Six other serials were produced: *Zorro's Fighting Legion*, 1939; *Zorro's Black Whip*, 1944; *Son of Zorro*, 1947; *Ghost of Zorro*, 1949; *Don Daredevil Rides Again*, 1951; and *Man with the Steel Whip*, 1954. Zorro's name appears in four of these titles even though the character Zorro was not even in the stories. Republic utilized extensive stock footage from the previous chapterplays, capitalizing on the public's fascination with the fox. The heroes of *Don Daredevil* and *Man with the Steel Whip* even wore Zorro-like outfits to match the older footage.

Zorro's Black Whip featured Linda Stirling, the reigning queen of Republic's serials. Even though the title was the only place Zorro was mentioned, McCulley did get an attribution in the credits for his character. The setting is the territory of Idaho in 1889, where law-abiding citizens favor statehood. Clad in a Zorro-like costume, Stirling portrayed the Whip, assuming the role from her brother, who was killed in chapter one. Her newspaper tries to campaign for statehood, making it a target of a reign of terror from the sinister forces opposed to the coming of law and order. Stirling relies on her leading man, George J. Lewis, to help run the newspaper. Lewis plays Vic Gordon, a secret agent of the government sent to investigate the trouble. In classic serial format, the heroine plunges off the road in a runaway wagon, headed toward jagged rocks far below; is almost blown up in a vault; falls off her horse while unconscious; is trapped in a shack buried by an avalanche; and becomes the object of a pitchfork attack, among other perils. In the final chapter, the villian is trampled to death by the Whip's horse. The reign of terror ends and the vote for statehood carries.

In *Son of Zorro* (1947), actor George Turner played the man behind the mask. How he became Zorro was explained away with one line in chapter one, "Zorro was an ancestor on my mother's side." The setting for this serial was the post–Civil War West, and Turner has returned home to resume his law practice. He finds a ring of crooks operating the county government, bleeding the people with exorbitant taxes, and protecting the bandits who raid the ranches. They follow orders from a mysterious indi-

Linda Stirling poses with her whip as the only female Zorro in the 1944 *Zorro's Black Whip*.

A REPUBLIC SERIAL IN 13 CHAPTERS

SON of ZORRO

featuring
GEORGE TURNER
PEGGY STEWART
ROY BARCROFT
EDWARD CASSIDY

Directed by SPENCER BENNET and FRED C. BRANNON

Chapter 2. THE DEADLY MILLSTONE

George Turner starred as Son of Zorro (1947).

vidual called "the Chief." Notable among Turner's hair-raising cliffhangers is the episode in which he gets pinned behind a wagon with blazing barrels of coal oil rolling down on him and his leading lady, Peggy Stewart. The tall, good-looking Turner had some boxing experience and tried to throw realistic-looking punches during filming, but the stunt team quickly showed him the error of his ways and made sure he performed the stunts as planned. Much of the footage was original, but some of the chapter endings came from earlier serials such as *Zorro's Black Whip* and *Daredevils of the West*.

Ghost of Zorro featured Clayton Moore, who later portrayed the Lone Ranger in the television series. He was a popular actor with a pleasant voice, and he effectively handled action sequences and rode well. Moore played an American grandson of Zorro named Ken Munson. He, too, masqueraded as something of a dandy to conceal the fact that, dressed as Zorro, he roamed the countryside fighting a ruthless gang who opposed the coming of the telegraph.

THE WEST'S FAMOUS MYSTERY RIDER BACK IN ACTION!

GHOST OF ZORRO

A REPUBLIC SERIAL IN 12 CHAPTERS

Chapter 11
RUNAWAY STAGECOACH

Country of Origin U.S.A 49-6841

Clayton Moore, later famous as the Lone Ranger, starred in the *Ghost of Zorro* (1949).

Don Daredevil Rides Again and *Man with the Steel Whip*, starring Ken Curtis (of later *Gunsmoke* fame as Festus) and Richard Simmons, respectively, used Zorro-like costumes so stock footage from the earlier Zorro serials could be utilized. *Don Daredevil* thwarted a land-grab scheme, and *Man with the Steel Whip* found the hero convincing a white man to leave a rich vein of gold alone in Indian territory.

Republic's only truly authentic Zorro serial was *Zorro's Fighting Legion*. It is generally regarded as one of the best of the Thrill Factory's early chapterplays. Released on December 16, 1939, this serial returned to McCulley's roots in the early 1800s. In *The Curse of Capistrano*, Zorro rallied the caballeros to his side, notifying them to be ready to ride in masks like himself. The caballeros called themselves the Avengers. The writing team of Ronald Davidson, Franklyn Andreon, Morgan Cox, Sol Shor, and

Barney Sarecky gave Zorro an equivalent of the Avengers, naming the fox's allies Zorro's Fighting Legions. They, too, rode with masks, hats, and matching short capes with a Z on them. The writers even took a line from McCulley when Diego asks Manuel, one of the crooked council members, for help: "These are troublesome times and I am a man of peace."

The story is set in Mexico after its war of independence from Spain. Benito Juarez needs a steady flow of gold from the San Medolita gold mine in order to establish foreign credit, but four villainous men on the ruling council oppose him. One masquerades as the Indian Yaqui god Don del Oro.[4] He attempts to rouse the Indians against the whites, to wreck the republic, and to make himself emperor of Mexico. A legion to fight these enemies of the republic had been formed by Don Francisco but upon his death, Francisco's nephew, who is visiting from California, takes the don's place. Zorro, as usual, conceals his identity by masquerading as the foppish Diego.

Reed Hadley played the dual hero, with Sheila Darcy as the female lead. She was cast as the ward of the deceased Don Francisco. Her brother, Ramon, played by William Corson, was Zorro's chief ally and avenger. Although Hadley's Zorro was devoid of Fairbanks's sly, playful sparkle, his Diego has been lauded. Reed all but raised his hands in mock horror when Zorro's name was mentioned and wielded his hankie in the best tradition of Diego imitators. Reacting to news of a five-hundred peso reward for Zorro's capture, Hadley's insipid Diego tells the ruling council, "Oh, but is that enough? I should think his capture would be worth much more than that—a thousand pesos at least!" And later, when accused by the council of being Zorro, he demurs that he's flattered.

Chapter titles for the twelve episodes were: *The Golden God, The Flaming "Z," Descending Doom, The Bridge of Peril, The Decoy, Zorro to the Rescue, The Fugitive, Flowing Death, The Golden Arrow, Mystery Wagon, Face to Face,* and *Unmasked.* The initial chapter ran for twenty-eight minutes, with subsequent chapters each being seventeen minutes long. Cliffhangers in *Zorro's Fighting Legion* include the masked hero swinging on the end of a cut suspension bridge, standing under a rapidly descending mine shaft elevator, being caught on a runaway stagecoach that explodes after colliding with a shipment of munitions, facing a raging onslaught of water released inside a mine shaft, getting trapped in a water barrel that

The only authentic Zorro serial starred Reed Hadley in Zorro's *Fighting Legion* (1939).

is sinking in a river, falling into a fiery pit, and even having a movable wall closing in to crush him.

Republic serials routinely used pulse-pounding music to enhance the action and William Lava's original score was no exception. Another feature

Zorro unmasks Don del Oro in Zorro's *Fighting Legion* (1939).

that kept audiences glued to their seats was the fantastic stunt work. Ya-kima Canutt's stunts again sparkled, particularly in chapter seven with one memorable maneuver on a stagecoach. Zorro/Canutt leaps on the two lead horses of the stage, and lowers himself under the rigging as the horses race along. He slides along the dirt road, flipping under the stage and coming up on the back of the coach. He then climbs onto the top, overtakes the stagecoach driver, fights with him, pushes the driver off the stage, and climbs back down on the horses as they separate from the coach, releasing the stagecoach to crash.

A number of Zorro's signature behaviors were created in this serial. Though the fox rides a white horse, for the first time audiences see the masked hero rear on his mount. Zorro leaps across a gorge on horseback to escape pursuers, an action sequence seen numerous times in the 1990–1994 New World Zorro television series. Zorro swings from light fixtures. He slices the waistband of an opponent, causing the man's pants to fall. All of these elements were later used in Disney's Zorro series.

The mask Zorro wore was a nose and eye shield that has since become associated with the Lone Ranger. It fit on his face like sunglasses with a mesh extension that hung down to cover Zorro's mustache. Zorro also wore a holster with two pearl-handled six shooters that were worn backward in their holster, a style emulated by boys all across America.

In 1938, the quality of films produced by Hollywood changed dramatically. Lavish productions like *Gone With the Wind, Casablanca, The Wizard of Oz,* and *Citizen Kane,* plus popular adventure films such as *The Adventures of Robin Hood,* met with huge audience approval. Twentieth Century-Fox was looking for a major adventure drama to produce. Exposure during the 1930s for the fox, Señor Zorro, provided them with the perfect vehicle.

TYRONE POWER
DONS THE MASK

*I*N 1940, the legendary fox reappeared on the silver screen in full verbal eloquence and dashing splendor. Twentieth Century-Fox could think of no better hero to garner their audience share of the day's successful adventure film genre than their namesake and McCulley's own fox, Señor Zorro. The actor chosen to play their masked hero was the romantic heartthrob Tyrone Power. Director Rouben Mamoulian was lauded for his stylish reinterpretation of the Fairbanks masterpiece. The notable pairing of Basil Rathbone (as Zorro's nemesis, Capitán Esteban) and Power drew raves. Their swordplay was as sharp as any in screen history. Power could not match Fairbanks's playful panache or his stunt athletics—these would be difficult for any actor to emulate—but the overall embellishments of the story gave this version of *The Mark of Zorro* its own distinctions.

Power spent considerably more time on screen without his mask, even in the climactic dueling scene. Consequently, his Diego persona was more polished than his masked hero. The studio might have wanted to showcase his impeccable looks, but Power was a serious, competent actor who came from a line of fine performers. His father and his great-

PRODUCED BY
RAYMOND GRIFFITH
DIRECTED BY
ROUBEN MAMOULIAN
SCREEN PLAY BY JOHN TAINTOR FOOTE
ADAPTATION BY GARRETT FORT
BASED ON THE STORY BY
JOHNSTON McCULLEY

TYRONE
POWE

Tyrone Power and Linda Darnell starred in the 1940 remake of *The Mark of Zorro.*

98   *Zorro Unmasked.*

Power as the dashing Zorro.

grandfather were both actors—and were both named Tyrone Power. His great-grandfather played major Irish roles on the London stage, and his father was an acclaimed Shakespearean actor on the American stage.

Tyrone Power was a protégé of Darryl Zanuck at Twentieth Century-Fox, one of many stars under long-term contract. His looks were not his only asset. He was an adaptable, versatile actor. Power was used consistently by Zanuck—in fact, some critics say he was overused—because he could do such a competent job with nearly everything he was assigned. He was Zanuck's most-favored star, with a chauffeured limousine and access to the executive steam room, one of few actors so honored. Zanuck cast Power in three categories of roles: swashbucklers in the athletic tradition of Douglas Fairbanks Sr.; film idol roles with the heavily scented feeling of Valentino movies; and breezy comedies.

Power's looks made him far more romantic than Fairbanks, and he was a much better actor than Valentino. He played comedies without a brash or cocky air. Due to the control the studio exercised over his image, his performances were always maintained within a delicate line of control. Neither rage nor passion could be released. His sarcasm was always fleeting so the audience wouldn't see the trait as ingrained in Power's character.

Power had higher aspirations that were held in check by the studio. His biographer, Fred Guiles, suggested that Power would have liked to become the American equivalent of Sir Laurence Olivier. He possessed the skills as an actor, along with the voice and the dash, to secure his place in American acting.

He was proud of his craft and was always well-prepared for work, always knowing his lines and being on time for every shoot. Years of high salaries sustained him through two marriages and two divorces, allowing him to live an extremely comfortable life.

In the end, these perks were too appealing to give up. He was never able to cut loose from the idol-makers of Hollywood who controlled his career, and the passion he needed to pursue Olivier's stature was eroded by the comforts of success. Moreover, his love life complicated his work life. His numerous affairs left the Hollywood landscape littered with broken hearts, among them Loretta Young, Judy Garland, and Lana Turner.

Doubtless there were countless broken hearts among his screen fans, too, for Twentieth Century-Fox churned up his fans to maximize his screen potential. He attracted crowds everywhere he went, even at the end of his career. Though the constant attention must have been an infuriating intrusion, he was cool and handled the adulation with aplomb. After World War II, he and his good friend Cesar Romero did a multicountry promotional tour in Latin America. (Twentieth Century-Fox had made him into an overnight idol by dubbing *The Mark of Zorro* into six idioms of Spanish. The studio wanted to capitalize on the Hispanic hero and expand its market share in the Spanish-speaking countries.) The two actors were mobbed everywhere by exuberant fans.

Tyrone Edmund Power was born in Cincinnati on May 5, 1914, to Francis Tyrone Power and Patia Reaume, a drama teacher and Shakespearean actress. He was a delicate child, and his doctor felt he would benefit from the mild climate of California, a fortuitous situation, since Tyrone's father had been offered work in silent films. The family moved to Hollywood, where the elder Power starred in the D. W. Griffth film *Dream Street* (1921). Tyrone's parents soon divorced, and Patia moved her two children back to Cincinnati. Tyrone became very serious about acting, and while working at a movie house during the summer between his sophomore and junior years of high school, he studied films obsessively. He kept a notebook in which he analyzed the structure of each movie he saw and the star's performance.

There was a tacit agreement in Tyrone's family that as soon as he graduated from high school, he would find his way in the theater. His mother had instilled in him a respect for the acting profession as a noble pursuit. He had great respect for his father's stage success, and at sixteen, he wrote to his dad confessing his desire to be a film star and asking for his advice. His father responded with words that lay the groundwork for Tyrone's future in acting. He recommended singing and dancing lessons, general calisthenics, learning to enunciate properly, speaking aloud formally once a day, studying facial expressions in the mirror, learning body control to move gracefully, and finally, listening intelligently to what another actor is saying.

Lloyds of London (1936) was Power's first starring film role. When the studio announced that Power was replacing Don Ameche, the slated female star, Loretta Young, opted out. After the film's success, Young realized her hastiness about working with a new face and subsequently became romantically involved with Power.

Tyrone was able to show the many talents he had polished by following his father's advice. By the time Zanuck decided to resurrect *The Mark of Zorro*, Power could dance, fence, enunciate, and control his facial expressions and gestures with grace and skill. He had attained sufficient skill with a blade to not require a stunt double in the fencing scenes. His wry, sardonic, natural wit was also finally exploited on screen. Power enjoyed everything about the film, from Diego's foppish magic tricks to the dashing exuberance of the masked defender of justice.

Zanuck hired Rouben Mamoulian to direct the picture in a moment of contrition because he had refused to loan Power to Columbia Pictures for Mamoulian's previous film, *Golden Boy* (1939). Their combined talents turned *The Mark of Zorro* into a successful box office hit. The actor and director formed a close friendship as well, and subsequently worked together in a remake of a Rudolph Valentino film, *Blood and Sand*.

Mamoulian shot *The Mark of Zorro* as a satire to capitalize on Power's flair for parody. However, some reviewers missed the satire, like the reviewer at the *New York Times* who noted that Power's performance "rather overdoes the swashing and the swash, (and) is more beautiful than bold." The director's opening scene in which fencers practice their swordsmanship while riding through posts, and severing surrogate heads from shoulders with their swords, remains as captivating today for its precision as it did over fifty years ago.

The supporting cast, particularly Basil Rathbone, garnered distinction for their fine performances. Rathbone's skill as a fencer was never more stunningly showcased than by Mamoulian's direction in the climactic duel between Diego and Capitán Esteban. Rathbone believed that the swordplay in *The Mark of Zorro* demonstrated the beauty and mastery of fencing as an art. His description of film duels offers an insight into the incredible artistry necessary to capture the power of sword combat on screen. Writer R. Jones noted,

> All duels are fought in exactly the same manner in which lines are
> learned. When you are duelling against someone in a motion picture

you are not making a response to his move. You know exactly what is coming next. Every phase of a fight is learned so that you're not guessing any moment. You know what your move against your opponent is. You are aware that you are holding in your hand a very dangerous weapon and, therefore, you are careful. I was never injured personally, and I never injured anyone. . . . These scenes take, Lord knows, how many set-ups. For instance, they will not take a long shot alone; they'll take a master shot, then a medium shot and then take some close-ups. Any fight that lasts five minutes on the screen could easily take two days to shoot.

Rathbone complimented Power, his on-screen opponent to journalist T. Weaver, "Tyrone could have fenced Errol Flynn into a cocked hat." Ever the gentleman, Rathbone neglected to mention the two deep forehead cuts that Power accidentally inflicted on him during the sword fight. Fred Cavens, the great Hollywood swordsman, who had trained Fairbanks for the 1920 version of *The Mark of Zorro*, also coached Power. In fact, he gave the actor the same sword Fairbanks had used in the silent film.

The gravelly voice of Eugene Pallette, as Father Felipe, gave a noteworthy dimension to his expansive character. Female star Linda Darnell played Lolita, providing the requisite dark-haired, dark-eyed beauty necessary to capture Zorro's heart. The memorable musical score for Power's *The Mark of Zorro* was composed by Alfred Newman. Zorro's theme song gives an upbeat vibrancy to his chase scenes. The dramatic screenplay was written by John Tainton Foote and was adapted by Garret Fort and Bess Meredyth.

Film Synopsis

Diego, reputedly the best student fencer at his program in Madrid, has been ordered back home by his father. At a farewell party, Diego portrays California as a "land of gentle missions, happy peons, sleepy caballeros, and everlasting boredom, where a man can only marry, grow fat children, and watch his vineyards grow." With no troublesome Indians to fight, Diego kisses his sword and heaves it into the ceiling, telling his friends, "Leave it there and think of me."

As he is rowed to shore in Los Angeles, Diego learns that the *alcalde*

Basil Rathbone and Tyrone Power engage in their classic cinematic fencing duel.

is a reviled man, and he sees the evidence when a mute driver takes him to town. The driver's tongue has been cut out for speaking against the *alcalde*'s taxes. But Diego's father is the *alcalde*!

The situation is clarified when Diego arrives at his family home in the plaza. Upon learning that his father has resigned, Diego assumes his foppish persona. He withdraws his handkerchief, and when queried by Capitán Esteban about his ability with a blade, Diego demurs that swordplay is a violent business. At the captain's insistence, Diego meets the new *alcalde*, Luis Quintero.

Inez, Quintero's wife, is enamored with the refined Diego. She invites him shopping with her on the visiting merchant ship. Dripping with sarcasm, Diego enthuses about choosing fabric: "I love the shimmer of satin and silk, the matching of one delicate shade against the other, choosing scents and lotions—carnation, crushed lily, musk."

When her niece, Lolita, questions Inez about Diego, she warns Lolita to cool her *hidalgo* blood or she'll put her in a convent.

Diego is greeted by his mother on his arrival home. The padre, a vocal rabble-rouser, colorfully describes Los Angeles as "a stench in the nostrils of heaven," in need of an avenging "angel with a flaming sword." The padre wants Alejandro to lead the caballeros in a revolt against the *alcalde*. Alejandro refuses to "rebel against the government I served for thirty years."

Diego's observation that the *alcalde*'s family was pleasant prompts the surly padre to utter, "Pleasant scorpions" and "Agreeable rattlesnakes." Diego urges calm amid the day's heat, but he is challenged by the padre to "be moved by injustice and cruelty." To divert the conversation, Diego demonstrates a magic trick with a fan.

Zorro rides into the plaza in daylight. He pulls down a new tax order, then carves a Z in a soldier's jacket before chasing the troops back to the barracks. He tacks up a replacement poster, which warns, "Luis Quintero is a thief and an enemy of the people and cannot long escape my vengeance . . . Zorro."

Zorro proceeds to rob the *alcalde* and his wife in their carriage, wearing a mask over his nose and mouth. He takes the money Quintero is hiding from Esteban plus Inez's necklace and leaves a Z in the carriage's upholstery.

That night, Zorro visits Quintero in his office, snuffing out a candle with the tip of his sword. He suggests that the *alcalde* resign, appointing Don Alejandro in his place. Binding Quintero to his chair, Zorro balances a sword with its tip in the *alcalde*'s neck, but vanishes before Esteban enters. The shaken *alcalde* points out a Z carved in the wall.

A search commences. In a friar's robe, Zorro takes refuge in the chapel where Lolita has come to pray. She doesn't want to be forced into a convent, to which Zorro replies, "The sin would be in sending you."

Zorro woos Lolita with brief words: "You are more radiant than a morning in June." She swoons: "Never have I heard such words before. . . . They make me lose my breath."

She notices the sword sticking out of the friar's robe as Inez comes looking for her, fearing that Zorro is on the loose. The fake friar inadvertently loses his mask before vanishing. A soldier retrieves it and is killed fighting Zorro.

Zorro escapes by jumping over a wall and onto his horse. He rears on a bridge, and seeing soldiers closing in on both sides, jumps with the horse into the water.

Zorro relieves Esteban of his taxes, after which he appears at Fray Felipe's as Diego. He gives the money to the astonished padre. As if beginning a magic trick, Diego pulls out his Zorro mask.

Zorro posts a new message in the plaza: "Luis Quintero will soon resign and leave for Spain or his blood will drip from my sword." Afterward, Diego appears in the *alcalde*'s office, where Quintero warily shows him Zorro's mark. The crafty fox suggests that it is "too bad your sense of duty keeps you here."

Esteban suggests an alliance between the Vega and Quintero families pairing Lolita with Diego. The *alcalde* offers Alejandro money as an inducement, but Alejandro won't consider such a match. Diego, however, wants to see Lolita.

He arrives late for dinner at the Quinteros', attributing his tardiness to bathwater that was too tepid. In an aside to Inez, Esteban extends the metaphor, anticipating a tepid married life. During an outdoor garden dinner, Diego does magic tricks with his hankie as mariachis play. Scorning Diego, Lolita expresses admiration for Zorro while the contemptuous Esteban jabs an orange with his knife.

Inez requests that Diego demonstrate the latest dance steps with Lolita. His ardor entices Lolita, but after the dance Diego feigns fatigue. Lolita flees angrily to her room. Within moments of Diego's asking the *alcalde* for Lolita's hand, Zorro tosses a flower into her window. He appears on her

Zorro surprises the *alcalde*, pointedly suggesting that he resign.

Hidden beneath a friar's robe, Zorro woos Lolita in the church.

balcony in the bandit-style mask, ready to make a confession. Interrupted by a knock at her door, Zorro retreats to the balcony. Quintero chastises her for running out on her fiancé. He is amused to find Diego hiding on her balcony. When Quintero leaves, Lolita berates Diego for pretending to be Zorro. Once he recalls his words in the chapel, she knows he is Zorro. The lovers kiss and Diego flees.

Inez selfishly promises to support Lolita if she refuses to marry Diego but Lolita demurs that she could "learn to tolerate Diego."

The *alcalde* subsequently hears that a priest has been lashed in the square for resisting taxes and sees Gonzales tossed over the wall with a *Z* carved on his chest.

Esteban appears at the mission, demanding the church money. Fray Felipe refuses, pulling a sword. They engage, but the padre is quickly disarmed, whereupon the captain threatens to hang him.

Lolita travels to the Vega hacienda to warn Diego about the padre's fate. Alejandro won't even welcome her, but Diego goes into action.

He surprises the *alcalde* that night. Diego compliments Quintero on putting his civic duty before his own safety. A servant summons Quintero to the flooded wine cellar, where open casks marked with *Z*s have been emptied. Footprints lead to a corner with no apparent exit.

The *alcalde* signs his resignation nervously, but Esteban rips it up. He challenges the "popinjay," Diego, to a duel. Stretching in preparation for the fight, Esteban takes a few swipes at a candle. He cuts it in two, knocking the candle off its base. Diego slices at a candle, too, but it remains unchanged. Haughtily, Esteban thinks Diego has missed completely, only to see Diego lift the top of the still-burning candle from its base. He has sliced it perfectly.

The duel begins. The fencing master has met his equal. Diego is shoved against the wall, bruising his shoulder, to which he responds, "I needed that scratch to awaken me!" He runs Esteban through the heart. The captain slides down the wall, a picture falling behind him and revealing the carved *Z*.

Meanwhile, the soldiers discover a secret stairway from the cellar and emerge in the *alcalde*'s office. Quintero orders Diego arrested as Zorro, since only he could have known about the secret stairway in his former

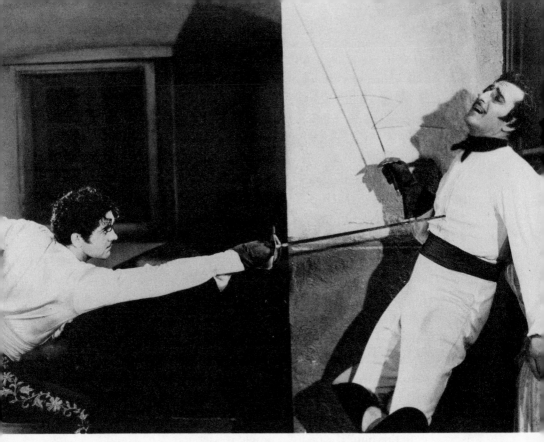

In the climactic duel, Diego kills Esteban, exposing Zorro's mark in the wall.

home. Also, Diego has mud on his boots and handles his sword like the "devil from hell."

Quintero summons the town to witness Zorro's execution. Jailed with Fray Felipe, Diego lures their guard close to the cell door with a magic trick, grabs his gun, and forces him to open the door. He hides the guard under the bed and puts the weapon in the padre's robe.

Quintero brings the caballeros into the jail to show off Zorro. Unimpressed, Alejandro calls Diego his "worthless, trick-playing offspring." Diego uses his magic trick ruse to garner attention, then swings open the cell door. He grabs a soldier's sword and leads the caballeros in battle. The padre escorts the *alcalde* through the fighting throng, whacking soldiers with his gun as he reverently offers, "God forgive me."

Quintero resigns, appointing Don Alejandro as his successor. The padre will accompany Quintero to San Pedro. Diego and Lolita plan to "marry, grow fat children, and watch their vineyards grow." In a final tribute to Fairbanks, Power tosses his sword into the ceiling.

Commentary

The Mark of Zorro starring Tyrone Power stretched the legend of Zorro, expanding and contracting characters and the story line.

Tossing a sword into a ceiling beam had become a signature statement of Zorro films, from the original Fairbanks *The Mark of Zorro* to *Don Q.* Another classic signature piece had become slicing the candles before a duel between the main characters. The audience witnesses the swing of an emotional pendulum that begins with Rathbone's smug, triumphant laugh when Diego's swipe seems to have missed the candle completely, and changes into his fury when he realizes that the "popinjay" has cut it so perfectly that the candle remains lit on its base.

Fairbanks introduced magic tricks to the Diego film persona. Sleight of hand continued to play significantly in this plot.

Alejandro has been a widower in previous versions, whereas his wife is present in this film. The padre, a rabble-rouser here, was a quietly defiant character in both the Fairbanks and McCulley treatments.

Zorro's first appearance is in daylight. He rides into the plaza without his classic cape rather than slinking into the tavern at night. He wears a bandit-style mask over his nose and mouth, but nothing over his eyes when he robs the Quinteros' carriage, and again when he appears on Lolita's balcony after the lovers dance.

Two references are made to the "mark" of Zorro. When Zorro robs the *alcalde* and his wife in their carriage, Inez asks, "You'd rob a lady?" The masked man responds, "Forgive me, I'd hate to mark such a lovely cheek." Later, Quintero sees a *Z* carved in the chest of Gonzalez, an innovation taken from Republic's *The Bold Caballero* (1936).

Diego woos Lolita in a chapel, not in a garden, as Fairbanks did, and his limited poetry pales in comparison to either McCulley's or Fairbanks's versions. This Lolita is an easier catch than her predecessors.

The horse rearing with Zorro astride him became a trademark of the Disney series, and later of the New World series.

The lascivious captain of the silent film and McCulley's story who forces himself on the young Lolita is absent in this film version. The love triangle between the captain, Lolita, and Zorro/Diego has been reconfigured to a less emotional game of cat and mouse between Diego, Inez, and Esteban. This captain vies for the attention of Inez, while the *alcalde*'s wife clamors after Diego.

In McCulley's story and in Fairbanks's film, Diego is forced to consider marriage at his father's insistence. In this film, Diego disdains the filial respect of previous versions and the tradition of the period. He flippantly replies to his father's rejection of Quintero's proposal, "I had no say in my father's marriage. Why should he try to instruct me on mine?"

While reference is made to the padre's lashing, a plot point in the earlier Zorro renditions, the lashing is not shown. When the padre is arrested by Esteban, his attempt to fight the captain is in the spirit of McCulley's Fray Felipe, who grabs the whip of the soldiers in the plaza before they lash him. Such fighting spirit was not exhibited by Fairbanks's padre.

Significantly absent from Power's version of *The Mark of Zorro* are the boastful Sergeant Gonzales; Bernardo, Zorro's mute ally and servant; and the Pulido family. The great sword duels do not occur between Zorro and his rivals but rather between Diego and Esteban. The sense of fun Zorro had in dueling and outwitting his pursuers is also absent, as is his use of a whip. Justice as a watchword for Zorro's work is conspicuously missing from the masked hero's lexicon. Only the padre voices this concern. The ending, however, returns to McCulley's original theme of saving the people from corruption, rather than to Fairbanks's focus on defending Lolita's honor.

Given that the Power version of *The Mark of Zorro* was produced after the action-oriented Republic serials of *Zorro Rides Again* and *Zorro's Fighting Legion*, this remake contained comparatively little action. The Production Code Authority refused to let the Twentieth Century-Fox script have Zorro cut the letter Z into an opponent's forehead, even though a similar sequence had been approved for chapter one of *Zorro's Fighting Legion* the previous year.

To some reviewers, Power's is the definitive version of Zorro, improving with age, whereas the Fairbanks version has become mildly amusing as an old-time screen melodrama. To others, Power was never at his best in action roles and didn't rise to the challenge of making the Zorro character believable. Because he was more an actor than a true swash-buckler, his performance suffered in comparison to Fairbanks's. The New York reviewer who missed Mamoulian's deliberate parody remembered Fairbanks "as a swashbuckler who swashed with magnificent arrogance and swished, when required, with great style." He thought Power reversed the role.

FRANK LANGELLA MISSES HIS MARK

The television department of Twentieth Century-Fox authorized an-other remake of *The Mark of Zorro* in 1974 as a made-for-television movie starring Frank Langella in the role of Zorro, with Ricardo Montalban in Basil Rathbone's role as Esteban and Gilbert Roland as Alejandro. Director Don McDougall essentially reshot the Power film, this time in color. Writer Brian Taggert inserted minor changes in the story, but generally, the film does not stray far from John Tainton Foote's 1940 script.

Commentary
The film begins with the familiar opening sword training sequence enhanced by the Newman theme music. Despite journalist Tom Weaver's opinion that this was the best thing about the film, the show did well in the Nielsen ratings.

The development of Diego's dual identity is foreshadowed in the opening sequence when a friend accuses him of wanting to right all the wrongs of Madrid. Another jests that Cortez might find a Z carved in his cheek. Still another soldier reminds the group that the Z is reserved for Zorro and he's dead. Zorro's role as the defender of justice is thus estab-lished as a legend, not as Diego's creation.

Diego offers the same toast to his friends and tosses his sword into the ceiling before leaving for home. When confronted with Esteban's exchange about swordplay, the captain tosses Diego his sword to feel its weight. Diego drops it, cutting himself as he establishes his feigned loath-ing of the blade.

Diego is more poetic, a return to the McCulley/Fairbanks character-ization. Complimented for being a poet, he flatters Inez: "A poet needs inspiration." Quintero defines his wife more fully, warning Esteban, "Inez cares no more for you than she does for me. She cares only for herself."

Alejandro again refuses to fight in a revolt he has no chance of winning. The padre's lines are less colorful and cantankerous, merely describing California as "a rose with two cankers." After declaring the need for an avenging angel, he recalls the de la Vega commitment to justice. "Remember the sword of the Vegas hangs in your home. The sword that first brought justice to this land is not to hang like a rusted memory." Justice becomes vested in the sword, much like King Arthur's sword in the stone.

Zorro, rather than Diego, gives the padre gold for the people; Fray Felipe observes that he had stolen "the sword of the Vegas." Shortly after, Diego appears. To raise his sense of moral outrage, the padre suggests that Diego spend a night in the village listening to children cry because they don't have enough milk.

Frank Langella donned Zorro's mask in the 1974 television remake of Power's version of *The Mark of Zorro*.

Zorro appears in the scene where the marriage alliance between Diego and Lolita is proposed. Alejandro notices that the masked man has his sword and worries that he has become an accomplice to Zorro's crimes, the same concern shown by Carlos Pulido in earlier versions. Zorro reassures Alejandro, "It's not theft to steal from a thief—it's merely irony," which infuriates Esteban. He fumes, "He pretends to be a savior but he is only a fool."

A new character, Maria, Lolita's *dueña*, cautions her not to seem too anxious about Diego during dinner because "to a man, there is only the hunt . . . don't take the challenge out of the sport." Lolita's disdain for Diego remains. In response to his query about why scoundrels like Zorro are remembered, but not well-bred men, she observes, "Perhaps because there's nothing memorable about scented bathtubs."

The distinction between Diego and Esteban is drawn more sharply in their exchange about the exhilaration of battle. Diego sees "only death" after battle, while for Esteban there's "also glory."

The dance between Diego and Lolita has been eliminated, as has Inez's offer to help Lolita get out of the match with Diego. Although the padre is again seized in the church, he makes no attempt to fight.

Lolita sees the friar publicly lashed on her way to the Vegas', where she reports the incident. Alejandro doesn't refuse to see her. She urges Alejandro: "Do something!" He rises to the occasion: "There's one sword left on my wall."

In this remake, Esteban follows the footprints in the cellar and finds the secret passage. Diego's sly verbal coercion to get the *alcalde* to sign his resignation has been bluntly replaced by a gun held by Zorro. Esteban enters through the passage as Quintero finishes, just in time to fight Zorro.

The ensuing duel between the captain and Zorro works better conceptually than the duel between Diego and Esteban in Tyrone Power's *The Mark of Zorro*. Though Mamoulian directed one of the premiere sword fight scenes in film history, Diego wasn't under suspicion as Zorro yet and he had been portrayed as a sissy who disdained swordplay. The main antagonists, Zorro and Esteban, never crossed swords. The Langella version corrected this flaw, but though their repartee is witty, their swordplay is lifeless.

Before the duel begins, Esteban and Zorro swipe the candles. In the middle of their duel, and for no apparent reason, Zorro takes off his mask. Esteban remarks, "So, inside the peacock we find a hawk."

Alejandro becomes the real hero of this film since he rallies the caballeros to fight and banishes the Quinteros back to Spain. The jail scene has been eliminated. When Zorro reappears, Alejandro proudly asserts, "The sword of the Vegas has never enjoyed such distinction," to which the masked man responds, "Thank you, father." They cross their swords in triumph.

The casting for this production did not have the strength of Mamoulian's cast. Langella's characterization is somber and humorless, and the dueling scene is dull. Quintero isn't played with the comic sensibilities of the superstitious, pompous fool. Inez and Lolita look nearly the same age. The resolution gives Alejandro, rather than Zorro, the distinction of defeating the corrupt administration, vesting the ideal of justice in the sword of the Vegas.

Typically, as McCulley's Zorro stories evolved through the decades, changes occurred. The author was as much a part of the character's reinvention as the writers who re-created Zorro stories for a variety of media. There is no denying that Zorro has left his mark. With each new production, actors who played the role and writers who gave him life put their individual marks on the fox.

GUY WILLIAMS
BECOMES THE FOX

*O*UT of the night, when the full moon is bright, comes a horseman known as Zorro. This bold renegade carves a Z with his blade, a Z that stands for Zorro. Zorro, the fox so cunning and free. Zorro, who makes the sign of the Z."

These lyrics were ingrained in the memories of a generation of baby boomers every Thursday night at seven-thirty on ABC. When the Disney television series first aired, on October 10, 1957, these words, their melody, and the visual image of Zorro rearing on Tornado against a lightning sky, echoing the word *Zorro . . . Zorro . . . Zorro*, provoked powerful imagery for an impressionable audience. Three previous generations had thrilled to the remarkable feats of the fox, from the silent film era of the 1920s through the Republic cliffhangers of the 1930s and the subtle satire of the 1940 Tyrone Power version. A new generation of eager viewers was now being captivated by Disney's adaptation of Zorro. The success of the series spawned a merchandising campaign and gave a previously unknown actor notoriety in America and around the world.

Writing for the pulp magazine *West*, Johnston McCulley generated more than fifty of his seventy-nine Zorro segments in the 1940s. Film exposure had infused Zorro in the public's consciousness. In the twenty-five years since McCulley had penned *The Curse of Capistrano*, his masked hero had been adapted, transplanted, even metamorphosed by writers taking advantage of the fox's popularity. Zorro's athleticism, his moral righteousness, and his adventurous spirit gave him the flexibility to function as well in the territory of Idaho as he did in the *pueblo* of Los Angeles.

Even broader exposure lay ahead for McCulley's creation with the energy, imagination, and resources of Walt Disney Studios behind it. First, however, Disney needed the rights for Zorro. Mitchell Gertz played matchmaker. Beginning on July 1, 1946, and extending through August 15, 1951, a series of agreements was signed between the author, Johnston McCulley, and Mitchell Gertz, a talent agent in Beverly Hills. Gertz represented McCulley's property, selling the rights to Zorro for radio, television, phonographic recording, and motion pictures. In exchange, McCulley received $1 and "other valuable considerations." These "considerations" included $30 per month for three years from May 1, 1947, to April 30, 1950, and 50 percent of all profits from Zorro deals. In addition, McCulley earned specified sums and a percentage of the net profits on every motion picture, record, or radio program Gertz negotiated.

A championship college wrestler in his native Rhode Island, Gertz had come to Los Angeles to try out for the 1932 Olympic team. However, he broke his leg in a pick-up basketball game, dashing his hopes for an Olympic berth. The father of one of Mitch's fraternity brothers had contacts in Hollywood and helped arrange a job for him with Nat Levine. Nat ran Mascot Films, which, in 1935, merged with Monogram Pictures and Consolidated Film Industries to form Republic Pictures. In 1936 Levine produced *The Bold Caballero* for Republic; it was the first talking Zorro film ever released. As head of the writing department at Nat Levine's company, Mitch was probably introduced to Johnston McCulley. With his relentless energy, he built his own successful talent agency, the Mitchell Gertz Agency, located on Rodeo Drive in Beverly Hills. "Hectic, harassed, and happy" was how a 1957 *TV Guide* feature article portrayed the agent. The most important deal Gertz consummated for McCulley was with Walt Disney, bringing McCulley's creation back to his origins—as the defender of justice in Los Angeles.

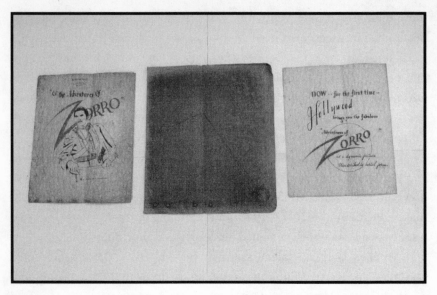

Mitchell Gertz presented Walt Disney with this leather-bound portfolio to sell Zorro.

Gertz presented Zorro to his friend, Disney, in a beautiful soft leather folder with a *Z* etched in the cover with a sword, the parchment pages within advertising the past triumphs and the promotional potential of McCulley's creation. A summary page included information about the Fairbanks and Power films. In addition, potential buyers learned that the 1924 edition of *The Mark of Zorro* had been translated into Spanish and Portuguese, selling over 100,000 copies. Over 800,000 copies of the book had been sold, and new stories were appearing in *West* magazine, which carried a circulation of 250,000 per month.

Zorro's exposure was assured to interested buyers. Gertz's pitch to Disney culminated in a deal that commenced on February 2, 1953. The agreement between Gertz and Disney required Johnston McCulley's notarized signature, for which the author received another dollar in "further consideration of anticipated benefits."

According to Gerry Dooley's extensive research on the Disney Zorro series for *Out of the Night,*

> Disney had tested the waters in television with Christmas specials in
> the consecutive years of 1950 and 1951. The first was a promotion for his

animated feature, *Alice in Wonderland*, entitled *One Hour in Wonderland*. The second was *The Walt Disney Christmas Show*. Following the success of these two initial television forays, Disney was ready to exploit the medium for live action.

Bill Cottrell became the producer on the Zorro series rather than Walt because Disney's own contract with the Walt Disney Studios prevented him from being the producer. WED Enterprises became the new moniker for Walt E. Disney, Inc. Casting began for *Zorro* in 1953, along with the development of scripts and the design of props. Walt and Bill pitched the series to CBS and NBC, but both networks wanted to see a pilot. At the time, WED's first priority was the building of Disneyland, consequently, *Zorro* was put on hold.

Huge financial resources were required to develop the Magic King-

7-Up's promotional activities for the Zorro show were inventive and ubiquitous.

dom, funds that WED lacked. Walt proposed a quid pro quo deal to CBS and NBC—a series in exchange for backing Disneyland. In the spring of 1953, Walt got a call from a third, quite small network, ABC. Kintner, an ABC executive vice president, proposed backing for Disneyland in exchange for Disney programming. If Disney gave ABC the shows, Kintner promised that within two years, his network would be one of the major broadcasters, right alongside CBS and NBC. The parties struck a deal. With WED's energies consumed by the design of Disneyland, Disney sold his rights in Zorro to the Walt Disney Studios.

Both sides kept their promises in the ABC/Disney deal. After its first two years, the *Disneyland* show finished in sixth and then fourth place. *The Mickey Mouse Club* was exceedingly popular, along with two other action features, *Davy Crockett, Indian Fighter* and *Davy Crockett and the River Pirates*. These successes eliminated the need for a *Zorro* pilot. Based on the previously developed script outlines and storyboards, thirty-nine half-hour episodes were green-lighted by ABC for the 1957–1958 season. Even though television was rapidly moving to become color, the Zorro series was shot in black and white, a decision that proved fatal to one of the most popular series in America.

Adult westerns were just beginning their rise in popularity. Some of the most popular western series were airing by 1959, including *Gunsmoke, Have Gun Will Travel*, and *Wagon Train*. The cast joked that *Zorro* was a "south" western rather than an actual western.

In the fall of 1957, *Zorro*'s chief sponsor, 7-Up, developed a flurry of promotional activity around the series' launch. As author G. Dooley noted,

"Lady Zorros" gave out Zorro hats, buttons, and six-packs of 7-Up in Los Angeles, New York, and Chicago. The "ladies" were even seen cleaning up chalk Zs on sidewalks and school hallways. Seven-Up published the monthly *Zorro Newsletter*, which was sent to their bottlers all over the country, and poured unprecedented amounts of money into advertising. A character called Fresh-up Freddie was featured in twelve one-minute cartoons for the first season of *Zorro*. AC Sparkplugs also became a sponsor, creating live-action commercials that featured an animated spokesman, a St. Bernard dog named Trapper, and a white horse called

Sparky. Zorro was allocated a print advertising budget of $175,000 between October 6 and November 14, 1957, the cost shared among 7-Up, AC, ABC, and Disney.

Character licensing was a burgeoning field before the *Zorro* craze hit. With the airing of *Davy Crockett*, every boy and girl in America desired a coonskin cap. Disney was caught off guard at the time, unprepared for the potential gold mine that licensing represented, but by the time *Zorro* was in the creation stage, Disney was geared up for the ride. The popularity of the fox translated into a mania that took the country by storm.

Companies produced various Zorro products, from lunch boxes to sword sets, and from costumes to wallets. Chalked Zs on fences, furniture, walls, garages, and kids' clothing were commonplace during the late 1950s. Demand for merchandise had been created by the extensive promotional efforts of Disney, ABC, and the show's sponsors, 7-Up and AC Sparkplugs, before the launch of the series. By April 1957, six months before the show premiered, retailers had already sold a large volume of Zorro merchandise. The products ran the gamut from playsets to puppets, puzzles, watches, swords, hobby horses, pajamas, and hundreds more. A brief resurgence of interest in Zorro merchandise developed in 1965 when the Disney series ran in syndication.

While the original retail prices of this Zorro merchandise were modest compared to similar products of the time, these vintage items command impressive prices among collectors today. Zorro lunch boxes from Aladdin now sell for $150. Zorro Pez dispensers command $100. The Hasbro Paint by Numbers Zorro set can cost $150. Dell Comics, which had issued Zorro stories based on McCulley's original *Curse of Capistrano* in 1949, revamped its covers and story lines to follow the Disney characterizations in 1958. Noted cartoonist Alex Toth drew the first six issues, and one other Dell Zorro later in the series. Even the Disney Dell comics, which originally sold for only ten cents, start at $10 today.

Topps, which produced its own series of Zorro comics in 1993, made a series of eighty-eight collectible Zorro cards similar to baseball cards from 1957 to 1959. Gund Creations made a hand puppet that children could change from Diego to Zorro by adding a mask and hat. Whitman made a Zorro board game. Jaymar made puzzles. The Ben Cooper Com-

The Marx playset was a favorite for children in the 1950s and 1960s, as well as a valuable item today for collectors.

pany made costumes, its biggest sellers ever; sales of the company's Zorro costumes outstripped sales for all other costumes by 60 percent during the 1958 Christmas season. Empire Plastics made the popular chalk-tipped sword and mask. Marx made a Zorro action set that included a whip, a mask, a hat, a pistol, a sheathed knife, and two fencing swords with chalk tips. It commands $400 in today's collector's market.

The Marx playset was a favorite in the 1950s and is a particularly cherished item to collectors. A complete set can now command $2,000, a far cry from its list price of $5.79 in the 1958 Sears Christmas catalog. Several series of the playsets were released, containing all or part of the following items: a fort and a hacienda with all the major characters in figurines—Zorro rearing on Tornado, Don Diego, Bernardo, Alejandro, and Sergeant Garcia—plus cacti, palm trees, fighting soldiers on the ground and on horseback, horses, a cannon, a well, a cave, a Zorro flag, a water pump, an anvil, and a sharpening wheel.

Disney did its own promotion prior to launching *Zorro*. Guy Williams appeared as Zorro on the *Disneyland* series, hosted by Walt Disney. As Walt explained the leisure park to the Mouseketeers, Moochie kept interrupting, asking about Zorro. To the delight of the littlest Mouseketeer, Zorro appeared, making his trademark "sign of the Z."

Writer/director Norman Foster took responsibility for fulfilling the expectations of not only the network, but the studio and *Zorro*'s sponsors. Foster had worked on Charlie Chan mysteries in the late 1930s, later directing Orson Welles in *Journey Into Fear* in 1942. In the mid-1940s and early 1950s he directed a number of films while living in Mexico but was lured to television in 1953 to direct some shows of his sister-in-law, Loretta Young.

Foster directed the successful Davy Crockett films that prompted his appointment to the Zorro challenge. His love of Mexican culture, along with a flair for action, and strong story sense, helped Foster set the tone of the show and shape the characters. Not only did he direct thirteen of the first thirty-nine shows, but he wrote five scripts and co-wrote two more. His biggest challenge was to meet Walt's desire for humor in the series, attempting to blend comedy with drama without turning it into farce.

Disney wanted an unknown actor to be cast as Diego/Zorro. Guy Williams, a model and actor, garnered the coveted role. His wife, Jan Williams, remembered

> When Guy was called to go on an interview for Zorro . . . he came home . . . so excited about it, because it was something that absolutely fit his personality and background and everything about him. . . . Before he heard who was going to do the role, they were building the Zorro set . . . we'd get in the car and we'd drive over to Griffith Park and park up high above the Disney Studios and watch them build the set . . . he'd watch gleefully and hopefully, thinking that was the thing he most wanted to do.

Guy Williams, born in New York City on January 14, 1924, to Italian immigrant parents, was actually Armando Catalano. According to Jan, Guy's father and his uncles were all fencers, a positive omen for Williams's future career as Zorro. One uncle had gained some notoriety in Italy for his fencing escapades. Guy's father, Attilio, began training his son to fence when he was seven. Williams studied acting at the Neighborhood Play-

Guy Williams did promotional work for the *Zorro* show at Disneyland.

house while he modeled to make a living. It was "a simple and profitable way of working around financial problems . . . it required little time and paid well," Williams recalled.

He changed his name to Guy Williams at a time when foreign-sounding names quickly typecast actors and actresses into a narrow range of roles. He picked Guy Williams because it was "about as non-specific as he could imagine." Williams first moved to California in 1948, under contract to MGM. In describing the roles he played, William classified them as "anonymous men leaning in doorways with cigarettes dangling from their lips. . . . There were times when I seriously doubted if I were cut out for this business."

He returned to New York, where he appeared in a few local television shows such as *Studio One*. He also continued modeling. While posing for a skiing illustration, he met model and future wife, Janice Cooper. After they married, a studio contract with Universal-International brought Guy back to California in 1952. Williams's first memorable picture was *Bedtime for Bonzo*, remembered not for Williams's role but for that of a future president, Ronald Reagan. Williams's starring vehicle was yet to arrive.

By the mid-1950s, his career constantly in ups and downs, Williams contemplated leaving the business. During this period, Guy was thrown from a horse and suffered a serious injury to his left shoulder and arm. He took up fencing with Aldo Nadi, a master teacher, in the hope that the exercise would restore the injury and within six months Williams had regained full use of his arm and had become a crack fencer. Unfortunately, his career had not taken off, so he and Jan returned to New York.

In 1957, California beckoned once again, this time with a small part in a low-budget thriller, *I Was a Teenage Werewolf*. Williams was cast as the policeman who eventually shoots the teen, while the lead was played by a young Michael Landon, who went on to star in *Bonanza*, *Little House on the Prairie*, and other successful television series.

This California journey proved auspicious for Guy Williams. On April 19, 1957, *Daily Variety* announced that Norman Foster was auditioning actors for the title role in *Zorro*, which he was set to direct. The new television series created a buzz in Hollywood. It was a choice role, given the pairing of the well-known character and Disney, and Williams found it tantalizing, aware that it could make an actor's career. Williams was now thirty-three, and television work looked like a promising move. Dark and handsome, with a brilliant smile, Guy Williams was perfect for the California hero. His athletic six-three frame could brandish a sword and he could handle the Spanish accent.

Foster initially liked Williams's looks but he had to make sure that the actor could fence, so even though he had seen film footage already, he had Williams do three difficult fencing scenes. Foster had suspected that his potential Zorro had been born with a foil in his hand but after seeing him in action, he was convinced. "Guy fit Zorro to a T," Foster claimed in a publicity release, promptly signing him to a one-year contract with a seven-year option.

Britt Lomond was cast as the series' villain, Capitán Monastario. Lomond's agent put him up for both the lead role and the evil captain, "to make sure our bets are backed." Like Williams, Lomond was an excellent fencer who had also studied with Aldo Nadi but unlike Guy, Britt had been a highly ranked college and amateur competitive fencer with fifteen years of experience under his belt. During the audition fencing scenes, Lomond gave Williams cues for which way his blade would go next. During the series, their duels were highly choreographed, first diagrammed on graph paper, then blocked out on the ground.

Fred Cavens, the fencing master, was so impressed with Lomond's ability that he offered to let Britt use Fairbanks's sword. Lomond said he felt incredibly honored.

> That's like handing . . . a commandment of God to me . . . and I took the
> sword and I must say that I respected it and I hope I did it honor for the
> first 14 episodes . . . at the end . . . I carefully gave the sword back to
> Freddy and they used another one . . .

In the very first fencing scene that Lomond and Williams filmed, Guy forgot one beat. ". . . instead of putting a point to my body," Lomond related, "he made a cut to my head and cut me right across the eye . . . which I still have the scar . . . Guy was horrendously apologetic . . ." As the series progressed, the two men developed an excellent rapport in their fencing duels.

Fred Cavens made dramatic use of Zorro's cape in the dueling scenes he choreographed. Disney's wardrobe department had recloaked McCulley's character in his black satin cape, made famous in the author's opening tavern scene. Though Fairbanks had worn a cape in the silent version of *The Mark of Zorro*, the Power version had dispensed with it.

Author Dooley attributed the excellent fencing and stunts on the series to the hiring of the best screen fencing master, Fred Cavens, along with the best stunt coordinator, Yakima Canutt, as the second unit director who had earned his reputation for remarkable stunt work in the Republic serials. Cavens brought his son, Al, into the business on the Zorro series, as did Canutt with his son, Tap. Williams did all his own fencing on the series but Buddy Van Horn doubled for him. Dooley noted that

Britt Lomond, as Monastario, confronts Guy Williams in his Diego persona.

Cavens thought Williams was his most difficult pupil, not because he was untalented or didn't work hard. In fact, the opposite was true. What made Williams difficult was that he knew too much. In film duels it was necessary to disregard classically correct guards and lunges. Of all the actors who played Zorro, Guy was the best fencer. Cavens' challenge was to make his latest Zorro forget so he could teach him the special thrusts and parries that made film fencing dramatic. Fencing sequences were shot on Fridays, or Fight Day, so if the actors sustained an injury, they had the weekend to recuperate.

The role of Sergeant Garcia was immortalized by the ample girth, excellent singing voice, and endearing buffoonish quality of actor Henry

Calvin. He brought an Oliver Hardy quality to his part. Wimberley Calvin Goodman had played a few parts in stock company productions during college. The experience shifted his career aspirations from journalism to acting. He moved to New York and entertained as bass baritone soloist at Radio City Music Hall in 1939. He appeared on Broadway after World War II, then worked on many television shows in the 1950s and even had his own radio show before securing his most famous role as Garcia.

The Sergeant Garcia of the Disney series was patterned directly on the character McCulley had depicted in the *West* stories of the 1940s. McCulley's Garcia was the second in command of the garrison, forever filling in until a new captain arrived. In *Zorro Races with Death* (1947), McCulley portrayed Garcia as "a jovial fellow at times and a stern disciplinarian at other times. The responsibility of attending to military matters in the district in the absense of his *capitán* weighed heavily upon him." He was "in the habit of bursting into a roaring song when filled with wine," flinging his "basso profundo into the air of Alta California."

Diego nurtured a friendship with Garcia by plying the sergeant with wine. Garcia's tongue then loosened and Diego learned valuable information about the army's troop movements. McCulley described a "strange friendship" between

> the uncouth soldier and Diego, the fastidious scion of a hildalgo . . . Diego bought the sergeant wine, and the sergeant regaled Diego with wild tales of his past experiences, many of which were the figments of his imagination. What Garcia did not know was that in his cups he often told the secrets of the soldiery, in which at times Diego was vastly interested, desiring to know what movements of the troopers were contemplated . . . Zorro certainly wished to know where the troopers were going so he could operate in an opposite direction.

The sergeant's physical appearance was described in *The Mask of Zorro* (1947) as a "mere mass of flabby fat . . . bulk but no muscle . . . and a burly sergeant." He bellowed commands as if commanding a regiment, despite the fact that only six troopers followed his orders. Regarding his pursuit of Zorro (in *Zorro Beats a Drum*, 1947), Garcia declared

I would have to take after the scamp with my troopers, of course, because we have orders to capture him, and also there is a big reward offered for the capture, but my heart would not be in the work. There are
times when I admire the rascal. . . . I confess, Don Diego, that I have a
measure of admiration for him, unofficially, of course. But he has been
declared an outlaw, and his liberty and life are forfeit if he is caught.
Since I am a sworn officer of the soldiery, I will do my duty and catch
him if I can.

Bernardo has elements that were set up in the *West* stories and carried into his Disney portrayal. But with Gene Sheldon's extensive talents,
Zorro's mute servant clearly evolved to showcase the actor's gifts. A superb
magician, Sheldon's talents were utilized on the series, following in the
tradition of Fairbanks's Don Diego in *The Mark of Zorro*. Sheldon learned
magic from his father, the actor and magician Earl Sheldon. Earl had invented a version of the trick in which a woman is sawed in half, often using
his son Gene as the woman. Gene's career progressed from radio to vaude-
ville and to musical comedy on the nightclub circuit before his foray into
television.

In both the McCulley and Disney interpretations, Bernardo was always ready with clothing and a horse for Zorro. He even rode as a relay or
decoy for the masked hero. McCulley's Bernardo, however, though faithful,
loyal, large, and strong, was dull-witted. In *Zorro Races With Death* (1947),
Bernardo was described as: "This mute peon, faithful and loyal, and not
any too quick in thinking." Diego's aide was slow to anger but would kill
anyone who threatened Diego. In the above story, Bernardo demonstrated
his protective instincts: "Bernardo gave a gutteral and sprang forward,
thinking Gomez was about to use the whip on Diego. Bernardo seized
Gomez by the shoulders and pressed down upon him, making the *capitán*
kneel in the dirt." Diego confronted Gomez for his mistreatment of Bernardo: "This man you struck is my personal servant. He was born a mute.
He cannot speak and answer you. If I had not jumped forward, he probably
would have seized you and choked you to death or snapped your neck, for
he has great strength."

The innovative differences between McCulley's version of Bernardo

In the first episode, Diego hones his skills on board while returning from Spain. Upon learning of the problems in Los Angeles from the ship's captain, he determines that he must become El Zorro, the fox. "When you can't clothe yourself in the skin of a lion, put on that of the fox."

and the character that Gene Sheldon portrayed in the series were threefold: first, Sheldon made Bernardo a clever mime with wonderful sleight of hand expertise; second, he was of small stature, rather than being the stereotypic hulking dimwit; and third, he was a quick and clever thinker, more Diego's partner and friend than a mere servant. Sheldon's comic timing, use of facial gestures, and magic skills made him a favorite of audiences.

The role of Diego's father, Don Alejandro, went to George J. Lewis, the only Hispanic member of the regular cast. Originally from Guadalajara, Mexico, his Welsh father and a Spanish mother fled Mexico with their family during the Mexican Revolution and settled in Coronado, California. During the 1920s Lewis worked at Universal under contract, but anticipating the change that sound would make in any actor's future, he moved to New York to get stage experience.

Lewis then returned to California where he worked regularly in Republic pictures. The Disney series was not his first experience with Zorro. He played the lead male in Republic's chapterplay *Zorro's Black Whip*. Lewis came to the attention of Zorro's casting group from his work on *Davy Crockett and the River Pirates*. He displayed the proud stature that Diego's silver-haired father, Don Alejandro, required.

The character Fray Felipe appeared at the beginning of the first *Zorro* season. After four episodes, the part was dropped. Romney Brent played the role as the moral conscience of the series, bringing Catholic ideology into his dealings with the commandante. Born Romulo Larrade, the Mexican stage actor was better known by his anglicized Hollywood name.

Modeled on McCulley's first Zorro stories, the padre was true to the author's characterization. In the Disney series, Fray Felipe did not know that Diego was Zorro. In McCulley's later *West* stories, the padre did know that Diego was Zorro.

Zorro's well-trained black stallion was given the name Tornado in the Disney series. In McCulley's stories, Zorro had such a steed, but the horse had no name. The Tornado used for Disney's publicity shots was Diamond Decorator, a seven-year-old quarter horse and former Grand National Medal Class winner of the 1950s. Three other horses took on the role during filming.

Foster wanted Lomond to play the heavy in the series with Williams as the lead, while Disney had favored Britt for the role of Diego/Zorro.

Foster went head-to-head with Disney over the casting decision and prevailed. He apologized when they were well into the first season. Foster explained that even though Britt was the better actor, with more experience, and he was absolutely the top fencer in Hollywood, he wanted Lomond to help Williams bring the show along.

Lomond pushed Foster to understand the motivation behind his character's villainy. "Greed" was the director's response. Nothing would stop captain Monastario from becoming the richest man in California. Without realizing it, Lomond prompted the definitive characteristic of most of the villains in subsequent Zorro media.

Ironically, after the thirteenth episode Monastario was written out of the series because Lomond's fan mail equaled Williams's. Walt told Britt that there could be only one star in the show. Since Lomond was under contract with Disney for three years, he continued to work on the lot in many other series. Playing Monastario helped Lomond's career. He said, "It did establish me as a fairly good name in Hollywood, and I went on to play many, many roles, usually heavies, of course, but good ones . . . good features . . . good television shows."

The Disney series was set in 1820 in Spanish California, the period historian Hoffman and film historian Reyes thought appropriate for McCulley's creation. A set costing nearly $500,000 was created on the Disney back lot and remained intact until 1983, when it was torn down to make room for more office space. The attention to detail for which Disney was renowned was evident on the *Zorro* set. The church was an exact replica of the original *pueblo* church in downtown Los Angeles. In addition to the church, Zorro Plaza contained the cuartel, the tavern, and the *magistrado*'s house. The de la Vega hacienda was outside of town, unlike its location in McCulley's original story. However, as McCulley further developed his character, the Vegas had also lived outside the *pueblo*.

Mission San Luis Rey in Oceanside became the San Gabriel Mission in the series with numerous ranches outside Los Angeles serving as locations, such as Corriganville and the Bell, Berry, Albertson, and Iverson ranches. However, the precipitous canyons that Zorro leaped across astride Tornado were actually created using matte paintings.

Filming costs per episode ran at over $75,000, the highest budget for a half-hour show in the industry. *Out of the Night* author G. Dooley noted that:

> In comparison, *The Lone Ranger* episodes were brought in at $25,000 per episode. Had the shows been shot in color, instead of black and white, the cost of production would have been prohibitive. But there was another factor besides cost. Walt Disney felt that Zorro should be a black-and-white character, a classic black-and-white hero. The decision created problems years later when he tried to sell the show into syndication.

William Lava created the underscoring for all seventy-eight episodes of the Disney series. His creative work on *Zorro's Fighting Legion* for the Republic serial gave a pulse-pounding sound to the episode. His contribution to the success of the Disney series was the type of attention to detail that greatly enhanced the characters and hence, the series. Each of the main characters had his own themes—heroic Zorro, the dashing brass section; mischievous Bernardo, the playful piccolo and flute; rotund Sergeant Garcia, the lumbering tuba and drums. Tornado even had a theme, a variation on the wooden soldiers from Victor Herbert's *Babes in Toyland*. Lava's scoring for sword fights and chase scenes was reminiscent of the swashbuckling scores of composers such as Alfred Newman, who wrote the music for the 1940 *The Mark of Zorro*.

Zorro's theme song, which has remained an identifying feature of the Disney series since its debut forty years ago, was written by director Norman Foster and George Bruns. Foster wrote the memorable lyrics and Bruns composed the music, and in the summer of 1958, a version of their *Zorro* theme song recorded by the Chordettes reached number seventeen on the national charts. Twenty-three other original songs were written for the series, several sung by Henry Calvin's character, Sergeant Garcia.

Walt Disney was thoroughly involved in the development of the series, particularly the first thirteen episodes, from reviewing scripts, to suggesting themes for the characters, to making suggestions to Guy Williams on his Spanish accent. Diego was not portrayed as the languid fop of the previous film version. The production team realized that not only had the times changed but also that the audience would tire quickly of the sissy Diego week after week. Williams's Diego became nonviolent and studious, but he was not a wimp.

The thirty-nine episodes of the first season fall into two categories. The first thirteen starred Britt Lomond as Monastario. The next twenty-six dealt with a mysterious character called the Eagle, who writer Lowell Hawley and director Bob Stevenson envisioned as a little Mussolini with plans to take over California's government. Writer Lowell Hawley came upon the idea after his research showed him how truly removed the province was from its colonizer, Spain. The Eagle was a capable, shrewd, and entirely unscrupulous villian. Like Darth Vadar, who turned to the dark side of "the force," the Eagle was a man whose natural leadership abilities became twisted to a truly villainous purpose.

During the Eagle episodes, people died while mysteriously clutching an eagle feather. Diego/Zorro's mission was, naturally, to stop the Eagle, but first he had to find out who the Eagle was and what he wanted. Numerous agents of the Eagle appeared over the remainder of the season, each having to be defeated. The Murrieta brothers were one set of villains in league with the Eagle. In episode thirty-five the identity of the Eagle is revealed—he is Jose Sebastian de Varga, the new *administrado* of Los Angeles—and in the season finale, episode thirty-nine, "Day of Decision," Varga is revealed to be in league with Ambassador Count Kolinko in attempting to take over California.

The Disney series sought to explain Diego's inspiration for his alter ego's name—Zorro, the fox—in the first episode. Diego is returning to Los Angeles from his studies in Spain, accompanied by his mute servant, Bernardo. After learning from the ship's captain that Los Angeles is now run by a tyrannical commandant, Captain Monastario, he decides to become the fox. He is inspired by an old proverb: "When you can't clothe yourself in the skin of a lion, put on that of the fox." Bernardo suggests that Diego play the scholar while he plays the fool, pretending not to hear. To reinforce their new identities, Diego's fencing trophies get tossed overboard.

The Disney studio's animation techniques were employed on the series for special effects. For instance, when Diego made the sign of the Z in the first episode, the tip of the sword was actually animated to give the appearance of moving over the paper.

Walt Disney confers with Guy Williams on the set for Zorro.

Zorro's secret passage was a favorite feature of the series. When he pressed a button under the fireplace mantel in his bedroom, a panel swung open to reveal a dark, dusty room with a table and a trunk. This was where Zorro kept his disguise. From this room, a stairwell led to the first floor of the house, and exits from the passage went into both the *sala* and the library. A short distance through the tunnel was a large cave that served as Tornado's corral. The secret hideout, which Diego had discovered as a boy, had been built by his grandfather as protection against Indians' raids.

Interestingly, Disney, like McCulley, chose not to take on the church regarding the missions' treatment of the Indians. Rather, the series took the same approach as the author and had the Indians mistreated by outsiders. In the case of the Disney series, Monastario forced them into slave labor.

Particularly memorable scenes from previous versions of Zorro made their way into the Disney version. In episode six, Monastario performed the sword and candle trick like the one Power had done in *The Mark of Zorro* (1940). Lomond slices the candle with the precision Power displayed as Diego. Garcia is forever getting a *Z* carved in his pants, like Gonzales in Fairbanks's *The Mark of Zorro*.

Killings were limited in the series, primarily because of its juvenile audience. But in the instances when Zorro was unmasked, those who discovered his identity naturally had to die. According to author G. Dooley,

> Initially, the producers felt the hero couldn't commit outright murder, so benign deaths occurred. In episode twenty-two, Zorro is unmasked in a struggle with Ortega, an agent of the Eagle. Zorro walks ominously towards Ortega, who edges backwards and falls to his death. In the very next episode, *The Secret of the Sierra*, Zorro is again unmasked and Perico, the man who unmasks him, is crushed in an avalanche. By the second season, however, Zorro overtly killed several bad guys. At the conclusion of episode sixty-five, *Manhunt*, Zorro stabs a rifle-wielding villian, and again in episode seventy-five, *Long Live the Governor*, Zorro delivers a lunge into the captain's gut.

The Zorro series received kudos from reviewers after the first thirteen episodes were aired. Its combination of action, quality production, clever story lines, and humor were lauded. Humor was an essential element of the series, so much so that when Monastario was retired in episode thirteen, *The Fall of Monastario*, a new comic relief character was introduced. Corporal Reyes, played by Don Diamond, served as Sergeant Garcia's foil, replacing the humorous dynamic engendered by the *capitán's* exasperated response to Calvin's incompetence. Their repartee had become comic scenes similar to Laurel and Hardy routines.

The first time Zorro carved a *Z* in one of his victims wasn't until episode twenty, "Agent of the Eagle." The mark wasn't carved in a cheek or a forehead but in clothing, as in the opening scene of the Fairbanks film. The gag became a regular feature of the Disney series—and later, of the New World Zorro series.

The second season's budget was smaller, consequently there were few location shoots and more soundstage/back lot filming. Stories targeted older viewers with more adult themes, including romance for Diego/Zorro. Zorro's first series kiss, which was supposed to last five seconds, took two hours to film and caused a big uproar among the executives, who didn't want too much of a kiss—and it didn't sit so well with young viewers either.

Three episodes in the second season featured popular Mouseketeer Annette Funicello. The shows were a sixteenth birthday present from Walt Disney, who knew that Annette had a crush on Guy Williams.

Wonderful camaraderie existed on the set, and the friendships extended off-screen. Britt Lomond remembered the fun the cast had together, especially the rapport among himself, Henry Calvin, and Guy Williams. Jan Williams recalled how they all went to Disneyland on the weekends to do promotions for the show, went on memorable sailing excursions aboard the Williams's yacht, the *Oceana*, and had wonderful dinners together. Even the set felt like a big party when she visited. Director Norman Foster and his wife became godparents to the Williamses' children. As a child, Guy's son, Steve, ate at the commissary with the original Mouseketeers, visited "Uncle Walt," and learned his first magic trick from Gene Sheldon. "It all seemed like normal family life . . . I remember the people associated with Disney's *Zorro* as friends, and almost family. The commissary was like a family dining room, warm and welcoming," he recalled.

The actors pulled pranks on one another regularly. Director Bill Witney often would have Gene Sheldon squirted in the eye when he looked through Zorro's peephole, but over time, Gene got so wary whenever he approached the hole that Bill developed a different strategy. Instead, he would sneak up from behind and squirt him. Lomond recounted a prank for which he and Guy were reprimanded.

> Guy and I were always playing practical jokes on each other because I always wanted to relax him; he was very uptight at times. Anyway, we both wore these skin-tight pants, so one day Guy comes out and he's taken a small towel and rolled it up and put it down the front of his pants. So I say . . . I'll fix him. I rushed into my dressing room and took a bigger towel and folded it up and put it in my pants. We shot the whole scene and we hear this tittering offstage when the director says cut . . . twenty-five nuns standing there watching. We got . . . chewed out for that one.

Guy Williams as Zorro.

Memorable mishaps for the actors occurred during personal appearances. Lomond recalled one occasion when he and Williams were doing a demonstration at Disneyland. Guy raced off the Mark Twain paddleboat, jumping onto his waiting horse. To his chagrin, Williams fell off the horse's other side.

Guy Williams's appearance on a float in Flint, Michigan, to commemorate the fiftieth anniversary of General Motors, the owner of AC Sparkplugs, one of *Zorro*'s sponsors, was memorable to many *Zorro* fans. The event was immortalized in the opening scene of the movie *Roger and Me*.

Although Johnston McCulley was not directly involved with the series, he was a frequent visitor on the Disney lot. He was very impressed with the *Zorro* set and with the series overall and he admired Guy Williams's fencing abilities. McCulley and Guy Williams became fast friends, often discussing Disney's treatment of the masked hero and reminiscing about past Zorro productions in between takes. Sadly, McCulley died during the second season of the *Zorro* show.

The second season wrapped on February 17, 1959, and the cast left for vacation, all expecting to return in July to begin work on another season. The show's ratings were good and they continued to win their time slot. Author G. Dooley explained what occurred:

> ABC had put Walt Disney in a creative bind. They wanted more westerns from him but Walt felt like he was in a creative straitjacket. The success of his shows had enabled ABC to compete with NBC and CBS but American Broadcasting no longer wanted to put money up for Zorro. It was more profitable for them to own the shows they produced rather than take ones from outside producers.
>
> Walt felt he had no choice and in effect canceled the show himself. *Daily Variety*, May 20, 1959, offered the obituary. "ABC Says Tag Too High So Disney Kills Zorro: Walt Disney will discontinue production of his Zorro series following the inability of the studio and ABC to get together on a price for the show."

For Williams, the cancellation was a particular blow. As his wife recalled, "He was so frustrated because the show was going so beautifully and he was enjoying it so much. It was really a shame." While many of the

Guy Williams with his son, Steve, raised the Zorro flag on the family yacht, the *Oceana*. (Courtesy of Guy Williams' family.)

principals in the series continued their careers in acting or in production, none achieved the recognition, satisfaction, or success they had realized working on *Zorro*.

Disney subsequently teamed up with NBC's Wonderful World of Color. This deal meant death for *Zorro* because a black-and-white series couldn't survive on an all-color network.

Eager to still capitalize on the *Zorro* mania, in 1959 the Disney Studios compiled several episodes of the Eagle saga into a ninety-minute fea-

Johnston McCulley, Zorro's creator, shares the spotlight with the show's star, Guy Williams.

ture called *Zorro the Avenger* and released it theatrically to the foreign market, where the series had not yet aired. In 1960, another ninety-minute compilation was released, this one called *The Sign of Zorro*, which drew from the first thirteen episodes. Gerry Dooley described the film as a "choppy patchwork with episodic pacing which is disappointing when one is expecting something more from a film." At the same time, Republic re-released *Ghost of Zorro* and *Zorro Rides Again* to cash in on the *Zorro* craze, and Twentieth Century-Fox re-released Tyrone Power's version of *The Mark of Zorro*.

The public appetite for Zorro brought ABC and *Walt Disney Presents* back together a year later in 1960. They agreed to produce six one-hour Zorro specials for the 1960–1961 season. Only four shows, however, were actually produced, with guest stars including Gilbert Roland, Rita Moreno, and Ricardo Montalban. Bill Witney, who had teamed with John English at age twenty-three to direct *Zorro Rides Again* for Republic Pictures, returned to direct the first two hour specials, *El Bandido* and *Adios El Cuchillo*. The shows aired in October and November 1960, then in January and April of 1961.

The *Zorro* series had been sold into syndication in 1965, experiencing another of the character's periodic revivals. The show ran for two years. When the Disney cable channel premiered in 1983, Zorro became a regularly featured series. Finally, Disney's *Zorro* went color in October 1992 when American Film Technologies colorized seventy-eight episodes, making it the only television series ever to have been colorized.

When asked how the colorization compared to his memory of the set, Williams's son, Steve, was very complimentary.

> I remember Zorro in color. I knew I would see them on TV in black and white, but my mind always filled in the colors. When I saw the first colorized episodes, it was just as I remembered the real colors. I would have to say that the colorization is extremely accurate.

Argentine television began airing reruns of the Disney series in 1973. The show became so popular that Buenos Aires's Channel 13 invited Williams down to do public appearances. That's when his love affair with Argentina began. Like a rerun of the enthusiastic reception Tyrone Power had received on his tours in South America after World War II, the streets were lined with fans for miles to welcome Williams. He started spending more and more time in the country, developing a Zorro script and his own circus based on a Zorro routine he had performed with the Argentine fencing champion, Fernando Lupiz, for the Real Madrid Circus. His show toured all of Argentina successfully.

One of the things Williams particularly enjoyed in Buenos Aires was going to the children's hospital. Jan Williams recalled,

> He'd put his costume on and go into the wards where the children were and talk to them and pick them up and carry them around and spend

time with them. It gave him a lot of pleasure and the children were just in seventh heaven when Zorro showed up.

Williams spent his later years moving back and forth between Buenos Aires and Los Angeles. He was considered for the father's role in *Zorro and Son*, a short-lived comedic series that aired in 1983, but the part went to Henry Darrow. Guy Williams died in his Buenos Aires apartment in early May 1989.

Steven Rubenstein of the *San Francisco Chronicle* wrote the following tribute, which exemplified what Zorro meant to a generation of fans:

> Guy Williams, the dashing hunk who played Zorro in the Disney TV series of the late '50's, was found dead in his Buenos Aires apartment. He was 65, an obvious misprint. A heart attack accomplished what the crummy commandante never could. It stilled Zorro's avenging sword.

The brief newspaper obituary hardly did Williams justice, as justice was Zorro's stock in trade, Rubenstein observed, and so he composed one to say good-bye to an old friend.

> Zorro isn't really dead, of course, because Mr. Williams wasn't Zorro. My brother and I were Zorro. Everyone else on the block was Zorro, too. Zorro was as big as Davy Crockett and the get-up was a lot more complicated. We sent away for the cape. We sent away for the hat. We sent away for the plastic sword. We would have sent away for the stallion if the back yard had been a little larger. The official sword came with chalk embedded in the tip. This was so a kid could leave Zorro's trademark "Z" on walls, doors and the backsides of unwitting brothers. My dumbstruck parents could not believe that the great Disney cartel would sanction what amounted to little more than graffiti, but they learned to follow behind us with a wet rag. We real Zorros galloped along on our thoroughbred bikes, rolling our R's, staying one pedal stroke ahead of the commandante, reaching down to pull the chintzy cape out of the spokes. Unable to ride in the street, we confined our search for bank robbers to the sidewalk.

Forty years after its premiere, *Zorro* continues to air on the Disney Channel and around the world. Viewed in black and white or in color, Guy Williams's winning smile still captivates Zorro fans and will do so as long as "the fox so cunning and free" still makes the sign of the Z.

DELON AND HAMILTON SNAP ZORRO'S WHIP

*D*URING the 1960s, over thirty foreign Zorro movies were produced, chiefly in Mexico, Italy, and Spain. Inexpensively shot, they would be classified in the genre of "spaghetti westerns."

McCulley's masked fox confronted Cardinal Richelieu with the Musketeers in *Zorro E I Tre Moschiettieri* (*Zorro and the Three Mousketeers*, 1961, Italy). Zorro returned the grand duchy of Lusitania to its rightful heir in *Zorro Alla Corte di Spagnia* (*Zorro in the Court of Spain*, 1962, Italy). He became king of Nogara in *Zorro Contro Maciste* (*Zorro Against Maciste*, 1963, Italy). In *Zorro Alla Corte D'Inghilterra* (*Zorro in the Court of England*, 1969, Italy), Zorro opposed a tyrant who ruled an English colony in Central America for Queen Victoria. *Zorro, Marchese di Navarro* (*Zorro, Marquis of Navarro*, 1969, Italy) found the masked hero opposing Napoleon's troops in Spain at the beginning of the 1800s. An extra named Sophia Ciccaloni who appeared in *II Sogno di Zorro* (*Zorro's Dream*, 1962, Italy) went on to a renowned film career as Sophia Loren. Another 1962 Italian film, *II Segno di Zorro* (*The Sign of Zorro*) launched the acting career of Sean Flynn, the son of romantic swashbuckler Errol Flynn. The fox didn't wear his characteristic black outfit and carve a *Z* on a wall only once. Directed by jour-neyman Mario Caiano, the remake was lackluster and forgettable.

ALAIN DELON'S ZORRO

The most notable of these foreign productions starred French actor Alain Delon. As with other productions, Delon's 1974 film takes great lib-erty in place and story, yet preserves the basic elements of McCulley's char-acter.

Film Synopsis

Diego visits an old friend who is leaving Barcelona for Nuova Aragona to take the place of his uncle, the governor. He believes the New World is an ideal place to create a model for justice and humanity in government. Unfortunately, the commander of Nuova Aragona, Colonel Huerta, has dif-ferent plans. He sends assassins to murder Diego's friend. Diego vows to avenge his friend's death and to keep alive his principles and ideals.

A reign of terror rules in Nuova Aragona. Colonel Huerta asks the ruling council for control over the army and the government in order to stop a revolution just as Diego presents himself as the new governor, Mi-guel Vega de la Serta. He is dressed as an exaggerated fop in a white wig and exquisite clothing.

Accompanied by his mute servant, Bernardo, Diego watches Huerta practice fencing. He wounds his soldiers as they spar, believing that only real danger and actual bleeding can teach a man to fight. In a display of skill, he slices the candles in a candelabra with the skill Tyrone Power showed in *The Mark of Zorro*. When he bangs on the table, the sliced can-dles fall.

Diego feigns fear of the impending revolution and asks Huerta to protect the people. Garcia, a big, fat soldier whose appetite is as great as his strength, is assigned to Diego for his personal protection.

A dog (I kid you not) has something to tell the new governor. The canine is seated in a chair with his paw resting on an arm of the chair. He presses the arm, which opens a secret passage behind a bookcase.

Cut to the bustling marketplace, where Chico, a young black boy, marks a chalk *Z* on fencing. Everyone is hungry and fearful. A padre gives

French actor Alain Delon cut a playful, heroic figure as Zorro.

a rousing speech to the populace, urging them to go to the new governor and protest, but the soldiers disperse the crowd. Diego and Bernardo have been in the market trying to get information, but no one will talk. They finally learn from Chico that Zorro will return to save the animals but not the people. They're too weak and don't deserve to be free. (This was a significant shift in the Zorro legend, elevating the fox to the level of myth. For Chico's oppressed people, Zorro is a mythical savior, almost like Christ himself.)

The soldiers arrest the rabble-rouser padre and the man who protected him for selling rotten hides, a device taken from the original McCulley story. Hortenzia, the female lead, protests their sentence of lashes.

Zorro rides into town, ordering the corrupt judge, the lying witness, and the murdering executioner to be lashed. His purpose? So the children will see that the law is fair.

Hortenzia rouses the people while Zorro fights with Garcia, humiliating him in the town square. The fox continues escaping from the other soldiers, dropping obstacles in their way, opening doors in front of them, knocking them off roofs and ladders, and carving a Z in the rear end of Garcia's trousers. He rides off to the cheers of the people with Chico behind him. This scene marks a return to the playful encounters Fairbanks had with soldiers. It reincorporates that sense of fun lacking in Power's characterization of Zorro.

Diego, posing as the fearful new governor, hides in his bed while Huerta explains his plan to imprison Hortenzia. She will be bait for Zorro. Naturally, Zorro has her escape planned. Hortenzia and Zorro are pursued by soldiers, ending up in the barracks, where Zorro sets off explosives.

Huerta is suspicious that the new foppish governor is really Zorro since they were the only two who knew the colonel's plan to use Hortenzia to lure Zorro. Each races to the governor's bedroom. Diego returns a split second ahead of the colonel.

Together, they hatch another plan. This time, Diego suggests that he be the bait. Garcia takes him fishing. When Diego tires, he naps in the carriage, warning the sergeant not to wake him unless Zorro is caught. Meanwhile, Diego slips out as Zorro. He attacks the soldiers and captures Garcia.

Meanwhile, Bernardo has gone to the padre's to get the children to help Zorro. In a field of tall corn, a stuffed Zorro is shot by Huerta.

Garcia thinks the real Zorro is in the carriage with the governor, ready to kill him if the sergeant does not follow his orders. Garcia drives the carriage, as ordered, to a labor camp. Zorro orders the release of the chained peasants and they escape.

Hortenzia warns Zorro that the soldiers are coming. As the fox drives the carriage wildly, pursued by Huerta and the soldiers, Hortenzia declares her love. The dog who showed Zorro the secret passage barks viciously, scaring the soldiers' horses. With a kiss, Zorro sends Hortenzia off to help the people. Then he drives the carriage over a cliff into the river, reminiscent of stunts in the Republic serials.

Huerta believes that Zorro and the governor have drowned. He convinces Hortenzia's father that it is in his best interest for Hortenzia to marry Huerta. Hortenzia arrives in the plaza for the wedding, escorted by Huerta. The padre leads the peasants, seeking justice. Zorro arrives and the rebellion begins.

A climactic duel ensues between Zorro and Huerta. In another tribute to Mamoulian's classic sword fight scene, Zorro again slices the candles in the candlebra. Not only are the tips cut perfectly, but one candle is split lengthwise. The sword battle rages through the castle, cutting curtains, knocking down armor, and creating general havoc. Zorro falls from a support beam inside the castle's rotunda. He grabs a curtain as he plunges through a glass window. Once again, Huerta is fooled into believing that Zorro has died. He rings the church bells, but his celebration over the demise of the fox is premature.

Zorro and Huerta continue their battle on the roof. After the colonel is wounded in the shoulder, he declares, "One of us must die."

"Well, then, let it be the moment of truth," Zorro responds. He removes his mask and proceeds to run Huerta through with his blade. (This sequence may have influenced the 1974 Frank Langella remake of Tyrone Power's *The Mark of Zorro*; where midway through the battle, Langella takes off his Zorro mask, revealing his identity to the captain.)

In the final scene of the Delon version, Zorro rears his horse before riding off to the cheers of the people. The horse rearing with Zorro astride him became a trademark of the Disney series and, later, of the New World series.

THE GERTZ HEIRS EXERCISE THEIR RIGHTS

Mitchell Gertz's heirs, twins John and Nancy, were drawn into active participation in their inheritance of the Zorro copyright as they closed in on their late twenties. Nancy, a budding screenwriter in Los Angeles, was contacted by Frank Paris, an executive story editor at Disney in 1978.

Disney was interested in doing a two-part Sunday night show called *Daughter of Zorro*. Nancy turned Paris's request over to her manager, Bob Thompson. Coincidentally, Thompson had been hired by Twentieth Century-Fox to produce the Frank Langella remake of the Tyrone Power *The Mark of Zorro* a number of years before.

Thompson spoke to Paris at Disney, and Paris proposed optioning the rights to Zorro for a year. They would make the two programs and perhaps turn them into a series. Thompson did not believe the deal was in his clients' best interest and consequently put feelers out to other studios, inquiring whether they might want to do Zorro. In addition, he informed Nancy about a European Zorro film that had just aired on television in the United States and that had also garnered a high Nielsen rating. That film was none other than Alain Delon's *Zorro*, dubbed in English.

With her brother, John Gertz, living in Israel at the time, Nancy took the lead in figuring out what exactly were their rights. In a lengthy letter to Thompson, Nancy reviewed the series of agreements between her father and Johnston McCulley, which were succeeded by the 1952 agreement between Mitch Gertz and Walt Disney. Because Disney had relinquished certain exclusive rights under the Disney-Gertz agreement, Nancy believed all of Disney's rights to Zorro were terminated. Disney, on the other hand, stood fast in its legal position that it had retained at least the nonexclusive right to use the Zorro character under certain circumstances.

Thompson found a better deal to option the Zorro rights for a series with Filmways. Nancy met with the company a number of times to discuss what would be presented to the networks as a new Zorro series, but meanwhile, she was moving on the legal front to get a determination of her and her brother's general rights to Zorro. Nothing came of the Filmways discussions, but in January 1979, an independent producer named Don Moriarty approached Nancy's agent for an option to do a comedic feature film version of Zorro.

ZORRO, THE GAY BLADE

Based on the success of *Love at First Bite*, a spoof on Dracula, starring George Hamilton, Moriarty struck a deal with the film's producer, Mel Simon. Mel Simon Productions took over as executive producers of what was to become the most outrageous version of Zorro—*Zorro, the Gay Blade*.

Simon arranged financing for the 1980 film and actor George Hamilton and C. O. Erickson took over as co-producers. George Hamilton had tackled the role of Count Dracula in Simon's *Love at First Bite* at the age of forty. He was born on August 12, 1939, in Memphis, Tennessee. In June

1979, flush with the success of his Dracula film, Hamilton appeared on the Johnny Carson show, where he announced that his next film would be a comedic version of Zorro. He then promptly demonstrated his character for the audience.

In a unique bit of Hollywood coincidence, Hamilton owned Greyhall, the estate that had belonged to Douglas Fairbanks, the original screen Zorro, before he built Pickfair, his home with Mary Pickford.

With his aptitude for farce, Hamilton played Diego, Zorro, and Diego's flamingly gay twin, Bunny Wigglesworth. The film was a spoof on Tyrone Power's *The Mark of Zorro*. Brenda Vaccaro starred as the wife of the *commandante* and Ron Leibman starred as Esteban, the *commandante*. Lauren Hutton, the supermodel for Revlon and *Vogue*, portrayed Charlotte Taylor Wilson, Diego's love interest. She agitated the people to revolt against Esteban's tyrannical rule. Ian Fraser's music was adapted from Max Steiner's *The Adventures of Don Juan*, and the theme sounds remarkably like the memorable score from the Tyrone Power version of *The Mark of Zorro* (music credit for that film had been given to Alfred Newman). Whether Newman adapted his work from the same Don Juan composition and failed to give Steiner credit is an issue for the Composers' Guild to investigate.

Vaccaro recalled how much fun the cast had shooting *Zorro, the Gay Blade* in Cuernevaca, Mexico, under Peter Madock's direction. They were encouraged to improvise, to "fly without a net," stretching the comic elements of their characters.

Vaccaro, a Brooklyn native, exploited her character's desire for attention with humorous flair, and she credits Bud Yorkin's film *Start the Revolution Without Me*, starring Gene Wilder and Donald Sutherland, with inspiring her comic pacing. Pouting like a spoiled child, she memorably blubbers, "You're going to ruin my party!" Vaccaro applauded Hamilton's use of an accent, phrasing, and timing that made his characterizations of Diego, Zorro, and particularly Bunny Wigglesworth unforgettable. The way Bunny declared "I want this for the peoples (pronounced "pip-oles")" had Vaccaro on the floor with laughter. She praised Hamilton for the way he handled each brother, pushing his characters into the arena of satire, of which Power had barely scratched the surface.

An outtake from *Zorro, the Gay Blade* featured on the television show

George Hamilton played Zorro in the spoof *Zorro, the Gay Blade* (1980). (©1981 Simon Film Productions, Inc.)

Pardon My Bloopers gave the flavor of Madock's directing style. Brenda was climbing up a very tall ladder in a long dress and satin pumps to surprise Hamilton with an illicit rendezvous. When she got to the top, she put her leg over the wrought iron balcony. Hamilton was supposed to pull her into the bedroom, but her heel got caught on the balcony. As Vaccaro explained

> He's pulling and he's pulling, and he's saying to me off camera, "What the hell is going on? Come on, come." . . . he starts to laugh and he fell, and I started to break up, and it's just terribly funny because I'm hanging . . . almost in space . . . with two hands. And finally he fell. He let go of me . . . and thank God I didn't fall backwards.

Zorro, the Gay Blade begins with a dedication to Rouben Mamoulian, the director of *The Mark of Zorro* starring Tyrone Power. Scenes that look like they are right from the Mamoulian film click past as the narrator explains,

Hamilton also played Bunny Wigglesworth, Diego's twin, as "the gay blade." (©1981 Simon Film Productions, Inc.)

> In the late part of the eighteenth century, the peasants of old California were oppressed by tyrannical landowners. To protect the poor and downtrodden people, there emerged a mysterious swordsman who pledged his life in the service of justice. To the people, he was a great hero who would live forever in their hearts. To the landowners, however, he was a real pain in the ass.

On screen, Zorro has ridden into the plaza, confronted soldiers putting up a notice, and carved a Z in one soldier's pants. Text appears: "In the House of Don Diego Vega in Madrid, Spain, 50 years A. Z. (after Zorro)."

Film Synopsis

Diego is in bed with a beautiful woman when her husband bursts into the bedchamber. Amidst the adulterous revelation, Diego's servant, Paco, enters, pantomiming a letter from California in which Diego is summoned home. Together they leap off a balcony into a waiting coach, fleeing the jealous husband and his four brothers.

In Los Angeles, Diego meets his old friend, Esteban, the hysterical *alcalde*, and Esteban's wife, Florinda. Diego learns that his father has died. As Esteban addresses the people a stagecoach brings beautiful Charlotte Taylor Wilson of the People's Independence Committee to town.

In a letter from his late father, Diego learns that his destiny is to be Zorro. He decides his Zorro costume is perfect to wear to Florinda's and Esteban's ball. Riding to the ball, Diego finds a peasant who has been robbed by a bandit with a silver patch over one eye. He chases the bandit down, sparing his life if the man will spread the word that a new bandit for the "oppres-sed and the trodden down" has arrived. He returns the peasant's stolen money, declaring he is back to "help the helpless, befriend the friendless, and to defeat the defeatless. *El Zorro* rides again!"

Zorro arrives at the ball just as Charlotte is being thrown off the premises for inciting rebellion. He escorts her into the party. While Florinda dances with Zorro, the silver-eyed bandit reports to the *alcalde* about his encounter with Zorro, mispronouncing the name as "Zero." Esteban challenges his masked guest to a duel, to which Florinda blubbers, "You're going to ruin my party." They exchange insults before Zorro disarms Esteban. Meanwhile, the peasants outside chant "Zorro, Zorro!" The fox further humiliates the *alcalde* by slicing his pants off because they bulge "with greed."

Zorro escapes to the balcony after swinging across the ballroom on a drape cord and riding up to a balcony on a chandelier rope. He leaps off the balcony, but he lands awkwardly, severely injuring his foot. The silver-eyed bandit reports the injury to Esteban.

Later that night, Florinda scales a ladder into Diego's bedroom, where he limps painfully. Begging him to make love to her, she confesses that she and Esteban only make love twelve times a year . . . all on the same night. As Florinda clutches Diego to her breast, he hears a horse approaching. She claims it's her heart, but they both know Esteban is coming. Diego hides Florinda in the casket that contained his Zorro costume.

Esteban is suspicious about Diego's absence from his party. He forces him through a painful routine of "walking and running and jumping in place . . ." with drill sergeant precision to prove that Diego's foot isn't injured. Claiming Zorro has upset him badly, the *alcalde* plunges his sword into the casket where Florinda is hiding. Esteban strides out, promising a reign of terror. When Diego throws open the casket, Florinda is cowering sideways, clutching her breasts. She exclaims, "Thank heaven for small favors!"

As Esteban's reign of terror enters its third week, a frustrated, limping Diego laments his inability to help. Suddenly a dandy British officer, Diego's long lost twin brother, Ramon, now known as Bunny Wigglesworth, rides up. Diego shares their father's letter. After trying on the costume and flipping profiles, from dark hair with a mask drawn around his eyes, to his blond wig and powdered face, Bunny accepts their destiny. The costume is not to his taste, however. He wants to make a statement so the world will recognize "Zorro, the Gay Blade!"

The "Gay Blade" goes into action—not with a blade, however, but with a whip. Each time he strikes, Zorro wears a new color, declaring, tongue-in-cheek, "There is no shame in being poor, only dressing poorly."

The *alcalde*'s agitation increases with each report of another escapade.

Charlotte declares her love after Bunny donates money to her work with children. They are like "partners in this great revolution." He is flattered but unresponsive, while Diego is obsessed with Charlotte.

Esteban again suspects that Diego is Zorro, forcing him to talk like a "sissy boy." He sees a hooded figure in the garden who claims to be a follower of Peter the dressmaker, Christ's tailor. Esteban requests that the padre (Bunny) pray for him.

Florinda wants Esteban to host another ball so she can show off her new necklace. Esteban agrees, seeing the event as an opportunity to snare Zorro. Diego has arranged for all the dons to come dressed as Zorro and Bunny arrives dressed as Diego's cousin, Marguerite. She captivates Esteban, charming the *alcalde* with an inane poem about Zorro.

Bunny succeeds in stealing Florinda's necklace. He turns the prize over to Diego and departs for England. Esteban is furious about the theft right under his nose. Esteban arrests Charlotte after a peasant reports seeing Zorro kiss her. However, he doesn't hear Charlotte confess that she knows Diego is Zorro. The *alcalde* is certain his nemesis will attempt to save his love. At the execution, the *alcalde* discovers Zorro hiding in a monk's robe. Zorro offers his life for Charlotte's freedom. Bunny returns at the climactic moment, in a lavish gold costume, to rescue Diego. Side by side, whip and sword flying, the twins battle the soldiers, aided by the peasants.

With Esteban out of power, Diego and Charlotte ride off into the sunset. She tries to convince him to give his land away to the people so they can live in Boston.

Fade

    to

       Z end.

Commentary

Zorro, the Gay Blade was an amusing, playful romp that showed a strong parallel between the Scarlet Pimpernel and Zorro. The poem Marguerite/Bunny recites at the party is strongly reminiscent of Sir Blakeney's rhyme about the Scarlet Pimpernel at Lord Grenville's ball. Also, Sir Blakeney's wife was named Marguerite. Bunny's Marguerite recites, "Ode to a bandit . . . His clothes are bold, his mind uncanny, give him your gold or he'll whip your fanny!" Sir Percy's ode in *The Scarlet Pimpernel* reflected the same mocking quality:

> We seek him here,
>
> we seek him there,
>
> those Frenchies seek him everywhere.
>
> Is he in heaven?
>
> Is he in hell?
>
> That demmed, elusive Pimpernel?

Donovan Scott's Paco is a rich combination of humor and mime. His performance is reminiscent of the girthsome gusto of Henry Calvin, who played Sergeant Garcia in the Disney series, combined with Gene Sheldon's Bernardo.

Florinda, Esteban's wife, is scornful of her husband, much like the distaste Lolita expressed for Diego in previous films.

In a recurring interplay that pokes fun at accents, Diego parodies the pronunciation of the words *sheep* and *peoples* with Charlotte. She can't understand him when he says "ships" for *sheep* and "pip-oles" for *peoples*.

Finally, when Charlotte reveals that she knows Zorro's identity, she is the first character in a Zorro story to see through Diego's disguise.

MINOR TELEVISION SERIES

The years between 1978 and 1981 marked a consolidation and clarification of the rights situation for Zorro, along with burgeoning interest in new projects. Nancy Larson continued her career as a screenwriter, branching into writing and directing for the stage. John Gertz returned to the United States to begin his doctoral studies in chronobiology at the University of California at San Francisco. Together, the twins formed Gertz-Larson Productions to shepherd their new business ventures while pursuing their other professions.

Two lawsuits were filed for copyright infringement on behalf of Gertz-Larson. One was against Allied Artists, who distributed Delon's film in the United States and Canada for airings on CBS on at least two occasions, December 30, 1977, and March 13, 1979. The second was against

Characters from the 1981 Filmation series, *The New Adventures of Zorro.*

David Friedman, the producer of a soft-porn film called *The Erotic Adventures of Zorro*.[5] Settlements were reached in both cases in favor of Gertz-Larson, recognizing their exclusive rights to the character of Zorro.

In 1980, Lou Schimer, head of the animation company Filmation, contacted Gertz-Larson Productions for the rights to produce a Zorro animated series. Schimer was already airing *Tarzan* and *The Lone Ranger* on CBS, but the broadcasting company wanted to expand Filmation's Saturday morning programming from an hour to an hour and a half. *Zorro* became the third segment of the company's action-adventure weekend lineup. Filmation produced thirteen half-hour episodes that ran for two years beginning in 1981. The following season, little blue Smurfs hit the airwaves and "cute" replaced "adventure." The *Zorro* series was shelved.

Filmation's animated series featured a significant variation on the traditional legend. Zorro's aide became a full partner in Zorro's fight for justice, much like the Lone Ranger's trusty Indian friend, Tonto. Bernardo was replaced by Miguel, who wore a mask, rode a palomino, and dressed in a tan outfit when accompanying Zorro. He was no longer mute or deaf and fought alongside Zorro with equal skill.

Diego introduces his role as Zorro in the opening voice-over. "As Diego, I pretend to be afraid, but with a mask as my disguise, I ride into the night and raise my sword in the name of justice, for I am Zorro."

Henry Darrow was featured as the voice of Zorro. Born Henry Delgado on September 15, 1933, he was the first Hispanic actor to play the Zorro lead. Darrow grew up in New York, inspired by the Tyrone Power version of *The Mark of Zorro*. As a youngster, he regularly imitated the fox with his friends, breaking apart fruit crates and nailing the boards together in the shape of crusaderlike swords. Darrow recalled whacking "the living daylight out of each other at the park . . . either you wanted to be Zorro or one or two . . . wanted to be the bad guy, Basil Rathbone."

After hearing Darrow's audition for the Zorro role, CBS was concerned that his inflection sounded like a come-on whenever he was doing a scene with a señorita. Lou asked Henry to redo his audition straight and he got the part.

Sergeant Gonzales, the character from the original McCulley and Fairbanks version, returned as the bumbling soldier. At the end of each episode, he would boast that if he'd been in charge, things would be different.

Captain Ramon was again the evil, greedy commandant; Don Alejandro was a righteous, white-haired, and bearded widower; but Zorro's horse was not Tornado, as in the Disney series—he was named Tempest.

An educational message was tagged onto the end of each episode. For example, Zorro sits atop his horse, looking down on San Pedro Harbor to his left and Santa Monica to his right. He explains to viewers that places named after men had "San" in front of them and that those named for women had "Santa." At the end of another episode, he explains that the explorer Balboa named the Pacific Ocean for its beauty and peacefulness.

In May 1981, Nancy Larson suggested that the time was right to try selling a concept for a Zorro live-action series. They could wait for a producer to option the rights, or they could take a concept to the network themselves. She had no interest in actually writing for a series, but she was interested in creating a show and working with the writers to develop it. Along with noted playwright Murray Mednick, Nancy created *The New Adventures of Zorro*, an hour-long adventure series. In her treatment, Diego was no longer merely a lover of poetry and a fop, rather, he was a renaissance man who used his knowledge to aid his work as Zorro. Diego also had an Indian mentor named Grey Owl who provided the mystical connection to Diego's transformation as Zorro and his fight against injustice. Nancy successfully pitched the concept to CBS, but although they loved the idea of doing Zorro, action-adventure series were out. Situation comedies and spoofs were in. CBS would happily do a funny Zorro.

With a network commitment from CBS, Nancy and John were in an enviable position. They didn't have to go pounding on studio doors to find someone to option the rights. Their phone literally began to ring off the hook with offers. Still, CBS was dictating a concept that neither John nor Nancy wanted to do. Though they had no great interest in doing another spoof after *Zorro, the Gay Blade*, Disney made an offer that ultimately became a deal between Gertz-Larson Productions and Walt Disney Studios to produce a situation comedy called *Zorro and Son*.

The CBS vision for *Zorro and Son* involved an aging Diego who brings his son into the "family business." Guy Williams, who was living in Buenos Aires and recovering from an aneurysm, read for the part of the older Zorro. However, Disney's original Zorro wasn't impressed with the new concept, and Williams returned to Argentina. He left quite an impression, however, on Paul Regina, the young actor chosen to play the younger Zorro. "I got to read with Guy Williams. . . . I was . . . twenty-four at the time and I'm in a room reading with Guy Williams."

Regina was cast as Don Carlos, Diego's son. He had been discovered by Derrick Cohen, the man who had found John Travolta for *Welcome Back, Kotter*. Henry Darrow was subsequently invited to audition and was then cast as the older Zorro, Don Diego. Working with Darrow was another highlight for Regina. Bill Dana, remembered for a character he created who announced "My name José Jimenez," played the role of Bernardo. Dana's Bernardo could speak, a significant adaptation from his predecessors in both print and film.

Paul Regina (*left*) and Henry Darrow (*right*) played a father and son duo in the 1983 series *Zorro and Son*. (©1983 Walt Disney Productions.)

Kevin Corcoran, the young actor who played Moochie in many Disney films, such as *Pollyanna*, produced *Zorro and Son*. Ironically, he had been the youngster who badgered Walt Disney about Zorro in the *Disneyland* promotional segment before the premiere of the original *Zorro* series.

Darrow wore Guy Williams's Zorro costume during the filming of *Zorro and Son*, though it had to be shortened due to the three-inch difference in their heights. Darrow was delighted with the opportunity to play a

Bill Dana, known widely for his José Jimenez character, played Bernardo on *Zorro and Son*. (©1983 Walt Disney Productions.)

man who was the same age as he was and who had similar problems. Zorro's feet hurt. Darrow's feet hurt. Zorro's back went out. Darrow's back went out occasionally. In the opening scene of the first episode, Darrow appears in the tavern on the interior balcony. As he looks down on the new commandant, he's ready to jump to the floor. On second thought, he announces that he might not be what he used to be but that what he's lost in youth he's gained in wisdom. He proceeds to explain that if "God had wanted people to jump, why did he invent stairs?"

The series reused the familiar Zorro theme song written by Foster and Bruns, with some slight changes in the wording. The lyrics became "the bold renegades both carve Zs with their blades . . . the foxes so cunning and free . . . Zorros, they make the sign of the Z."

In the first episode, the slapstick humor and ribald wordplay set the pace for what was to be a short-lived (five episodes) season. The new commandant is introduced in the tavern as Paco Pico. His second in command is Sergeant Sepulveda. *Zorro and Son* tried to replicate the exasperating interactions between Monastario and Garcia that had delighted viewers of the old Disney *Zorro* series. In response to Pico's query about the Curse of Capistrano, Sepulveda advises him to boil the water and he won't have to worry. Annoyed, Pico tells Sepulveda that the curse is Zorro, not Montezuma's Revenge. Pico muses further on the Scourge of El Camino, as if Zorro were a disease, to which Sepulveda again makes an inane remark about a scourge he'd picked up leaving San Francisco. Pico chastises his sergeant again, telling him the Scourge is also Zorro.

By this time, Zorro has trotted down the stairs, instead of jumping, to confront the commander. Zorro insults Pico by calling him Pico Paco and refers to himself as the "black blight of San Bernardino." Zorro makes his exit by attempting to jump from the balcony to the chandelier, but he misses. His pride is bruised. Throughout the entire episode, Diego refuses to admit he's lost any skill. He keeps insisting that the innkeeper raised the chandelier. Bernardo suggests that perhaps the innkeeper lowered the floor.

Diego's son, Don Carlos, returns home from college in Spain, having been summoned by Bernardo. Padre Napa has been strung up by the wrists and is to be tried for "selling a wine before its time." His twin brother, Father Sonoma, brings the news to Don Diego, hoping he will help. Diego refuses, but Don Carlos offers to help, especially since Father Sonoma has brought his lovely ward, Señorita Anita. When asked where she's from, Anita tells Don Carlos that she was found floating in a reed basket in the Valley of San Fernando. "Ah, a valley girl," he replies. With lines like that, it's no wonder the series didn't last long.

Don Carlos was portrayed as a teacher and a scientist. In the first *Zorro and Son* episode, Don Carlos begins making onion gas in Zorro's cave to help his father rescue the padre and Señorita Anita. Zorro won't hear of it. He needs only his sword and his courage because he has righteousness on his side. But when Zorro is surrounded in the cuartel, Don Carlos's onion gas canisters save the day.

A running gag between Diego and his son, Carlos, throughout the five episodes is who gets to kiss the girl at the end. Diego gets hugged by the padre or has to schlep the mother from Mexico, while Carlos gets the kisses. Each time, Diego reminds his son that the next time he gets the kiss. A humorous character, a soldier named Cassette, functions just like a cassette recorder. He repeats conversations verbatim—and can even be run on slow.

Carlos finds out that his father is really Zorro when he returns home. He's frustrated that his attempt to defend Father Napa has been thwarted. A true miscarriage of justice has occurred, and Carlos fumes that someone ought to do something. Seated with a shawl over his shoulders, Diego rises. He draws his foil and etches the legendary Z on the screen.

"I had a good time doing that one," Darrow later declared.

Carlos confesses that he never thought his father loved him. He was always out at night. His mother thought Diego was spending time with other women. Diego admits that he can't be Zorro forever but says he still has some Zorro left in him. Then he proceeds to show Carlos how to carve a Z. Carlos, however, takes forever, carving an elaborate Z.

Unlike the original Disney version, the fencing in *Zorro and Son* is minimal and the action is slow. And although *Zorro and Son* was shot on the Disney back lot in the old Zorro City, it is difficult to recognize the set in this series. Most plaza scenes were shot in front of the Casa de Cops, where the latest victims of Commandante Pico's brutality were strung up by the wrists. Location shots were limited to a few grassy, tree-lined locales. The show ran for only five episodes in 1983, and after that, the rights to produce new Zorro productions belonged to Gertz-Larson.

REGEHR EXTENDS
ZORRO'S LEGACY

*T*HE old Disney series hit the airwaves in France, airing on FR-3 in 1985, causing a nationwide sensation. Zorro fever struck France with a force equal to the one that captivated Americans during the heyday of *Dallas*. The Disney show aired in the most desirable time slot in France, Friday night at nine o'clock. The interest spilled over to merchandising. Kiosks featured new comic strip Zorro stories in Edimonde's *Le Journal de Mickey*. Products ranging from puzzles to chocolates to bedsheets and everything in between were marketed.

Over the previous two years, John Gertz had been running the Zorro business part-time while he completed the coursework for his Ph.D. Nancy Larson continued screenwriting and was selected to attend the prestigious Sundance Institute to develop her film *The Wizard of Loneliness*. Gertz-Larson Productions had evolved into Zorro Productions, Inc. Now, two roads diverged before John. He could devote his energies full-time to reviving Zorro as a classic character, or he could write his doctoral dissertation. John took a year's leave of absence from school to see how he'd fare in the business world and saw the leave extend as he grew Zorro into a successful international property.

Riding the wave of success in Europe, Gertz interviewed agents in early 1987 to see if they could generate interest in a new live-action series. Along with Bob Cristani of the William Morris Agency, John pitched Nancy's treatment to seven production companies in two days. Twenty-four hours later, all seven came back with offers to do the show. They closed a deal with New World Television, which was willing to commit to a minimum of twenty-five episodes, the number required for European participation. A network sale would have been more lucrative but it also would have meant a limited production order. Gertz didn't want to see the show cancelled again after only five episodes.

John had insisted on creative consultation rights for the series, but he found himself in conflict with the producers over how much they would be willing to accept him as a creative partner. The problem he confronted with Goodman-Rosen, the line producers, was to be revisited with each new Zorro project. Hollywood producers have a notorious reputation for paying rights holders and expecting them to disappear once the contracts are signed, but rights holders must exercise controls to protect the integrity of their characters to insure the property into the future. John's concerns regarding the pilot were summarily ignored by Goodman-Rosen. His chief complaint was the violence. The plot involved numerous killings and generally lacked humor, a critical part of the Zorro formula. Gertz felt that the music was terrible and that the original casting was by and large a disgrace.

Nancy's treatment had again been abandoned in favor of the concept of the producers, Goodman-Rosen. Antonio de la Cruz, the nephew of Don Diego, takes up the mantle of his boyhood hero when Zorro is killed by the commandant, Monastario. One element of Nancy's treatment was retained: Antonio played a clumsy scholar with glasses whose heroes were da Vinci and Cervantes.

The pilot featured Patrick James as Zorro and Patrice Martinez as the female lead, Doña Maria Constansa Arrillaga, a spoiled, rich girl to whom Antonio was betrothed. Antonio does not endear himself to his arranged marriage partner, harboring memories of Maria as a fat and homely child. Yet she has grown into a feisty, dark-haired beauty. Maria's feelings about Antonio echo his own about her. She is, however, very impressed with Zorro. In the climax, Antonio uses his knowledge of da Vinci's principles of flight to build a hang glider, which he dramatically sails into the plaza to rescue falsely convicted men from execution.

Location shooting took place on the southern coast of Spain near Almería in November 1987. Many of the extras were retired Brits who had abandoned their foggy isle for the warmth of the Mediterranean coast. Almería had been the location for filming many spaghetti westerns, possibly even some of the European Zorro films from the 1960s and 1970s. Gertz fumed on the set, watching a nightmare unfold before his eyes.

Based on a disastrous pilot, interest in the revival of Zorro as a live-action hero fell short of attracting the required funding partners. The fox once again seemed headed toward a short-lived revival. Although Patrick James looked the part of Zorro, his limited acting experience had not prepared him to meet the challenge of playing the fox. The producers went back to the drawing board, revamping the concept and addressing some of Gertz's concerns. The story line reverted to a traditional Zorro scenario without the oppressive violence. The fox had partially been rescued.

The reworked concept attracted French partners, Ellipse Programme, the production arm of the French broadcaster Canal Plus, Germany's Beta TV, and Italy's RAI. In addition to New World Television, the Family Channel, an American cable operator, joined as a producer. A true international co-production took shape. The show was shot outside Madrid with a crew from Spain, England, and the United States. A total of eighty-eight episodes were filmed over four seasons.

The only cast member to survive the face-lift was Patrice Martinez. The rest of the cast was completely new. Martinez, who was born in New Mexico, played the female lead in Steve Martin's *Three Amigos* and had a small role in Tim Burton's *Beetlejuice*. She was trained at the Royal Academy of Dramatic Arts in London on scholarship, and upon graduation she received a number of the academy's prestigious awards.

In her newly fashioned role, Patrice became Victoria Escalante, the tavern owner. She was not only Zorro's long-term love interest, but a feisty advocate for justice as well. Martinez described her excitement about the role.

I never had an interview where somebody with the production, where the writer, producer, or in this case, John Gertz, wanted to know my input on a character.... I was thrilled. They wanted to know how I saw it and they even let me give her the name. We gave her Victoria... we talked about how we saw her and it was great because we were able to come to a character that was much more interesting. She was feisty, fiery, headstrong, ahead of her time... I was thrilled to play that character.

Victoria's characterization gave an updated bent to the traditional female lead in a Zorro story. Rather than the traditional daughter of a don, Victoria was an independent businesswoman.

A Mexican actor named Ferdinand Allende was offered the lead as Zorro/Diego. He declined the part, however, because the shooting schedule conflicted with his wedding.

The nod was finally given to Canadian actor Duncan Regehr, who was tall, dark, and handsome. Like Guy Williams, Duncan could fence and ride. Born in Lethbridge, Alberta, and raised in Victoria, British Columbia, Duncan entered show business as a figure skater at age ten with local and regional ice shows. He began acting at the age of fourteen, hosting a talk show on cable TV in his hometown. He attended the Bastion Theater School, Vancouver's Julliard, spending two years studying voice, movement, acting, and fencing, along with his academic load. Duncan undertook several years of acting in regional theater, moving on to the Ontario Shakespeare Festival before jumping into television and films. He had trained for a spot on Canada's Olympic boxing team from 1976 to 1980 and had learned to fence at school in Ontario. While living in Los Angeles, he raised horses. At six-five and 196 pounds, Regehr cut a commanding image as the Spanish California hero.

Regehr had been considered for the pilot but was tied up with another

Patrice Martinez updated the role of Zorro's female love interest as an independent businesswoman in New World's 1989 *Zorro* television series. (Courtesy of New World International.)

Canadian actor Duncan Regehr brought a powerful pantherlike quality to his role as Zorro in the New World series. (Courtesy of New World International.)

series at the time. He was called again when Patrick James was abandoned. This time, schedules clicked. Duncan, who had played the swashbuckler Errol Flynn in *My Wicked, Wicked Ways*, was in England working on *The Last Days of Pompeii* when he got a call from one of the Zorro producers. Gary Goodman went to meet him. Since Duncan had already seen the script, casting was a snap, and as he explained, the producers were "very keen to get me for the role. So, that's it! I graduated to Zorro."

At age thirty-six, Regehr portrayed a man—or rather, two men—roughly ten years younger. He played Diego as an educated man, well versed in the arts and sciences, as in the Larson-Mednick scenario. He did many of his own stunts and fencing. To stay in shape for his grueling schedule, Regehr got up at four in the morning for a two-and-a-half-hour workout in addition to an eight-mile run every day. Despite the heavy volume of work, Duncan found the role extremely fulfilling and a great challenge.

The stunt coordinator, Peter Diamond, was often Zorro's sparring partner on screen. Diamond was well-known for his excellent work choreographing the spectacular laser light sword fights in the Star Wars trilogy and the swashbuckling in *The Princess Bride*. He also trained Bob Hoskins for his physically grueling role in *Roger Rabbit*.

Along with his stunt coordinating role, Diamond acted in the series, too. He played Sir Edmund Kendall, Diego's fencing instructor in Madrid, in the two-hour show, *The Legend Begins*. Regehr explained how the fencing scenes were shot.

> Very often, the stunt coordinator is my opponent and we used him as the villain. In fact, you only usually see his arm or hand. Sometimes, we put in the other actor for a couple of quick pops, but nothing really complicated. Then, we switch back to me or the stunt coordinator's arm. It's very cleverly done . . .

Ray Austin directed many of the episodes from the second through the fourth season and functioned as producer and director during the last thirteen episodes. Austin had a good feel for action, having come up in the business as a stuntman and then a stunt director. Regehr had worked with Ray previously and was delighted with his appointment.

The shooting schedule was intense. Two episodes were shot in a week, each requiring three days. Regehr described the work schedule and how he approached his character.

> The days are long and very physical . . . I also have lots of speeches in my dual characters. I must say that I do get a lot of support from the other actors. People ask all the time if I based my Zorro on any of my predecessors, such as Guy Williams. I never even saw any of those guys. I don't follow anyone's ideas except my own.

> The image that I used for Zorro . . . was the panther, the black panther. The guy moved like a cat. He was fluid and he could disappear in and out of shadows. . . . I purposely stayed away from watching any of the other Zorros before taking off on my own journey with it. In fact, I really never did get to play the character that I wanted . . . I ended up playing what the network wanted me to play. The version I would have done was entirely different. . . . There was a tendency, I think, to take Zorro in the direction of self-righteousness. He was very puritanical, which was the mandate of the network. When I signed on, I wanted to make him much sexier, much darker, much more of a visceral character because when you think about it, there has to be something a little quirky with a guy who's going to not only deceive his father but all the people around him and put on a mask . . . you know, he's a kinky guy. . . . I wanted to make Don Diego into much more of a nerd, if you will . . . play him with blonde hair, long blonde hair . . . because you never actually see Zorro's hair. It's kept under a scarf . . . then put on some Benjamin Franklin spectacles and make him totally nonathletic so that you would never guess in a million years that this guy could make the jump to the super-hero . . . that would make the definition of three characters for Zorro. There's the masked crusader, there's the nerd at home who is also not the real don, not the real man, but the man who is also deceiving or hiding from his father and the woman that he loves. And then there's the real guy, whoever that is.

Like Zorro's alter ego, Diego, Duncan is an artist and a poet. His abstract paintings have commanded one-man gallery shows, and his poetry has been published in literary magazines.

James Victor was cast in the role of Sergeant Mendoza, the comic relief character with a heart. Born in the Dominican Republic, Victor moved to New York City with his family as a child and eventually grew up to work in the publicity department of Disney sending out Zorro publicity. Victor never imagined he'd be playing Henry Calvin's successor in a new Zorro series. He trained with John Cassavetes's workshop in New York and was featured in the Oscar-nominated film *Stand and Deliver*. After four auditions, James won the part, despite a disagreement with the producers over using an accent, which he felt was an important comic element for the character. He won out. Working on the series was an experience he will always treasure as a highlight of his career. James portrayed Mendoza with the same sympathy for Zorro that had characterized McCulley's Sergeant Garcia. He enjoyed food, was superstitious, and boasted shamefully. Not only was he the most convenient object of the *alcalde*'s fury, but Zorro regularly humiliated him by slicing Zs in his pants or making him drop his drawers.

Juan Diego Botto, a Spanish teenager, was cast as Felipe, a re-envisioned Bernardo role. The producers wanted to provide a youthful character with whom a young audience could relate. Honing his miming skills proved useful, since Botto spoke no English and like Bernardo, played the role of a deaf-mute. An orphan who lived with Don Diego and his father, Alejandro, Felipe became Zorro's aide.

Michael Tylo played the role of the wicked *alcalde*, Luis Ramone. With his deep, cultured voice, Tylo captured the caricature of the part. The comic dynamic between Tylo and Victor was modeled after the relationship between Montastario and Sergeant Garcia in the original Disney series. Tylo wore his hair long and dressed elegantly and as an extra touch, added gloves to his costume.

Besides the language barrier of filming in a foreign country, Tylo missed his family. His sons were young, nine and two, at the time of the filming, and his wife was an actress. With her working, Tylo was on his own in Spain. As a result, he left after the second season. John Hertzler, a stage actor, ably took over the role of the new *alcalde* with Tylo's departure.

The location shooting took its toll on Patrice Martinez's life also. Between the original pilot and the first season, Patrice got married. For the first three seasons, her screen credit was "Patrice Camhi." By the fourth

James Victor played the inept but endearing Sergeant Mendoza, shown here with Regehr as Diego. (Courtesy of New World International.)

season, she and her husband had divorced. She returned to using Martinez for her credit line. Another actor who left the show after the first season was Efrem Zimbalist Jr., who played Don Alejandro. The former star of *The FBI* found living abroad undesirable at his age.

The departure of Zimbalist opened the door for Henry Darrow to participate in his third Zorro series. Darrow holds the distinction of being the only actor to have three lead roles in *Zorro* series. Darrow enjoyed doing some of his own fencing in the show, as well as using the skills he had learned wielding a whip for his role on the series *High Chaparral*. Darrow had met producer Goodman at the LA Polo Lounge. Asked if he'd like to play the father, Darrow answered in the affirmative.

According to James Victor, camaraderie among the cast and crew was great during the first season—except for relations with Regehr. Filming in a foreign country for five months out of the year put pressure on the cast in a manner unlike shooting a series in the States. Transportation during their off hours was a concern for all the principals. Working within a constrained budget, the producers told the series stars that no one would have a personal car. When the cast found out that Duncan had been promised a car, it became a thorn in their sides since they all worked equally hard. Compounding the problem was Duncan himself. During the first season, he was standoffish with the other cast members. His snobbish, inaccessi-

Michael Tylo, the *alcalde* during the first two seasons of the Zorro series, was continually humiliated by his nemesis, Zorro. (Courtesy of New World International.)

The cast assembles in the de la Vega salon in the episode, "The Buccaneers." John Hertzler (*right, facing the camera*) replaced Michael Tylo as the *alcalde*. The other cast members (*from right to left*) include: Duncan Regehr as Diego, Juan Diego Botta as Felipe, Henry Darrow as Alejandro, Patrice Martinez as Victoria, and James Victor as Sergeant Mendoza. (Courtesy of New World International.)

ble, Hollywood airs did not endear him to the other cast members or to the crew.

James Victor remembered one occasion during filming in which Duncan tried to tell him how to say a line. Actors take direction from the director, not from other cast members. Duncan's suggestion pushed the wrong button on Sergeant Mendoza's tunic. The two men went outside, as Victor tells it, "like two high school kids, ready to duke it out." Henry Darrow and Gary Goodman smoothed over the dispute. Regehr never gave Victor another pointer on dialogue. But it was either guts or foolhardiness for Victor to even think about taking on Regehr. Besides the difference in their heights, Duncan had been in sixty-five amateur boxing bouts, losing only three. Victor hadn't thought through the consequences of engaging in

Veteran Zorro star Henry Darrow replaced Efrem Zimbalist Jr., as Diego's father in the second season. (Courtesy of New World International.)

fisticuffs with Duncan, just as Duncan hadn't thought through the implications of what a blow to his nose in a fistfight might do to his screen career.

Relations between Duncan and the crew were tense that first season also. James recalled another occasion when the crew put cow dung in Regehr's dressing room. Ten minutes before Duncan arrived, they took it out. The smell made a lasting impression on the fox. Over the course of the series, however, Regehr made a complete turnaround in his rapport with the cast and crew. He became charming, ate with the other actors, and invited them to visit him and his wife at their home in Vancouver. James even attended a book signing for an art book Duncan wrote called *The Dragon's Eye*.

The entire cast and crew did become like a family over the four years. Actual family members joined the cast, too, garnering roles in the series. Patrice Martinez's brother and sister, as well as James Victor's brother, were seen in feature roles or bit parts. Even rights holder and creative consultant John Gertz appeared in one episode, "The Reward," in season four. Visiting the set with his family during the last week of filming for the series, John Hertzler, the *alcalde*, and James Victor, Sergeant Mendoza, convinced director Ray Austin to give Gertz a Hitchcock-like cameo appearance. Dressed in caballero attire, a sombrero hanging down his back, Gertz sat unobtrusively at one of the tables in the tavern, quietly listening to a stranger dispel Mendoza's fanciful tale of crossing the Yucatán.

Ignacio Carreno served as Duncan's stunt double for the four years of New World's *Zorro*. He did the riding sequences during chase scenes, swung from chandeliers, jumped off buildings, and did the whip work. Carreno's role was not limited to stunts. He had occasional speaking parts in episodes like "Pride of the Pueblo" (season one). Ignacio was shorter and stockier than Regehr, but he had been ably trained for his stunt work with *Rocky* action hero Sylvester Stallone.

Reference material from the California Historical Society and the Spanish National Archives helped the set designers re-create a model of the Los Angeles *pueblo* in 1820 on a thirty-four-acre parcel at Colmenar Viejo, outside Madrid. Built in seven weeks by a crew of fifty carpenters, fifteen craftsmen, thirty-six laborers, and twenty-five painters, the set included practical interiors to accommodate interior filming, along with Victoria's tavern and the cuartel, jail, church, and blacksmith shop. A sign that read PUEBLO LOS ANGELES hung above the entrance to the plaza. The exterior of the de la Vega hacienda was nearby. A ravine behind the outdoor *pueblo* provided the setting for many of the chase scenes, as well as an exterior cave that was used in a number of episodes.

Indoor sets were located at San Sebastian de los Reyes, in the outskirts of Madrid. They were designed utilizing sketches and information from the historical reference materials. Diego's ornately carved desk chair in Zorro's cave, as well as the *alcalde*'s chair, are examples of the fine period pieces that graced the set. Costume designers created original wardrobes from textiles that approximated the look of the historical period. Weapons and uniforms followed designs in the reference materials.

Zorro's secret cave could be accessed through the salon of the de la Vega hacienda by pushing a panel on the right side of the fireplace which opened a door behind the fire grate and led down stairs into Zorro's laboratory. A desk and Zorro's experiment table filled the dark cavern. Beyond, Tornado stood in wait. In this cavern, Diego put his scientific training to work to complement his deeds as Zorro. One example of his ingenuity was demonstrated by the method in which the cave entrance opened. Zorro would guide Tornado to step on a pad buried in the ground that activated a system of gears and pulleys which opened a boulder camouflaging the outside cave entrance. Another pad was buried outside the cave and also triggered the gears to move the boulder. A control on a wall sconce on the stairway inside the cave opened the fireplace door back into the *sala* of the de la Vega hacienda. A peephole allowed viewing from inside the cave into the salon in the hacienda, and another one offered a view outside the cave. This secret entrance was a far cry from the simple double-door cellar entrance used by Fairbanks in his 1920 *The Mark of Zorro*.

Science played a significant role in the series. Diego applied the principle of levers to opening a caved-in cave entrance. He played with Ben Franklin's kite experiment on electricity and incorporated a boomerang in his work; he took water samples for analysis; he analyzed handwriting to determine that a signature was a forgery; he utilitzed da Vinci's principles of flight in designing his hang glider; and he created tons and tons of explosive devices.

Executive story editor Phillip John Taylor and supervising producer Robert McCullough had time to explore the characters, as well as to bring in guest stars over the course of the four seasons. Taylor and McCullough wrote fifty-two of the eighty-eight episodes either together or individually. Adam West, television's Batman, guest-starred as a traveling inventor who offers to capture Zorro by scientific means ("The Wizard," season one). Philip Michael Thomas of *Miami Vice* starred as a freed slave who becomes a boxer ("Pride of the Pueblo," season one). Andre the Giant guest-starred in "Big Brother" (season two). Playing Nestor Vargas, Andre uses his physical strength to defend his brother, Enrique, a short, skinny weasel of a fellow who has been accused of robbing the Bank of Los Angeles.

In other stories, prejudice, superstitions, environmental issues, historical figures, and aging all became themes explored from the perspective of the characters in the series. New immigrants face accusations of witchcraft. Zorro discovers that lead sulfate, used to stop weed growth, has contaminated a creek, causing the deaths of two landholders. Annie Oakley comes to town, posing as a teacher, determined to earn the reward for capturing Zorro. Mendoza inherits a hacienda inhabited by a ghost. Alejandro hooks up with his old gang to revenge his brother's death. Unfortunately, the four men were like the "Over the Hill Gang" and desperately needed Zorro's help to complete their mission.

Love themes naturally found their way into the series. The ever-present tension in Diego/Zorro's underlying relationship to Victoria was a subtext to many stories. While traveling together to deliver a message to the governor, Victoria and Diego spend a rainy night in the grain storage area of a windmill à la the Clark Gable, Claudette Colbert classic It Happened One Night. Though Victoria is unaware that she was with her true love, Zorro, Diego is very much aware of his uncomfortable dilemma ("One Special Night," season two).

In "An Affair to Remember" (season four), Zorro asks Victoria to marry him, even though for her protection he must not disclose his secret identity. As a token of his love, Zorro slips his mother's gold ring on her finger. Later, in the tavern, Diego devilishly prods Victoria to reveal why she is looking so radiant. She etches a Z in the air. Victoria lures Diego into thinking she'll tell him. "Can you keep a secret?" she whispers. He can. As wily as her love, the fox, she smiles and replies, "So can I." Victoria leaves Diego dangling, but the audience knows that her loyalty gives Zorro more reason to love her than ever.

Felipe fell in love, too, with an Indian girl, and was forced to engage in a battle of honor with her Indian fiancé ("Rites of Passage," season two). Sergeant Mendoza became the object of the affections of a female thief in "The Whistling Bandit" (season two). Even Alejandro relived an old romance with female guest star, Donna Bakala, in "A Love Remembered" (season three). He'd had a romantic relationship with the same actress on the High Chaparral series in 1967. The Zorro episode features footage from their past romance, as well as her death in Darrow's arms in both series.

In "The Legend Begins" (season one) Diego learns that Felipe actually can hear. He conceals the fact from Diego and Alejandro, not certain they would still care for him. In "The Word" (season three), Felipe's inability to speak is explained. Caught in a battle during the Mexican Revolution, his parents were killed. When Diego found him, the boy was traumatized. He brought Felipe back to live in Los Angeles. He speaks one word, "Zorro," to save his mentor from an attack.

Most episodes in the series were self-contained, twenty-three-minute stories with budgets for each episode running between $400,000 and 450,000. There were, however, some notable exceptions. The two-part story, "The Legend Begins," explained how Diego became Zorro. The story is told as a flashback as Zorro lies injured in a canyon. It was a further embellishment of Disney's previous attempt to draw a connection between Diego and his symbol, the fox. Concealing his identity to not endanger those he loves, Diego combined two ideas to become Zorro. In the tavern, he listens to Mendoza explain how soldiers fear the unknown. Later, he sees a fox hiding in what would become Zorro's cave. The two experiences coalesce into a vision. Like the clever fox who travels at night, eluding the hunters who covet its pelt, Zorro, too, will ride at night, preying on the soldiers' fears as he accomplished his daring deeds of justice.

Observant viewers will notice that when Zorro dramatically hang glides into the plaza to rescue his father, he is launched from the back of a wagon. The driver of the wagon is not Juan Diego Botta, who played Felipe. Rather, it is the young actor who appeared in the series pilot. Footage of the rescue was edited into "The Legend Begins." The plaza is also different in the rescue scene, edited into the episode from the pilot which had been shot in Almería, on the coast of southern Spain, two years before.

In "Devil's Fortress," another two-parter, the cast went on location to a Spanish castle that doubled as a notorious prison where Victoria's father lay dying. The story provided Michael Tylo's exit as the *alcade*. He falls to his death after desperately grabbing Zorro's mask. As he hurls through space, he exclaims, "De la Vega . . . I should have known."

A four-parter in the last season reveals that the royal emissary of the king, Risendo, is Diego's twin brother. Veering toward soap opera, the story details how Risendo was stolen at birth by the barren midwife of Alejandro's wife. Since he was not present during the birth, Alejandro had no knowledge of his other son. Now Risendo wants his inheritance, at Diego's expense. To prove the blood ties between Diego and Risendo, the midwife discloses an unusual, corresponding birthmark on both the twins' inner thighs. During a final duel, between Diego and Risendo, the *alcalde* intercedes to protect Diego from his twin's blade. Risendo dies by the *alcalde*'s blade. Referred to as the Brothers Quartet, the episodes were titled "The Arrival," "Death and Taxes," "Conundrum," and "The Discovery."

In "The Three Musketeers," a two-parter, Diego joins the descendants of the original trio to fight against an evil vicomte during a vacation in France. The show was used as the pilot for a series about the Musketeers, but it was never produced.

Zorro premiered in the United States on the Family Channel on Friday, January 5, 1990, at six P.M. It also aired at eleven P.M. Fridays, with repeat showings on Saturday and Sunday nights at six-thirty P.M. In addition, it was broadcast in thirty-five countries around the world. In the United States, young families made up 56 percent of the audience, the prime target market for advertisers. After the first season, an analysis of the viewers revealed that over 650,000 households watched the show during any particular episode. Not only children were watching *Zorro*. Women were the show's single biggest viewing audience, at 43 percent and the biggest block was baby boomer women aged thirty-five to forty-nine.

To captialize on and tantalize the show's female viewers, the producers marketed Duncan's fine physique by having him change his shirt several times on screen in the fourth season.

The theme song began with a *swish, swish, swish* sound as a silver *Z* was etched across a black screen. Zorro streaked across a bluff on Tornado, cape flying, as the lyrics echoed the tale of the Spanish fox. Jay Asher wrote the pulsating music with lyrics by Joel Siegel.

When daggers are pointed at innocent hearts and muskets
are ready to fire,
When tyrants ride high and govern with fear and the forces
of evil conspire,
Then from out of the night a hero must ride with courage
that even a mask won't disguise
They turn to . . . a man called Zorro (echo—Zorro).
One who's larger than life and defender of all is this man
who the people acclaim.
He's the one who strikes back for the poor and oppressed,
A hero, whose name is Zorro,
   his name is Zorro,
    his name is Zorro.

Regehr received high marks for his athletic prowess and charming portrayal of the dual character from M. Demarco, writing for *Movie Collector's World*. The *New York Post*'s David Bianculli called the show

> an instant hit in my household. . . . I loved the original "Zorro" as a kid but watching tapes of it now, which I did to compare the Zorro series . . . The "New Zorro" is that rare TV remake that is more fun than the original—and it's in color, too.

Don Freemen of the *San Diego Union* praised the series.

> The years pass and now what we have on television is . . . a spanking new Zorro. And that is thrilling news, is it not? . . . Regehr's Zorro has dark, good looks, sleek black hair, a pencil-thin mustache, a lean frame, a big smile and legendary skills with horses and whips. He has a ton of derring-do. He also has a señorita named Victoria Escalante and what a señorita! . . . What does she look like? Tell me what is the Spanish word for "knockout"?

Tom Walter of the *Commercial Appeal* reviewed the new Zorro series, calling it

> fun stuff, with Zorro jumping off buildings onto his horse, carving a Z onto people's shirts and using his whip to snag a roof tile he's accidentally knocked off. . . . And the dialogue is as ripe as the story lines. As he carves a Z on the Alcalde's desk, he says, "Your office is so drab. Why don't we re-decorate it?" Oh, that Zorro. Such a kidder.

The series garnered the attention of many fans, including one special educator in Covington, Kentucky. Alma Burnette, like Zorro, has been on a mission. Her cause wasn't injustice in the *pueblo* of Los Angeles but rather high-risk kids in her school. The First District School of Covington is an inner-city elementary school with 97 percent of its children on the government's free lunch program. In addition to living below the poverty line, most of her students were underachievers who saw no need for education. Children who got good grades were ridiculed. Some of the students

Alma targeted had learning problems. Others were suicidal or had police records.

Alma knew what these streetwise kids were like because she had been one of them herself. Television shows had opened her eyes to a better life and changed her attitude toward education, showing her "how life should be, not how bad life can be. It showed ideals to shoot for, not problems to wallow in." For three years, she searched for a program that would inspire her students to learn, and when she saw the new Zorro series, she was impressed, particularly with the interpretation of Diego as a scholar who put his learning to use. Based on episodes in the first season, Alma developed a pilot teacher's guide for her school, choosing the hardest students to reach, and assumed that if the program worked with them it would work anywhere.

Her guide was so successful that teachers around the district wanted access to it. In Alma's report, after only four weeks of using the Zorro Teaching Program, students were expressing amazement at the self-confidence Diego possessed. They saw that it did not bother him to be considered a nerd and that he never gave in to peer pressure. These were major lessons the staff had been trying to teach their pupils for years. Students talked about how Zorro treated Felipe with kindness and as an equal, even though he was handicapped, while some of the older students who were suicidal or had police records were proud of the Spanish words they had learned. Kids who had even refused to make Christmas ornaments suddenly wanted to construct a *pueblo* or draw a life-size picture of Zorro for their classroom.

After word of her work spread, April 26, 1991, was declared Zorro Day in Kentucky and Alma was honored in a special ceremony at her school by the governor and the mayor of Covington. The producers of the series attended, thrilled with the impact Zorro was having on children's lives.

Alma received a letter from then–First Lady Barbara Bush, complimenting her as "a shining example of what George Bush means when he talks about 'a thousand points of light,'" and the National Education Association (NEA), which endorses very few television programs, officially recommended the new Zorro series for viewing.

The Family Channel hired Alma to develop a comprehensive Teachers' Guide for *Zorro*, and eventually several hundred booklets were distributed to teachers, who were encouraged to make as many photocopies as they could use. The Family Channel estimated that 140,000 students were impacted by "Zorro in the Classroom." Teachers could tape specific, commercial-free episodes off *Cable in the Classroom* and show them to their students in order to follow the activities across subject areas in Alma's guide. It motivated students to emulate a dashing role model who used his education to solve problems.

Alma realized the important influence the program had on children's lives when she asked students to respond to the following statement: "Zorro has helped me discover many new ways to see the world in which I live. If I could use this knowledge to change one thing in my life, it would be . . ." One fifth-grader wrote:

> . . . alcohol and drugs. I would help people to say No to alcohol and by helping I will say No, too. And the way Zorro encourages me to say No is by him saying No to alcohol and drugs, too. And by watching him say No gives him a good life and if I say No I could get a good education and lead a great life too.

In response to the question "If a friend offered you something alcoholic or drug-related that you would prefer not to do, how would you respond?" another child wrote:

> I would say No and tell them I don't do that kind of stuff. Then if they keep trying to get me to do it, I still wouldn't. Then I'd say exactly what Zorro said, No thank you. I'd prefer to keep a clear head. They might think I'm stupid, but I know I ain't.

Zorro didn't get all rave reviews. In fact, United Hispanics of America considered the Family Channel's Zorro to be another example of a "legendary Spanish hero . . . being portrayed by a non-Hispanic actor" and charged discrimination. Though they did not call for cancellation of the series, they used the protest to "enlighten the country to the injustice in discriminatory hiring practices in the film industry." Their goal was to pro-

Today he's teaching elementary school in Covington, Kentucky.

The First District School in Covington is an inner-city school filled with kids who used to think education wasn't cool. Then along came media specialist Alma Burnette with an unlikely solution to the problem: Zorro.

Using tapes of the masked hero's most recent adventures on The Family Channel, Ms. Burnette created teaching guides designed to motivate students to stay in school. Suddenly, they began to see how education could help them solve problems

and become leaders like Zorro.

Zorro's success in Covington is but one example of how local cable companies like yours are helping teachers bring subjects to life. Through a national program called Cable in the Classroom, cable companies provide free service and a wealth of commercial-free programming to over 43,000 elementary and secondary schools.

Cable's contributions to the classroom today can help teach lessons that last for a lifetime.

Cable contributes to life.
National Cable Television Association

The *Zorro* series was recommended for viewing by the National Education Association.

vide visible, positive Hispanic role models for children and future generations.

John Gertz, who had engineered the revival of the character, bristled at an editorial by Angelo Figueroa, published in the *San Francisco Chronicle*. Figueroa took issue with casting Regehr and Zimbalist as father and son. John pointed out in his letter to the editor that a Mexican actor had turned down the role that Duncan subsequently accepted. Zimbalist bowed out after the first season, to be replaced by Henry Darrow. Of the six principals in the series, Darrow, Victor, Camhi/Martinez, and Botto were all Hispanic. Darrow and Victor had anglicized their last names, as Guy Williams himself had done.

The merchandising campaign that accompanied the New World series did not cause the same Zorro fever that had run rampant in the late 1950s, but dozens of worldwide licensees covered a broad spectrum of products and commercial endorsements. Notably, Marvel Comics produced a series of twelve issues based on New World's Zorro shows, while seven novels by S. R. Curtis for middle-age readers were published in Germany, Poland, Sweden, Holland, Finland, the Czech Republic, Hungary, and Russia. At this time Zorro even became a spokesman for drug education and crime prevention.

The success of the New World series encouraged Gertz and Larson to begin thinking about a feature film, and in 1990, they set a plan in motion, utilizing the model that had worked so well to sell the New World series.

HOPKINS AND BANDERAS
SLASH THEIR ZS

*T*RISTAR Pictures and Amblin Entertainment joined forces to create *The Mask of Zorro*, a blockbuster action-adventure film starring Antonio Banderas, Anthony Hopkins, and newcomer Catherine Zeta Jones. This movie, the biggest Zorro feature film ever undertaken since Johnston McCulley created his legendary character, brought together the elevated star quality of Oscar winner Hopkins with the sex appeal of Banderas, under the consummate direction of Martin Campbell. The sweeping story plumbed the depths of human anguish across twenty years of tragic loss, thievery, imprisonment, and greed, emerging with measured triumph in rescue, love, and redemption.

As Doug Claybourne, co-producer on the film, noted, "The *hard* ones are always the best pictures." Audience responses to research screenings reflected Claybourne's optimism about the picture. The studio's enthusiasm for the director's first cut prompted their decision to move the film from a spring release to become their 1998 mid-summer blockbuster.

As Don Montero, the despised Spanish governor, prepares to leave California for Madrid, he has planned a parting execution. His goal is to lure his nemesis, Zorro, the masked defender of justice, into a trap. In a characteristic display of cunning and athletic skill, Zorro foils Montero's execution plot, but receives a small wound in his arm. He is aided in his escape by two admiring orphaned youths, Joaquin Murieta and his younger brother, Alejandro. As a token of his appreciation, Zorro gives the older boy a valuable medallion. Zorro confronts Montero before his final escape, marking him with a lasting momento—three quick strokes of his blade, which etch a Z in the governor's neck.

Zorro returns to his secret cave beneath the home of his alter ego, Diego de la Vega. Peering into the crib of his darling infant daughter, Elena, he amuses her with a fanciful story of heroic deeds while his lovely wife, Esperanza, joins him, relieved that he has returned home safely. Suddenly, they are surprised by Montero and his men, intent on arresting Diego as Zorro and, with the obvious wound on his arm, the evidence of Diego's dual identity is undeniable. Driven by jealous revenge, Montero reveals his unrequited love for Esperanza, but in the duel that ensues, the object of both men's passion is mortally wounded. Montero kills the soldier who unintentionally shot her and the grieving Diego is captured. In an act of retribution that drives a dagger through Diego's anguished heart, Montero steals the young Elena and banishes Diego to a living hell in Talamantes Prison. Heartbroken, de la Vega promises Montero that he will never be rid of him.

Twenty years later, life in California has become desperate. Families have disappeared without a trace while Diego has languished in brutal prison conditions. Joaquin and Alejandro Murieta, now grown, have become wanted *bandidos* and work with an accomplice named Three-Fingered Jack, stealing from the soldiers who have stolen from the people. The callous Captain Love sets a trap for the Murieta brothers and Three-Fingered Jack after they rob his soldiers. Three-Fingered Jack is wounded and captured, but Joaquin, surrounded by Love and his men, kills himself. Furious that he has been denied the privilege of killing Joaquin himself, Love beheads the *bandido* as Alejandro watches in horror from his hiding place. Zorro's medallion goes flying. Bereft, Alejandro finds the medallion later that night and drowns his sorrow in drink.

Meanwhile, Montero returns to California. Haunted by the fear that Diego has somehow survived, the former governor is escorted under cover of night by Love to Talamantes Prison. In conditions worse than grim, all the prisoners claim to be Zorro—except Diego. He deftly arranges an escape by substituting himself for a dead man. Buried alive, he digs his way out of a grave and makes his way to the seashore where Montero has disembarked to a less than enthusiastic reception. Intent on murdering Montero in broad daylight, Diego maneuvers through the crowd, looking for an advantageous position. As the former governor announces his pledge to fight for a free and independent California, Diego positions himself to strike. At that very moment he sees his daughter, Elena, come on shore. She is the vision of her mother, Esperanza. It is instantly clear to Diego that this lovely young woman is the apple of her "father's" (Montero) eye and there is no way he can kill him.

Diego wanders into the cantina where Alejandro is about to trade his medallion for another drink, but recognizing the necklace, he disrupts the purchase. Alejandro protests but then spots Captain Love across the plaza. He starts to pursue his brother's killer, only to be stopped again by Diego, who warns Alejandro that he can't win when he's drunk and angry. Diego offers to teach Alejandro to fight, remembering the help Joaquin and Alejandro gave him twenty years before. In great awe, Alejandro understands that this broken old man is his childhood hero, Zorro.

Diego takes Alejandro to Zorro's secret cave under the old de la Vega hacienda, where his training begins. It is strenuous, demanding intense discipline and concentration. Diego trains Alejandro to follow the medallion's etchings, which are inlaid on a raised marble dais in the cave. His method brings the combatants closer and closer together until one can strike at the other's heart.

In town to trade Diego's old trinkets for food and supplies, Alejandro and Diego see a gorgeous black stallion. The horse suddenly breaks loose in the plaza, but Alejandro calms it down before it charges Don Peralta and his wife. The don rewards Alejandro with a peso and, in turn, Alejandro discreetly relieves the don of his valuables, including an invitation to Montero's upcoming banquet.

HOPKINS AND BANDERAS SLASH THEIR ZS

As Alejandro Murieta, Antonio Banderas readies himself to fight the soldiers in the barracks. (Stills copyright © 1998 by TriStar Pictures, Inc. All Rights Reserved.)

That night, unbeknownst to Diego, Alejandro strikes out on his first Zorro exploit. This new fox needs a horse, and Alejandro decides that the black stallion would be perfect. Wearing a crude mask and cape, Alejandro sneaks into town at dusk, but he is startled by Elena, who is riding to the church for confession. After an interlude in which he warns her about dangerous men, both go their separate ways, each smitten with the other.

In the subsequent sequence, Alejandro daringly steals the black stallion, in the process causing the destruction of the barracks. Pursued by soldiers, Alejandro seeks a hiding place in the church. The padre conceals him in the confessional where an unwitting Elena sits on the other side. Awkwardly, Alejandro listens to her confess her sins, but his unorthodox responses prompt her suspicion. When Captain Love enters the church with his soldiers, Alejandro escapes through the roof of the confessional.

Alejandro proudly returns to Zorro's cave astride the horse, only to find Diego furious. The young man had no right to assume he has become

Zorro. The fox was not a show-off, but a servant of the people. Diego challenges his pupil to choose a weapon. Alejandro draws his sword. Diego, however, pulls out a spoon and the invitation to Montero's banquet. He wants Alejandro to attend as a spy, but the young man declines. While he can pass as Zorro, he would never pass as a don. Diego disagrees and announces his intention to teach Alejandro the keys to Montero's world— charm, nobility, and breeding. Alejandro's goal will be to convince Montero that he is a gentleman of stature, worthy to be invited into his inner circle. In this way Diego can learn of Montero's plan for California.

Alejandro arrives at the banquet on his black stallion, Tornado. Dressed elegantly, he is accompanied by Diego, riding on a donkey, who has assumed the role of Alejandro's servant, Bernardo. At the fiesta in progress, Alejandro wins Montero's confidence and competes with Captain Love for Elena's affections. He cuts in on a sedate dance between Love and Elena, moving into a second number, a wild, erotic fandango.

Meanwhile, Diego steals into a guarded room that is Montero's private study and witnesses Don Luiz take a carved wooden box from a locked chest in the room.

Montero invites Alejandro to join Love and the dons at a private gathering, where he unveils his map of an independent California and reveals his plan to buy the territory from Mexico's General Santa Anna. He also discloses the contents of the wooden box. Inside lies a solid bar of gold bearing the Spanish insignia. He then invites the men on an excursion the following day.

The dons travel in carriages with black, drawn curtains to a secret gold mine being worked by slave labor. Among the slaves are Three-Fingered Jack and Fray Felipe. Alejandro watches Love shoot Jack, his former accomplice, but his reaction raises Love's suspicion. He demands to meet Alejandro when they return to Montero's estate. Afterward, the captain nonchalantly cuts off Three-Fingered Jack's hand.

Back at Montero's stables, Elena joins Bernardo, who is grooming Tornado. She finds his singing comforting but is sure she's heard his voice somewhere before. Painfully, Diego must deny such a possibility to his daughter.

When the dons return, Alejandro meets Love in his office. Love offers him a drink from one of two containers. The first has Joaquin's pickled

head floating inside while the second has Three-Fingered Jack's hand. Love watches for Alejandro to crack and reveal his true identity. Controlling his rage, Alejandro drinks from the jar with Joaquin's head.

In town, Elena visits the marketplace where she learns from her old nanny that she is the daughter of Esperanza and Diego de la Vega.

Alejandro returns from the mine consumed with anger. Diego cautions his protégé to conceal his hatred for Love and when Alejandro asks,

Banderas impersonates a don to discover Montero's secret plans. (Stills copyright © 1998 by TriStar Pictures, Inc. All Rights Reserved.)

An erotic dance between stars Antonio Banderas as Don Alejandro and Catherine Zeta Jones as Elena. (Stills copyright © 1998 by TriStar Pictures, Inc. All Rights Reserved.)

Captain Love, played by Matthew Letscher, invites Alejandro to have a drink from a jar holding the pickled head of his brother. (Stills copyright © 1998 by TriStar Pictures, Inc. All Rights Reserved.)

"How?," he is presented with the mask of Zorro. At long last, the pupil has earned his place as the legendary fox.

To save the people, Zorro must get back to the mine. But first, he must steal Montero's map to discover its exact location. Diego lights a flaming *Z* on the hillside outside Montero's estate to announce Zorro's return and to signal Alejandro into action. The new Zorro steals the map and in a breathtaking, adventurous series of feints, offensives, and counter-offensives at the estate, his intelligence and athleticism are put to the test against Love, Montero, and the soldiers. The masked man even crosses swords with Elena in a seductive battle before managing his escape from Montero's estate.

Zorro's not out of the woods yet. Sergeant Garcia leads the soldiers in pursuit of Tornado. Zorro, however, has missed his mount. In a dazzling display of trick riding, he overtakes the galloping soldiers, moving from the last horse up to his own. When he finally returns to the cave, Zorro expects Diego will join him at the mine, but Diego has other plans. He has waited twenty years to confront Montero for the murder of his wife and the theft of his daughter. Alejandro tries to convince Diego to see beyond personal revenge, as Diego has taught him to do, but his arguments fall on deaf ears. Diego has given the people a new Zorro to fight for them. The two men part ways, Diego heading for Montero's estate while Alejandro goes to the mine.

Diego reveals himself to Montero by exposing the scar he etched into

Elena crosses swords with Zorro in a sexy sword fight. (Stills copyright © 1998 by TriStar Pictures, Inc. All Rights Reserved.)

the former governor's neck so many years before. He demands that Elena be told the truth directly from Montero's lips, but the former governor refuses. Elena, however, has become suspicious of her true heritage and is confused when she hears her father call Bernardo by the name Diego de la Vega. In a near replay of Esperanza's death scene, Elena protects Diego from Love's pistol shot. Montero has Diego seized and locked in the wine cellar and then rides off to the gold mine with Love. Time is critical. The gold shipment must meet Santa Anna at the designated hour. Elena releases Diego from the cellar and they hasten after Love and Montero.

In the thrilling climax, Montero and Love attempt to destroy the slave laborers along with the gold-mining operation. They want to prevent Santa Anna from learning of their scheme to buy California with what is really his own gold. Zorro appears, battling with the soldiers to foil Montero's plan, while the slave laborers are herded into cages as the gold wagon is loaded. Montero, wanting no evidence of his wicked scheme, orders fuses laid to blow up the entire mining operation.

Diego arrives just in time to save Zorro from Montero's rifle. Love and Zorro then engage in a fierce battle along the mining ramparts, as do Diego and Montero. Diego disarms Montero, holding him at sword point, but Elena pleads for his life. The instant Diego hesitates to act on his advantage, Montero takes Elena as his hostage. He puts a pistol to her head and Diego drops his sword. At that moment, Elena knows which man is her real father. Montero levels his pistol at Diego.

Meanwhile, Zorro pursues Love into the gold smelting room. Love cranks the steam valve, causing the room to explode, which sets the mine on fire.

Montero squeezes the trigger but Elena knocks his shot askew. Diego charges him as Montero tosses Elena aside. She slams her head, collapsing to the ground. When she comes to, she sees not only Diego bleeding from a wound in his side, but also the immediate peril of the caged prisoners. Diego tells her to help the people.

As Elena races to release them, Zorro and Love continue their cat and mouse sword fight on burning ramps. Zorro slashes a Z in his adversary's cheek, then adds a fourth slash, an M—for Murieta. They battle against time as the burning fuse gets closer to exploding the mining operation and the workers. Zorro ultimately runs Love through with his sword, pulling off his mask to reveal his true identity.

Diego continues to battle Montero beside the gold wagon. He releases the brake, sending it rolling toward a precipice. Montero's legs get entangled in the wagon's harness and the cart careens over the edge, dragging Montero, screaming, with it and crashing down on Love.

Meanwhile, Elena frees two groups of the caged prisoners and is aided by Zorro in time to uncage the remaining workers before the entire mining operation explodes.

As Alejandro and Elena cradle the dying Diego, he cautions Alejandro that the need for Zorro will continue. Alejandro understands his responsibility. In his few remaining moments, Diego blesses his daughter's relationship with Alejandro, but to the couple's grief, Diego dies.

Justice has triumphed, though. The people have been saved and the new Zorro lives to fight another day.

Bringing the Film to the Screen

As is often the case with many Hollywood films, the development process took years to reach principal photography. Eight years passed from the first conversation John Gertz had about doing a new Zorro movie until the film appeared in theaters around the world. In those intervening years, Gertz devoted his time to building the worldwide Zorro license through the development of plays, a comic book series, product promotions, and a major museum exhibit. Rejuvenating classic properties had become a major trend in licensing and Zorro was the quintessential nostalgic hero.

The long journey of *The Mask of Zorro* began while filming was under way on the New World television series. John convinced Nancy to focus her creative skills on McCulley's version of the character. Almost ten years had passed since the last Zorro movie, George Hamilton's satire, *Zorro, the Gay Blade*. Nancy agreed and the two met with her agent, Michael Siegel, to advance their strategy. They decided she would take six months to write an original script, which would then be made available to a list of the top studios and producers in Hollywood.

In the spring of 1991, nineteen A-list producers and studio executives were selectively called, each being informed that his or her personal copy of the hot new Zorro script would be awaiting them at Siegel's office Friday afternoon at 4:45 P.M. By 5 o'clock, eighteen of the nineteen had been picked up. The one remaining script was designated for Steven Spielberg at Amblin Entertainment but his associate, executive producer Kathleen Kennedy, had called with regrets, indicating that she was sure Steven would not be interested in Zorro.

Gertz had been discussing possible deals with both Warner Brothers and Columbia Pictures when he received an urgent call from Siegel while on his way home from a European business trip. Michael urged John to re-route his flight to Los Angeles for a meeting with TriStar. The studio was prepared to make an immediate deal, assuring both Siegel and Gertz that they had a filmmaker who will "knock your socks off!"

After seven hours of negotiation, the jet-lagged Gertz had hammered out the fundamental deal structure. Their agreement, however, hinged on the name of the filmmaker. Everyone left the room except John, Mike Medavoy, the chairman of TriStar Pictures, and two other top studio executives. In a hushed tone, Medavoy leaned over to John and whispered the filmmaker's name.

"Steven Spielberg."

John was naturally surprised, given Kathleen Kennedy's expressed disinterest. Medavoy, however, told John that Spielberg loved Zorro. After TriStar had picked up their copy of Nancy's script, Medavoy passed the idea by Spielberg on the set of *Hook*. He responded enthusiastically. Spielberg had grown up around the block from a movie theater where old Republic serials, including *Zorro's Fighting Legion*, played during Saturday matinees. These action-packed cliff-hangers later infused much of Spielberg's filmmaking. Zorro had been a particular favorite.

Medavoy wanted to set the deal with Gertz in motion immediately but Nancy had to be consulted first, since it was her script. She had some concerns that she wanted to discuss with the filmmaker. After meeting with Spielberg, Nancy advised John to "make the deal . . . he'll make a great film." Spielberg's vision was not a traditional Zorro story like the one she had written. Instead, he wanted to create a "passing the mantle" story with a Gold Rush subtext.

As Nancy was leaving the meeting, she asked Spielberg to consider a friend of hers for the male lead. Reaching into her briefcase for a casting photo, Nancy described him as a dark, handsome, strong, outdoor type. Impishly, she pulled out a picture of her black gelding, Horus. Despite his family connections, however, Horus did not get a starring role as Tornado.

On April 23, 1991, *The Hollywood Reporter* announced,

> Spielberg to make sign of the Z for TriStar's "Zorro." Steven Spielberg is set to direct the latest version of the classic swashbuckler "Zorro" for Tri-Star Pictures. The studio recently acquired Nancy Larson's (*The Wizard of Loneliness*) completed "Zorro" screenplay as well as the underlying film and allied rights on Friday. "It's a genre adventure I've loved since I was a kid . . ." Spielberg said through a spokesman.

By 1994, after two previously aborted scripts, Ted Elliot and Terry Rossio, the team who wrote *Aladdin*, were hired to work on the Zorro film. Spielberg was intimately involved in story development sessions and was very influential in creating a strong plot line and the major character conflicts. *The Mask of Zorro* benefited from his remarkable skills at visualizing the action and fashioning a dramatic adventure tale. Elliot and Rossio's first draft was submitted on July 6, 1994.

A casting call for "Zorro" appeared in *Back Stage West, the Performing Arts Weekly* of June 9–15, 1994:

> TriStar/Amblin is accepting submissions for Zorro . . . Breakdown—
> *Young Zorro:* 24–30, male, Hispanic, to play the hero, a masked man with deep expressive eyes, must have a macho charisma as well as an abundance of boyish charm, strong and confident man with great sense of humor and comedic timing, the defender of the weak and oppressed, a daring outlaw and a fighter of injustice, a relentless warrior, a gentle soul, animated, expressive, full of life, handsome, physically agile, a classic hero in every sense, must speak fluent English, acting experience is not necessary.

By that fall, Spielberg's new studio, Dreamworks SKG, a partnership with music mogul David Geffen, former Disney executive Jeffrey Katzenberg, and himself, was announced. Spielberg passed the task of directing the Zorro film on to former cinematographer Mikael Salomon (*A Far Off Place*). With Hispanic actor Raul Julia slated for the lead as the older Zorro and Andy Garcia favored to become Zorro's protégé, the film appeared to be coming together. On October 24, 1994, however, tragically, Julia died from a stroke. He was only fifty-four years of age.

Sean Connery was rumored to become the older Zorro, teamed with Garcia, but as the year passed, the scenario shifted. The hottest Spanish actor in Hollywood, Antonio Banderas, was in discussions to play the younger Zorro. On September 14, 1995, *Daily Variety* announced a new actor/director pairing with a classic headline: *"Desperado" duo due to redo 'Zorro.'* That same day, Stephen Galloway reported in *The Hollywood Reporter* that Robert Rodriguez would direct an

> all-Hispanic Zorro with his *Desperado* star Antonio Banderas . . . About a month ago, Spielberg decided not to do a big studio movie, but an all-Hispanic version with Hispanic actors and a Hispanic director. Rodriguez had created a stir in Hollywood with his tongue-in-cheek action film, *El Mariachi*, about a guitar player turned vigilante. The movie was shot on a shoe-string budget of $7000. Rodriguez remade the film under the Hollywood banner of *Desperado*, starring Banderas. While the $40 million dollar projected budget for the new Zorro film was small by contemporary action feature standards, it represented more than a five-fold increase over Rodriguez's budget for *Desperado*.

Elliot and Rossio submitted their rewrite of the script on April 22, 1996. Shooting was scheduled to commence in July. In early June, however, Rodriguez quit the project and the film was put on hold.

With Raul Julia's death and Rodriguez's departure, prospects for principal photography seemed bleak. However, Banderas remained attached to the project and within two weeks, TriStar announced that Martin Campbell had agreed to direct the Zorro film. His latest film, *Goldeneye*, had brilliantly revived the moribund James Bond franchise. Shooting for *The Mask of Zorro* was rescheduled for October.

Campbell requested a further rewrite to simplify and clarify the story. He tightened the action, revamped the opening sequence, deepened the character development, and restructured the climax. He strove to enrich the mythic quality of Zorro, enhancing the film's appeal to both children and adults. John Eskow rewrote the script, followed by a second overhaul by David S. Ward. Shooting was pushed back to January 1997.

At the end of September, a management change at the head of Sony Pictures put every film on their plate under scrutiny. Even though the new chief, John Calley, would be reviewing every film deal, Zorro's prospects seemed good. Campbell had directed *Goldeneye* for Calley at United Artists, which was a huge success, grossing over $350 million worldwide.

In short order, Calley greenlighted *The Mask of Zorro* with a $20 million budget increase, production was set on a fast track, and casting proceeded. Academy Award winner Anthony Hopkins (*The Silence of the Lambs*, 1991) agreed to play Diego, the older Zorro, boosting the star power of the film. Stuart Wilson (*Death and the Maiden*, 1994) signed to play Montero, Zorro's nemesis in love and cunning. Following screen tests in Mexico, Catherine Zeta Jones (*The Phantom*, 1995) was cast as the female lead, Elena.

Shooting extended over a six-month period from January 27, 1997 to June 15, 1997 with a ninety-nine-day schedule. Filming in and around Mexico City evoked an authentic feel of Spanish California for the mythic hero in black. The landscape and architecture set the tone for an historic age gone by.

ANTONIO BANDERAS—ALEJANDRO/YOUNG ZORRO

Antonio Banderas was an ideal choice to play the Spanish California hero. Dubbed the "Spanish Heartthrob" by fan magazines and "A Neo-Latin Lover" by the mainstream press, Banderas possessed the passion, intensity, and physical prowess to become Zorro. He grew up watching Guy Williams as Disney's Zorro and reading Zorro comics. Banderas is the first authentic Spaniard to play Spanish California's defender of justice for the American cinema. Consequently, he brought a particular vision to his portrayal of the fox.

"Zorro must be a classic hero," Banderas explained. "When he [Diego]

Banderas as an intent Don Ale-
jandro. (Stills copyright © 1998 by
TriStar Pictures, Inc. All Rights
Reserved.)

is passing the torch, here is the opportunity to explain what it means to be Zorro. He has a chance to teach me that being Zorro is about changing revenge for justice. It's about discipline, respect, and centering oneself."

The fact that Zorro was the first Spanish hero invented by Hollywood did not escape Banderas. "There is an important message here in 'Zorro' for the entire Hispanic community. He fought for justice. He fought against poverty. This is an especially important model for kids, especially today and especially here in Mexico," Banderas remarked to Mark Fineman of the *Los Angeles Times*.

Nor was he unaware of being the first screen Zorro to appear without a mustache. Though Banderas wanted to sport one, the decision was made to present the new Zorro with a naked upper lip. As he becomes the defender of justice, taming his impulsive instincts and honing his skills, the scraggly Alejandro Murieta becomes clipped and trimmed into the refined Zorro. The loss of his unruly, unkempt hair serves as a metaphor for the physical and emotional transformation that occurs in his character.

"If ever there was a perfect Zorro," noted producer David Foster, "it is Antonio." His co-producer Doug Claybourne lauded Banderas in his role, observing that Antonio had a "special feeling for the character" along with a "very romantic idea of the movie." Crew member Kim Marks, second unit director of photography, characterized Banderas as "living Zorro." Banderas was extremely cooperative, always willing to give an extra effort. When not working on the film, he spent all his time with his family.

Born on August 10, 1960, Jose Antonio Dominguez Banderas began acting in theater and television in Madrid. Before he was a regular performer, Banderas wanted to play soccer professionally, but his dream was crushed when he broke his foot at the age of fourteen. The child of a policeman and a teacher, Antonio recalled the grim years of Franco's postwar Spain, when he sat transfixed in front of the family's black-and-white TV watching hours of Hollywood classics dubbed in Spanish. He told M. Walker of the *Los Angeles Times*,

> I was always fanatic about American movies—I love George Cukor, Orson Welles, Raoul Walsh, Billy Wilder. Seeing Americans using washing machines in the '40s—the first washing machine my mother bought was in 1970-something. It was like a dream of a faraway world.

Banderas attended the School of Dramatic Art in Málaga, Spain, and performed with the city's independent theater company. He moved to Madrid by age twenty-one to work in television and theater and eventually became a member of the prestigious National Theater of Spain. His film career took off when director Pedro Almodovar chose him to be in *Labyrinth of Passion* (1982), but his first big splash with American audiences was in *Mambo Kings* (1992) as the sensitive songwriter Nestor Castillo. Director Arne Glimchers took a risk by casting Banderas since the Spanish actor spoke no English when he made the film and had to pronounce his dialogue phonetically. To make his transition into Hollywood cinema permanent, Banderas told his agent to get him just a few minutes on screen with top actors, directors, and projects. He began as Tom Hanks's lover in *Philadelphia* (1993), landing subsequent roles in *House of the Spirits* (1993) and *Interview with the Vampire* (1994), among others. He went on to star in an impressive number of films, including *Evita* (1996), *Too Much* (1996), *Four Rooms* (1996), *Assassins* (1995), and *Desperado* (1995).

After a romance with his *Too Much* co-star, Melanie Griffith, that filled the pages of popular magazines, the couple was married in May 1996. Griffith gave birth to a baby girl in September in Marbella, Spain, and early shooting schedules for *Zorro* included a few days off for Banderas around his child's due date.

The proud father of Stella del Carmen nuzzled his seven-month-old child between takes during a visit to the Mexico City set in April 1997. Griffith gazed on as the proud, doting mother, while the infant charmed the crew with her gurgles and smiles. She was fascinated by the mask her daddy sometimes wore when he held her. Producer Foster described Banderas as an "out of his mind first time daddy" who thoroughly enjoyed fatherhood.

Banderas reteamed with his female lead of *Truth or Dare* (1991), Madonna, in the 1996 film release of Andrew Lloyd Webber's musical, *Evita* (1996). Ironically, the star had lived in a boardinghouse in Madrid a few doors from where a lavish stage production of *Evita* played and could hear the music every night when he went to bed. As a struggling young actor, he had scraped the money together to buy the record of *Evita*, but was so poor in those days he didn't even have enough for the subway. He would often walk to auditions with his eyes glued to the ground, looking for loose change. Banderas's financial situation has dramatically changed since the early days of his career.

Banderas's work style has been described as intense and his ability to completely focus on his work was evident on *The Mask of Zorro* set. Banderas listened carefully to Campbell's direction, accepted the input, then added his own ideas on how to portray the part. In the sword fighting scene between Diego and Elena in Montero's stable, Campbell suggested that Banderas "make it feel like a competition with her." Banderas agreed, but added that he "must do it with a smile. Zorro is always the gentleman."

The actor frequently checked the monitor after takes to assess his performance and conferred with writer David Ward, offering numerous suggestions for his character. Banderas proposed that Diego bless Alejandro and Elena's relationship at the end of the film. He also thought Alejandro should react angrily when Diego admonishes him after his first exploit as Zorro.

Banderas was at times reflective and at times playful on the set during filming. Toying with his sword between takes, he would spin its tip in the palm of his hand or on the top of his boot, displaying his adroit soccer skill. He joked with crew members between takes of the sword fighting sequence in which female star Catherine Zeta Jones cuts him. "I'll be accused of sexual harassment anyway, even though she started it!"

To prepare for his role as Zorro, Banderas began fencing lessons at his home in Marbella, Spain, in July of 1996. He worked two hours a day with fencing master Bob Anderson. Both he and his assistant, Mark Ivie, raved about Banderas's swordsmanship. Having trained the likes of Mandy Patinkin and Cary Elwes for *The Princess Bride*, Anderson credited Banderas's exceptional skill as the actor performed almost all of his own sword fighting routines in the film.

Anderson described Banderas as an athlete who "picks things up remarkably quickly and has a real feel for the blade. He is undoubtedly the best I've ever worked with." Upon hearing Anderson's praise, Banderas joked to Elizabeth Snead of *USA Today*, "I think that he is becoming nuts. The best sword fighter that I have seen on the screen was Gene Kelly in *The Three Musketeers*, but he could have done anything with his body."

Now one of the foxiest male leads in Hollywood has taken on the role of the California fox. As Alejandro Murieta, Banderas is out for revenge against Captain Love for the death of his brother, Joaquin. Through Diego's training, Alejandro turns revenge to the service of the people, ennobling himself as Zorro in the cause of justice. Banderas is certain to become an icon in the cinematic mythology of the Spanish California fox.

ANTHONY HOPKINS — DIEGO/ZORRO

When queried as to why an Academy Award–winning actor who had portrayed such famous men as Richard Nixon (*Nixon*, 1995), John Quincy

Adams (*Amistad*, 1997), the artist Picasso (*Surviving Picasso*, 1996), and even a notorious criminal, Hannibal Lector (*The Silence of the Lambs*, 1991) would want to do *Zorro*, Hopkins laughed: "I get to wear black and have a lot of fun!"

He had been thinking of retiring after a slipped disk operation, but once he recovered from surgery, he found himself quite fit for a man of fifty-nine years of age. Though Hopkins had been a favorite choice early on to play Diego, according to producer Claybourne his back problems precluded his consideration. Following his surgery, Hopkins became the lead candidate. He was simultaneously offered the role of a James Bond villain or of Zorro, and after weighing the roles, Hopkins opted for Zorro. He chuckled as he shared his thoughts:

Anthony Hopkins as Diego prods Montero to tell Elena the truth about her parents. (Stills copyright © 1998 by TriStar Pictures, Inc. All Rights Reserved.)

All the young girls love Banderas . . . he's the most sexy young star . . . I thought I'd get in on his coattails . . .

I've had a busy, broad career playing many roles, wonderful parts, but I'm not like any of those characters I've played who are half dead from the waist down. I've always loved adventure. I'm not interested in doing Masterpiece Theater . . . I don't take acting seriously. It's fun.

Prior to shooting *Zorro*, Hopkins shot an action-adventure film with Alec Baldwin entitled *The Edge*. His stunt double, Alex Green, who also served as the whip master on *The Mask of Zorro*, gave Hopkins a gift from his line of deluxe bullwhips after shooting the Alaskan wilderness film. The handle contained a silver ring engraved with Hopkins's initials, A. H. Green explained,

I had a whip made up for Tony as a gift to hang on the wall. I gave it to him at the end of the picture and ten days later, he calls me and says, "You'll never guess what's on my table." I've got no idea. Tony says, "They've just given me the script to play Zorro. You've got to teach me how to use it now." Hopkins used his special whip in the cave-training sequence as Diego instructs young Alejandro.

Green praised Hopkins's whip-cracking skills: "He learned to crack the whip in three weeks. Now I have him doing a horizontal crack and a vertical circus crack." Hopkins does his own whip work in the film, along with much of his sword fighting.

Hopkins does not ride in *The Mask of Zorro*, however. Thirty years ago he almost killed himself on a horse in his first picture and he decided then and there that "it wasn't worth risking life and limb for a picture."

Hopkins began serious sword training in December 1996 with Bob Anderson's partner, Peter Diamond. No stranger to Zorro swordplay, Diamond had served as stunt coordinator for four years on the New World *Zorro* television series. He worked with Hopkins once a week, then Anderson spent Christmas working with him. Their serious training began in January 1997. During filming, Hopkins practiced every day, either with Anderson or his assistant, Mark Ivie. "Tony is so determined," admired Anderson.

Tony, as he's known, was born Philip Anthony on December 31, 1937, in Port Talbot, Wales, to baker Richard Hopkins and his wife, Muriel. Hopkins was a slow learner in school and a solitary child, but at age seventeen, he wandered into a YMCA amateur theatrical production and knew immediately that he was in the right place. With his proficiency at the piano, Hopkins won a scholarship to the Welsh College of Music and Drama in Cardiff. He studied there for two years, from 1955 to 1957, after which he did his mandatory military service as a clerk in the Royal Artillery unit at Bulford.

Hopkins joined the Manchester Library Theatre as an assistant stage manager, then moved to the Nottingham Repertory Company, where he was advised to study acting further. Hopkins auditioned for London's Royal Academy of Dramatic Art in 1961 and was accepted on scholarship. In 1963, he graduated as a silver medalist and immediately joined the Phoenix Theatre in Leicester. From there, he went to the Liverpool Playhouse and Hornchurch Repertory Company.

In 1965, he was invited to audition for Sir Laurence Olivier, the director of the National Theatre at the Old Vic. Hopkins served as Olivier's understudy in Strindberg's *Dance of Death* two years later. In his film debut, playing Richard the Lionheart in *The Lion in Winter* (1968), starring Peter O'Toole and Katharine Hepburn, Hopkins received a British Academy Award nomination for his work. The film won an Oscar for Best Picture. His cinematic résumé has been further augmented by august roles in such films as *Legends of the Fall* (1994), *The Remains of the Day* (1993), *Shadowlands* (1993), and *Howard's End* (1992).

In 1996, Hopkins made his directorial debut with *August,* an adaptation of Chekhov's *Uncle Vanya*. He also starred in the film and composed the musical score.

The highly decorated actor has been married to Jennifer Ann Lynton since 1973. He has a daughter, Abigail, born in 1968, by his first marriage. He is a self-proclaimed Amerophile who lived in Los Angeles from 1974 to 1984, but since returning to England, he has resided in London. Anthony Hopkins was named Commander of the Order of the British Empire in the Queen's Honour List, June 1987. On December 31, 1992, his knighthood was announced and his investiture was held at Buckingham Palace on February 23, 1993. He has received numerous other commendations and awards for his acting, including an Oscar for Best Actor for *The Silence of the Lambs* (1991), the Best Actor award for *The Remains of the Day* (1994) from the British Academy of Film Arts and Science, Commander of the Order of Arts and Letters in 1996 from France, and two Emmy awards for his television work on *The Bunker* (1981) and *The Lindbergh Kidnapping Case* (1976).

CATHERINE ZETA JONES—ELENA

Joining fellow Welsh countryman Hopkins in *The Mask of Zorro* is Catherine Zeta Jones in the role of his daughter, Elena. She was born on September 25, 1969, in Swansea, West Glamorgan, Wales, and is one of the United Kingdom's up-and-coming popular actresses. Jones starred in

Catherine Zeta Jones as Elena. (Stills copyright © 1998 by Tri-Star Pictures, Inc. All Rights Reserved.)

the West End production of *42nd Street* before landing a starring role in the Yorkshire hit television series, *The Darling Buds of May* (1991), based on the novels of H. E. Bates, but gained prominence with American audiences through her roles in both feature films and television dramas. Her credits include the CBS mini-series *Titanic* (1996), Hallmark Hall of Fame's adaptation of Thomas Hardy's *The Return of the Native* (1994), the title role in the mini-series, *Catherine the Great* (1994), *The Young Indiana Jones Chronicles*, and the feature film *The Phantom* (1996).

As Elena, Jones portrays Diego's daughter, who has been raised by Montero. Her mother is accidentally killed during a skirmish between Diego and Montero, and with Diego imprisoned, Montero decides to take Elena back to Spain to raise as his own. Since he had been in love with Esperanza, Diego's wife, Montero deludes himself into believing that Elena should have been his child all along. Elena falls for Zorro, admiring his defense of the people. But she must come to terms with the truth about her family and the evil intentions of the man who raised her. In the end, Elena frees Montero's indentured slaves, at the encouragement of Diego and with help from Zorro. She loses both the father she knew and the father she did not know, yet captures her noble heritage and the heart of the hero.

STUART WILSON—MONTERO

Stuart Wilson has an impressive breadth of experience in film, television, and theater, which he brought to his role as Diego's nemesis, Rafael Montero, the Spanish governor in *The Mask of Zorro*. Wilson has worked with Hollywood's top directors, including Roman Polanski (*Death and the Maiden*, 1994) and Martin Scorsese (*The Age of Innocence*, 1993), and high-profile actors like Mel Gibson in the popular action film *Lethal Weapon 3* (1992). Wilson appeared as Helen Mirren's love interest, the psychiatrist Patrick Schofield, in *Prime Suspect 4: Scent of Darkness* and *The Lost Child* (1995). Previous television credits include *Anna Karenina* (1997); *I, Claudius* (1976); *Madame Bovary* (1975); *The Jewel in the Crown* (1984); *Wallenberg: A Hero's Story* (1985); and the *Return of Sherlock Holmes* (1986), along with a sizable list of theater credits in England.

As Montero, Wilson takes on the villainous character who not only

Stuart Wilson played the villainous Montero. (Stills copyright © 1998 by TriStar Pictures, Inc. All Rights Reserved.)

plots to take over California, but imprisons slave labor to mine gold for his imperious plans, locks up Diego, steals Diego's daughter, and deliberately deceives her as to her true parentage. Montero is the quintessential evil, greedy, reprehensible blackguard. Wilson's challenge was to find that ounce of humanity in his character that would take him out of the realm of a two-dimensional villain by conveying the emptiness that would drive this man who seeks to replace the loss of his unrequited love for Elena's mother. By playing Montero as Elena's indulgent father, Wilson was able to find the spark of empathetic warmth in his character.

MATTHEW LETSCHER—CAPTAIN LOVE

Youthful-looking Matthew Letscher captured the role of Montero's henchman, Captain Love. Not only does Love murder Alejandro's brother, Joaquin, making him the object of the young Zorro's revenge, but he is an accomplice in Montero's plan to take over California. Letscher trained for

Matthew Letscher played Montero's accomplice, Captain Love.
(Stills copyright © 1998 by TriStar Pictures, Inc. All Rights
Reserved.)

film and theater at the University of Michigan, working at the Heartlande
Theatre Co. in Detroit and other regional theaters. He appeared in Ron
Maxwell's film *Gettysburg* (1993), while television audiences saw Letscher
in *Long Shadows* (1994) for PBS's American Playhouse, and *Stolen Inno-
cence* (1995), a movie of the week. Letscher also appeared in the TV series
Ellen, the *Larry Sanders Show*, *Dr. Quinn/Medicine Woman*, and *Almost
Perfect*. Specializing in dialect and accents, sports and stage combat,
Letscher was eminently qualified for his role as Captain Love in *The Mask
of Zorro*.

His character is based on the actual Captain Love, a figure from California history who was contracted by the state legislature to track down Joaquin Murieta and did so by forming a posse based on the Texas Rangers and hiring former rangers to pursue Murieta. In the film, though Alejandro transcends his initial motive of revenge for Love's murder of his brother, Love remains consumed by his pursuit of Murieta to the bitter end.

MARTIN CAMPBELL—DIRECTOR

New Zealand film director Martin Campbell is no stranger to big-budget action thrillers. At the helm of *Goldeneye* (1995), a sophisticated James Bond thriller, he put United Artists back in the black with the film's phenomenal $350 million box office success. For John Calley, then head of UA, it was a coup. Hoping to pull off the same type of success for Sony, Calley and Campbell were again teamed up on *Zorro*. Previously Campbell had directed *No Escape* (1994), along with *Cast a Deadly Spell* (1991) for television. He directed several TV series: *Homicide: Life on the Street* (1993), *Edge of Darkness* (1993), and *Charlie* (1984). His other feature films include *Defenseless* (1990), *Criminal Law* (1989), *Eskimo Nell* (1975), *Three for All* (1974), and *The Sex Thief* (1973).

Campbell's vision for Zorro enhanced the legend of the fox, ennobling both Alejandro and Diego. "Although our film is based on the well-known character of Zorro, our story is very different from anything previously done with him. Ours is not the traditional story of Zorro being a nobleman's son. It has much more to do with a Merlin/King Arthur–type relationship where the older Zorro hands over the mantle to a younger Zorro." Diego ensures that Alejandro will carry on his work for the people, thereby perpetuating the myth of Zorro as the defender of justice. Campbell told Elizabeth Snead of *USA Today*, "We're not a generic movie. We have a plot, a dense story, rich characters, good actors, and it rises above the comic strip stuff of some of the earlier films. And we've got Zorro." For Campbell, "Zorro is the perfect hero. From a moral point of view, he doesn't go out to kill as many bad guys as he can—he cleverly disables them, embarrasses and makes fools of them. I thought it would be interesting to bring such a character to the screen today."

Director Martin Campbell (*Goldeneye*) (*left*) conferred with his lead actors, Anthony Hopkins (*middle*) and Antonio Banderas (*right*). (Stills copyright © 1998 by TriStar Pictures, Inc. All Rights Reserved.)

Campbell wanted to make *The Mask of Zorro* look "like one of those big Hollywood epics—with tremendous action, romance, and a lot of fun." When he stepped into the role of director, Campbell was "very happy with what Robert [Rodriquez] had done. The production designer, wardrobe designer, the whole art department, and most of the locations were very good."

The sword fight scene between Jones and Banderas was Campbell's favorite. "It's really delightfully sexy. Off goes her dress. Off comes his cape. But it's really about the competitiveness between them. She proves she's equal to him . . ."

He praised his two Zorros. "Antonio has all the attributes I wanted for Zorro," Campbell said. "He is a very fine actor, dashing, physical, easily conveys compassion, and has a great sense of humor." As for Hopkins, Campbell noted, "Tony is the nobility of the film. He brings tremendous weight and depth to the character and serves as the anchor. He is the voice of reason and experience."

Working right through filming with writer David Ward, they revamped scenes from previous drafts. For the opening sequence in which Montero oversees an execution prior to his departure from California, Campbell sought to evoke the panic and chaos of the fall of Saigon. An extraordinarily rigorous yet humorous dimension was added to the montage in which Diego trains Alejandro to become Zorro. Rather than having the climactic confrontation between Love and Alejandro/Zorro and Montero with Diego begin at the mine and then continue at the hacienda, the order of the scenes was reversed. Diego's confrontation with Montero begins at the hacienda and moves to the mine, allowing the final conflict to be resolved at the mine, right where the enslaved peasants, who are Zorro's raison d'être, can be freed.

Campbell's contributions succeeded in making a film that is more than just another action-adventure movie. He has effectively rewritten Zorro's legacy by deepening the mythical legend of the fox.

STEVEN SPIELBERG—EXECUTIVE PRODUCER, AMBLIN ENTERTAINMENT

Steven Spielberg has been regarded as one of the most creative forces in the modern film industry. His films are among the highest grossing in Hollywood history. Like Orson Welles, he was both celebrated and chided for being precocious; like Alfred Hitchcock, he has been both praised and cursed as a master of emotional manipulation; and like D. W. Griffith, Charlie Chaplin, and Frank Capra, he has been criticized for sentimentality. He is perhaps most like Walt Disney, another creative producer who made himself into a brand name as he developed frivolous entertainment into serious business.

Largely self-taught, Spielberg made his first feature film at the age of sixteen. A local theater in Phoenix, Arizona, agreed to run his two-hour science fiction movie, *Firelight* (1965), for one evening. His short film *Amblin'* (1969) was shown at the Atlanta Film Festival, earning him a job with Universal Studios' television unit at the tender age of twenty. Spielberg's debut directing task starred Joan Crawford in a TV pilot movie for Rod Serling's *Night Gallery* (1969). From there, he went on to direct weekly series such as *Columbo* and *Marcus Welby, M.D.*, along with three television movies. One of these films, *Duel* (1971), was a suspense story of a salesman, played by Dennis Weaver, pursued by a giant diesel truck. The driver of the truck was never seen, nor was the pursuit motive explained. *Duel* was released theatrically in Europe, garnering critical acclaim and commercial success.

Spielberg's first feature film, *The Sugarland Express,* came out in 1974, but it was his second feature, *Jaws* (1975), the classic adventure tale, that propelled Spielberg to the A-list of Hollywood directors. His *Indiana Jones* trilogy, in collaboration with George Lucas, was in the mold of the action-adventure serials of the 1930s and 1940s. *Close Encounters of the Third Kind* (1977) set the stage for naive trust in the space aliens that marked his later success with what may be his signature masterpiece, *E.T.* (1982).

In the mid-1980s Spielberg shifted his emphasis from directing to producing, forming Amblin Entertainment in 1984. He diversified into television with the series *Amazing Stories* (1985) and the animated *Tiny Toon Adventures* (1990). Spielberg undertook riskier directorial projects, including *The Color Purple* (1985) and *Empire of the Sun* (1987), before returning to fantasyland with *Hook* (1991) and then *Jurassic Park* (1993), which grossed more than his own record-breaking *E.T.* In 1986 he was awarded the Irving G. Thalberg Award for lifetime achievement in film.

Schindler's List (1990) marked a dramatic break-through for the filmmaker and his craft. After making his mark in films that celebrated childlike wonder, *Schindler's List* showed the filmmaker's remarkable maturity and restraint. Shot in bleak black and white, Spielberg's Holocaust film garnered every top award in the industry, including the Director's Guild of America, the Golden Globes, and seven Academy Awards, most notably for Best Picture, Best Director, and Best Adapted Screenplay.

With profits from *Schindler's List*, Spielberg created The Righteous Persons Foundation, which funds Jewish cultural programs. The foundation's projects range from filming the oral histories of Holocaust survivors to the Genesis project, a four-week camp at Brandeis University for Jewish teenagers to explore their roots through the arts.

In 1994, Spielberg parlayed his remarkable success in Hollywood by forming a new studio, Dreamworks SKG, in partnership with record mogul David Geffen and former Disney executive Jeffrey Katzenberg. By age fifty, Spielberg had achieved recognition and success unequaled among his peers. As the cameras rolled on *The Mask of Zorro*, Spielberg was on another set directing *Amistad*, which was based on a true story from 1839, when African slaves mutinied on a Cuban slave ship. They killed the crew, and ended up imprisoned in New York, charged with murder. John Quincy Adams, played by Anthony Hopkins, comes out of retirement to argue the Africans' case in the Supreme Court.

The powerful theme of justice races through *The Mask of Zorro*, as it does for *Amistad*. The Zorro film, however, will most likely be remembered for its action sequences. After viewing the first director's cut of the *Zorro* film, Spielberg praised director Campbell's work as the best of this action genre since *Indiana Jones*. Spielberg's alliance with the fox and the director who revived James Bond will leave a legendary mark on the masked hero, passing him on to a new generation.

WALTER PARKES—EXECUTIVE PRODUCER, AMBLIN ENTERTAINMENT

Walter Parkes's first foray into the film industry began with a documentary about the American Nazi party's activities in San Francisco, *The California Reich*, which played at festivals all over the world and was nominated for a Best Feature Documentary Oscar in 1978. Parkes studied acting and worked as a studio musician for two years in Los Angeles before turning his attention to screenwriting. His first script, *WarGames*, written with Lawrence Lasker, became one of the most successful films of 1983 and garnered his second Oscar nomination for Best Original Screenplay. Parkes and Lasker went on to write and/or produce a number of feature films over the next several years, including *True Believer, Sneakers,* and *Awakenings*, which garnered Parkes's third Oscar nomination for Best Picture.

In 1992, Parkes teamed with his wife, Laurie MacDonald, and the two were named president and executive president of Steven Spielberg's Amblin Entertainment in 1994. At Amblin they served as executive producers on such films as *Twister* and *How to Make an American Quilt*. Later that year, Parkes and MacDonald were named co-heads of the motion picture division of Dreamworks, the new studio founded by Steven Spielberg, Jeffrey Katzenberg, and David Geffen. Besides supervising Dreamworks's initial slate of movies and producing its first release, *Peacemaker*, Parkes and MacDonald produced the 1997 summer blockbuster *Men in Black*, which became the most successful movie in the history of Columbia Pictures.

LAURIE MACDONALD—EXECUTIVE PRODUCER, AMBLIN ENTERTAINMENT

Laurie MacDonald began her producing career as a documentary and news producer at KRON, the NBC affiliate in San Francisco. She later joined Columbia Pictures, where she served as a vice president of production for five years. In 1994 she was named executive vice president of Amblin Pictures, where she executive-produced the films *How to Make an American Quilt*, *Twister*, and *Trigger Effect*.

Currently MacDonald serves as co-head of Dreamworks Pictures with her husband, Walter Parkes. MacDonald produced Barry Sonenfeld's blockbuster science fiction buddy comedy *Men in Black* in the summer of 1997. She also served as an executive producer on Dreamworks's inaugural feature film release, *The Peacemaker*.

BOB ANDERSON—FENCING MASTER

Now seventy-five, fencing master Bob Anderson has trained the top actors in Hollywood, starting with Errol Flynn in *The Master of Ballantrae* (1953). He competed in the 1952 Olympics for the British fencing team, and rendered years of service as the coach for the British Olympic, and later, the Canadian Olympic fencing teams. Besides training stars to fence, Anderson has dueled in many films himself. His most famous screen persona is Darth Vader, for which he dueled inside the dark lord's suit in all three Star Wars films.

Among *The Mask of Zorro* cast, Anderson found others who impressed him in addition to Banderas. Hopkins's determination and Jones's talent, along with Letscher's skill, prompted him to observe, "This will not only be the best Zorro movie, but it will be the best sword fighting movie ever."

When asked to compare the swordplay in *The Mask of Zorro* to that of the comic fantasy *The Princess Bride*, Anderson explained,

> The sword dialogue was so integral to the sword fight in *The Princess Bride*. Here, Campbell's direction is very fast. Catherine is fabulous. Banderas is better than both Patinkin and Elwes. Hopkins is so determined. He practices every day. Letscher will astonish people. This is sword play with finesse.

Anderson got into screen fighting by a fluke. He was on a ten-day break from the World Fencing Championship in 1952 when a sword store recommended him for *The Master of Ballantrae* (1953). The star, Errol Flynn, liked Anderson and invited him to Palermo to finish shooting the film. Bob is a finesse fencer who stresses style, not slashing strength. There was no question in his mind as to which came first on his priority list— coaching commitments or film assignments. It was coaching.

Bob chose Mark Ivie as his fencing assistant from 150 other swordsmen who auditioned for a film entitled *By the Sword*, and since then they have worked together on and off for the last eight years. Ivie took up fencing at age twenty-eight. He was looking for a competitive sport to replace his college skiing. As Anderson's heir apparent, Ivie compared film fencing to competitive fencing.

> If you try to do competitive fencing moves on film it wouldn't look very good. Moves have to be choreographed so you know what to expect. The Italian, French, and Spanish schools stressed style. The aristocracy was concerned about how they looked. But it wasn't functional. They would get killed.

Anderson and Ivie have choreographed some consistent moves to connect the younger Diego with the movements of Alejandro as he becomes Zorro. Ivie demonstrated the hang parry, in which the blade is dropped behind the back. "We repeat the hang parry. It's used to protect the back."

Anderson summarized the reverence he holds for his sport, the essence of which he has imparted to his students over many years: "The sword is the ultimate weapon. When a blade is at your throat, you've got only your skill to rely on."

ALEX GREEN—WHIP MASTER

Australian-born whip master and stuntman Alex Green has followed a dream he nurtured from a very young age. He has been playing with a whip for over fifty-two years. Beginning when he was all of four in Queensland, Cattle and Sheeps Station, Alex would put on his mother's black hat, step into his wellies (black knee-high rain boots), pull his raincoat on backward and crack his whip, imitating Reed Hadley as Zorro. Not only did Alex tear the flowers off his mother's hat to make it look like Zorro's, but he flicked all the flowers off her bushes in the backyard.

After seeing the movie *Red River* at the age of seven, Green told his mother that when he grew up, he was "going to America to be a cowboy."

In 1966, Alex spent eight months in Los Angeles, training to be a stuntman. He went from stuntman to stuntman, trading his skill with the whip for an entree into the stunt world. Veteran stuntman and second unit director Yakima Canutt introduced Green to another stunt veteran, David Cashner, who subsequently introduced him to Rod Redwing, the gun coach of Hollywood, who was known for his fast draw and gun-twirling expertise. Green taught Redwing the whip, and Rod taught Alex guns. Green promised to return to his home in Canada, so the two would not compete for jobs and formed Stunts Canada, which has been active for thirty years and boasts fifty-two members.

Green has done over 100 pictures and 250 television shows and has the distinction of being designated by Anthony Hopkins as his permanent stuntman. They met during filming of *Legends of the Fall* (1994) and were reunited on Hopkins's recent action film, *The Edge* (1997). From Green's perspective, having given Hopkins the engraved whip after working on *The Edge* fortuitously sealed their fate to work together on *Zorro*.

Green bubbled enthusiastically as he noted his remarkable good fortune. Douglas Fairbanks Sr. had been trained by Snowy Baker, another Australian, for his whip work in *Don Q, Son of Zorro*. Green owns two of the stock whips used in *Don Q*, gifts he received from David Cashner. Alex noted that like Baker,

> I'm from Australia and now I'm doing Zorro. And there's a second paral-
> lel. It's a second-generation Zorro story, like *Don Q*. . . . Nearly seventy
> years have gone by and here I am on the best Zorro probably ever
> made. Snowy Baker taught Fairbanks and growing up with all that, go-
> ing to all the serials, living it, and I'm here . . . It's absolutely magic! . . .
> It's done a full circle. All my dreams have come true.

STORIES FROM THE SET

As the new year dawned, the stars began assembling for filming in Mexico. Banderas and his family moved from their home in Málaga, Spain, to Mexico City. Other key crew traveled down for a month of pre-production. Casting sessions began for the role of Elena, the female lead. Spielberg had seen Catherine Zeta Jones in the mini-series *Titantic* and sent a videotape of her for Campbell and Foster to see. Jones was eventually chosen for the role from among three other actresses. Campbell held the first full cast read-through on January 13, 1997. Actual filming began on January 27. The first scenes shot were in the cuartel where Alejandro confronts the soldiers and steals the stallion from the stable.

Preproduction for *The Mask of Zorro*'s production designer, Celia Montiel, began two years earlier than actual filming. She started research-ing the period, costumes, and architecture, filling two large bookshelves with historical volumes. A thick research binder was then developed with background material for use by art director Michael Atwell's department and costume designer Graciela Mazon. Each strove to base their designs on historical facts. Paintings of Mexico from the late 1700s to 1860s were very influential, as were engravings, lithographs, and photographs.

Working with her crew of up to 400 people, that included artists, sculptors, iron workers, and carpenters, Montiel planned the look and feel of each soundstage at the Churbusco Studios in Mexico City, as well as each location site. She worked closely with the director and the art de-partment, moving from the easiest to the hardest designs, with the mine

The impressive gold mine location site designed for *The Mask of Zorro* was exploded in the dramatic finale. (Stills copyright © 1998 by TriStar Pictures, Inc. All Rights Reserved.)

Zorro effectively used his whip to escape after rescuing the prisoners in the opening sequence filmed at the refurbished town square in San Blas, Mexico. (Stills copyright © 1998 by TriStar Pictures, Inc. All Rights Reserved.)

and Zorro's cave proving to be the most difficult. Interiors in which horses were involved had to be created with period floors designed out of latex to cushion their crashing hooves. The major soundstages included the soldiers' cuartel, Montero's stable, and Zorro's cave.

The production crew was drawn to Mexico primarily for its location possibilities. Producer David Foster explained that "finding the right locations was critical since eighty percent of *The Mask of Zorro* was filmed outdoors. It was important that the locations reflected the era in which our story is set. We needed great expanses of the land as it existed in Southern California, circa 1820, and we needed several classic haciendas of the period." Producer Doug Claybourne added that "the view seen through our camera lens is the same as it would have been for Zorro a hundred years ago."

The locations selected for the shoot were each within a few hours of Mexico City. The town square scenes, including the cantina, were filmed in San Blas, in the rural state of Tlaxcala. The de la Vega hacienda ruins were at Zotoluca, near Pachuca. Montero's estate was in Tetlapayac at a former agave plantation, where a liquor called *pulque* is made from the agave cactus plants. Talamantes Prison was in Santa Maria Regla. Colonel's Farm, about an hour out of Mexico City, provided the exterior setting for the horse-chase sequence. The Lady Luck Goldmine became the site for Montero's slave-operated mine. Finally, the Guaymas beach area in the state of Sonora was used for the watering station where Alejandro, Three-Fingered Jack, and Joaquin met the soldiers. For a few short hours, three streams were diverted into one above the waterfall cascading over the entrance to Zorro's cave to increase the waters' flow.

In her previous film, *From Dusk to Dawn*, Montiel based her designs on Aztec and Mayan culture. For *The Mask of Zorro*, she worked within the time frame of 1820 to 1840. For the film's overall look, she strove to match director Campbell's vision of the cinematic appeal of old Monterey. The monumental architecture of the area around Mexico has remained unchanged since the 1600s, and rather than rebuilding outdoor locations, Montiel's construction crew patched and painted actual buildings, giving them an upscale face-lift.

She integrated architectural elements of the period in the windows of Montero's stable so that when lit from behind, the apertures looked very much like the "eye of the bull." Her primary goal in the party scene at Montero's estate was to create the feeling of a garden. To that end she designed a flower tapestry with four arches, dominated by bougainvillea, then extended the floral theme to the exterior of the hacienda by filling the fountain with petals.

The Mask of Zorro was Montiel's third film paired with costume designer Graciela Mazon. Mazon's background as a sculptor and painter, along with her studies in Paris of Jacque Le Coq's mime techniques, are integral to her designs. She combined her artistic talents to create the expression of movement in color and space.

Montiel and Mazon developed a color chart from which to select fabric for the costumes. To create a rich, textured look on screen, they chose heavy materials. Mazon saw Zorro as a *guerrillero*, a Che Guevara type, and strove to retain his mystery as part of his outfit, keeping it at once elegant and traditional. This new Zorro was one of the townspeople, "growing up like a bandit fighter who had a big heart and who believed in the justice of the people." She created his outfit from the textures of the town, always thinking of how his clothing would flow with his movement to make it part of the surrounding space. She mixed the *Chinacos* style of the 1850s, a combination of *mariachi* from Mexico and Spain, with a touch of the pirate—the open lace shirt and boots worn outside the pants. As accents, she went for very traditional engravings on his belt and hat. The outfit Alejandro wears in his first attempt as Zorro is an improvised version of his real Zorro outfit, employing rough colors and textures.

Mazon adapted the traditional *rebozo* around Zorro's face to add mystery to his expressive eyes, and tried to capture the strength of the bull fighter's magnetic, unyielding gaze as he attempts to control the bull.

For Elena's costumes, Mazon sought to show the transitions in Catherine Zeta Jones's character. At first, as a baby, she wore the Indian style of her nanny. On arriving in California, Elena was dressed as a traditional young woman from Spain. As she walked through the open market, Mazon clothed her as a *Chinaco* woman in a white shirt with a red skirt, looking like one of the people. Elena's party dress had to be sensual but not delicate. Mazon employed the bullfighter imagery here, too, with the passionate colors of red and black to portray a strong personality. In designing Elena's nightgown for the sword fighting scene with Zorro, Mazon had to contend with piecing the gown back together for repeated takes. She resorted to a series of Velcro patches, so that when Banderas's sword slashed the puffy sleeve of Elena's nightgown, it could quickly be reattached.

For Diego's costumes, Mazon wanted to contrast the humility of the Diego character Hopkins played with that of Banderas's character, Alejandro. For Diego's peasant image, she employed a mix of Spanish traditions in the 1820s, using the same strong colors she used in her designs for Alejandro.

Director Campbell was delighted with Mazon's wardrobe, but since Zorro's costume was designed for its look, not for actual sword fighting, it presented Banderas with quite a challenge. As Campbell admiringly observed, "The cape chokes him. The bloody gloves make it so he can't pull the sword out. He can't see to the sides because of the mask. But somehow, he manages to make it all work."

Audiences won't be aware of these practical problems. Filmmaking is, after all, the creation of illusions. Viewers will see Zorro sweep his flowing cape to begin his battles, or move sinuously onto his horse. To their eyes, Mazon will have succeeded brilliantly with her goals, for Zorro's attire moves with him through space as he moves with the grace and elegance of a dancer.

Shooting in Mexico was beneficial to the production as well as to their hosts. Overall, the studio got much more for its money than had it been filmed in the States. Producer Doug Claybourne (*Apocalypse Now, Black Stallion*) observed that in the states the cost to build the sets would have doubled. The arrangement was good for the locals, too, since over 7,000 Mexican extras were employed on the film, along with hundreds of other crew members. As the man responsible for the day-to-day concerns, Claybourne negotiated with Mexican officials and townspeople at location sites, got equipment for construction, arranged drivers, plus attending to myriad other details.

Despite his daily challenges, Claybourne had nothing but praise for those associated with the film. L. Q. Jones (*The Wild Bunch*), who played Three-Fingered Jack, connected them to Wild West films of the past. Banderas's entire attitude was "How can I help get the movie done?" Catherine Jones even befriended Clayborne's nine-year-old son, who had developed a crush on her. That praise continued for many months after filming had been completed. At promotional screenings, the stars, producers, and directors reminisced about the dedication, professionalism, and mutual enjoyment they experienced working on *The Mask of Zorro*.

Producer David Foster (*The River Wild, McCabe and Mrs. Miller*) joined the production, along with Martin Campbell, at Spielberg's invitation. His long, respected career began with his own public relations agency, then moved into producing at the suggestion of his client Steve McQueen. He carried the ball on *The Mask of Zorro* through the final stages of post-production, with his efficient, experienced hand. Foster lauded the efforts of executive producers Parkes and MacDonald as the driving force behind the scenes, moving the production along to completion. He noted the strength of Spielberg's influence at numerous stages, including the hiring of Oscar winner James Horner (*Braveheart, Titanic*) to do the music.

Foster recalled a vignette that demonstrated the camaraderie among the principals. *Show West*, a Las Vegas trade show where studios promote their films, took place in March, right in the middle of filming. Sony sent a company jet to pick up the stars, director, and producers at 5:30 A.M. one morning. They took off from a pitch-black runway. After a three-hour flight, the Zorro group was taken by van to the Bally Hotel, where they showered before their presentation in the main ballroom. Film clips were shown as hundreds of stars milled about with their studio representatives. After three hours, the Zorro crowd was scheduled to get right back on the plane to return to the set for filming that night. Though they had risen early, spent hours in promotional work, and had a long flight back before a long night of work, spirits remained high. They requested one stop before taking off. After almost two months of eating Mexican cuisine, they craved deli food. The group picked up corned beef and pastrami and ate all the way back.

Second unit director of photography Kim Marks found filming in Mexico added a special quality to the experience. Working with his all-Mexican crew made the shoot "more Zorro." Campbell expressed a similar sentiment to Mark Fineman of the *Los Angeles Times*. He praised his Mexican extras for "adding a special touch . . . they are fantastic. They're far better than the professionals; they're totally believable."

The physical demands of an action film with horses and sword fighting created unique challenges for the crew in charge of action sequences.

The extensive flying leaps in the fight sequences proved to be very hard work. Stunt coordinator Glenn Randall used a couple of favorite sayings to get his stuntmen ready: "OK, guys, cowboy up," and "Son, just hit the ground."

Marks recalled that the two-day shoot for the scene in which Alejandro steals the black stallion was like being in the middle of a rodeo arena. Bull pens were built inside the stable to protect the cameramen from the hooves of the bucking horses. For the mine scene, extensive stunt rigging was utilized for the safety of the stuntmen. Deaccelerators were put on the safety attachments to slow down the stuntmen's return to terra firma after catapulting off high platforms.

Tad Griffith, the son of a circus rider and rodeo star who earned his living as a trick rider in Las Vegas, performed an astonishing stunt-riding sequence in the film that had Banderas bubbling with enthusiasm. Emerging from a trailer on location at Colonel's Farm after viewing a rough cut of the sequence, Banderas spotted Zorro's owner, John Gertz. He eagerly requested that it be shown for Gertz. Both men agreed that Griffith's riding was spectacular.

As Zorro, Griffith bounded out of the saddle, hit the ground with his feet, and rebounded with a backflip, landing backward in the saddle. Then he whirled around to face front in the saddle, overtaking soldiers in front of him and knocking them off their mounts. The most amazing trick Griffith performed entailed standing astride two galloping horses. He appears to ride over the head of an astonished Sergeant Garcia, then leaps a log stretched across the road, and lands back on the two horses while still standing.

The shot riding over Garcia was particularly difficult to capture. The horses were skittish and the maneuver was challenging. Tad Griffith's groom, already familiar with the horses, had a camera strapped to his chest. He was to ride a motorcycle down the dirt road as Griffith came charging after him, balancing on the two horses. The groom's job was to keep the camera squarely horizontal as Griffith rode over him, steering the horses on either side. It was a masterful piece of riding and camera work.

Location shooting frequently presents problems for film crews because scenes are dependent on weather conditions. *The Mask of Zorro* was no exception. Filming close-up shots for Griffith's stunt-riding sequence kept the crew watching the sky. Rain and clouds obliterated the sun for long stretches over several days. Marks had to match the light of his close-ups shots of Banderas to the bright light of the sunny days during which the stunt-riding sequence had been shot. Each time the sun popped out for longer than a few seconds, the crew rushed into action, filming Banderas as Zorro's cape billowed in the wind.

Stuntmen and -women are used to hitting the ground as part of their job, but whip master Green humorously shared a personal bone-crunching experience in the prison burial scene. When Diego escapes from Talamantes Prison, he substitutes himself for a corpse and is buried alive. Green doubled for Hopkins during filming of this scene. Two locals were hired to carry him in a burial bag to the grave. These men were of small stature and staggered under Alex's weight, plopping into the grave with him. After the third take, director Campbell replaced them with two larger locals. These men dropped Green with bone-crushing thuds another three times. They then proceeded to dig around his head with shovels. Inside the bag, Green was in complete darkness. All he could hear were the shovels working conspicuously close to his head. The sound indicated that the shovels were getting closer and closer, such that Alex thought he was going to end up "like Van Gogh, one ear short!"

Hopkins brought his own playful sense of humor to the production. After returning from filming his role as John Quincy Adams for Spielberg's *Amistad* (1997), a mysterious sign appeared outside his trailer with the abbreviations "Etc., etc., etc." Since no one had yet seen Hopkins, hushed whispers pondered the meaning of the message. When Tony finally emerged, all became clear. He had shaved his head, *à la* Yul Brynner in *The King and I*. The "etc." sign was a reminder of Brynner's skinned *tete* as the king of Siam.

Despite heat hovering over 110 degrees during the last weeks of filming, some equipment problems, rain delays, illness, and the idiosyncrasies of shooting in a foreign country with an international cast and crew, great excitement surrounded the filming of *The Mask of Zorro*. The Hopkins/Banderas version of the mythic fox of Spanish California is expected to leave a high-water mark on the cinematic legacy of Zorro.

Banderas elegantly continues Zorro's legacy. (Stills copyright © 1998 by TriStar Pictures, Inc. All Rights Reserved.)

10

*T*he *Mask of Zorro* might have commanded the bulk of media attention about Zorro over the past year, but the animation, toys, publishing, and stage productions have had a life of their own, with no relation to the film. Great excitement was generated in the toy world as Playmates, Zorro's master toy licensee, geared up to launch its line of action figures for the fall of 1997, coinciding with the fall premiere of a new animated television series from Warner Bros. International. The successful Zorro Topps comic series published in 1993–94, will be republished and new comics are in development with veteran comic writer, Don McGregor.

The success of the Topps Comics rested on the able shoulders of Don McGregor, who was originally approached in 1992 by Jim Salicrup, the new editor-in-chief of the comics company. Zorro was to be Salicrup's first project, and McGregor was surprised, figuring Jim would choose something more contemporary for his initial exposure. McGregor, however, was delighted, for Salicrup always looked for writers who identified with their characters. A Zorro fan from the early days, McGregor meticulously researched the historic setting, delving into the fascinating period of the early 1800s for inspiration.

He created a panoply of villains who brought Zorro not only into the 1990s but dealt with the darker motivations in his character. He added depth to Zorro's adversaries, pulling the comic figures from their earlier two-dimensional existence, and gave them complex motives that sometimes brought the hero and the villains together on the same side. McGregor also brought unlikely figures from classic literature into Zorro's domain. In the premiere edition, a tense, two-part drama, Zorro battled Dracula in Notre Dame as gargoyles loomed ominously in the background.

McGregor turned Diego into the first comic strip artist. From personal experience, he knew the tension that existed between comic book readers or artists and their parents. Tension had always existed between Diego and his father in Zorro stories, but Don made it dynamic. He pinpointed the father-son conflict to Diego's satirical drawings, which he sketched instead of running the rancho. Tying Alejandro's criticism to Diego's art established a bond between the main character and the Topps readership.

The stunning artwork of Tom Yeats and Mike Mayhew pushed the comics into revealing more of the characters than had ever been imaged. Titillating adolescent fantasies, McGregor created a female adversary named Lady Rawhide whose revealing, scanty attire rocketed Lady Rawhide's popularity so high, she was spun off into her own series.

Don wanted to build on the wonderful legend of the masked defender of justice while retaining his sense of humor and righteousness. He worked to maximize the visually dynamic qualities of Zorro, setting the man in black against orange terra-cotta rooftops. Zorro could blend into the shadows or leap out at the reader from the rooftops. When the hero was juxtaposed next to Lady Rawhide, in her skimpy outfit, the passionate side of Zorro was evident—a facet of his character often hinted at but never explored. McGregor exposed the sexual dynamism of both characters, igniting erotic sparks between them.

When McGregor was a child, he had been mesmerized with the roguish zest Guy Williams gave the character, but he always felt that Zorro defeated his foes too easily. Consequently, McGregor created truly formi-

Original art by Tom Yeats for the innovative 1993 Topps comic
Zorro versus Dracula.

dable, multidimensional opponents. For example, Lady Rawhide's threat
was physical as well as sexual. She was Zorro's equal, a character in the
thick of the action with the fox. Exploring gender roles hadn't been a domain of Zorro stories before McGregor began writing them. McGregor
grappled with sexual stereotypes new to his legend—the gentleman fighting a barely clothed woman whom he finds exciting, yet who can really
harm him. Since the fox had never fought a woman before, each of their
interactions set up dramatic consequences. McGregor, however, was al-

ways careful to retain an element of humor between the characters to relieve the dramatic tension.

Some readers hated Lady Rawhide; others were enticed by her appearance. McGregor felt that the rigid roles maintained by both men and women during that historic time period compelled Lady Rawhide to take on a secret identity. She needed a dual personality, just like Zorro, in order to do things she couldn't in her day-to-day life.

Machete was McGregor's master manipulator. He was designed as a very physical character who had lost a hand to molten lava after a confrontation with Zorro. Consequently, Machete wore a cover on his stump that concealed weapons he used against his nemesis, the fox.

McGregor's interest in integrating history with character development was best exemplified by Zorro's Native American antagonist, Moonstalker. The Indian carried on a personal battle against the Spanish establishment. McGregor presented Moonstalker as a complex, virile character who rebelled against the missions' control over every aspect of the Indians' lives. Even though Zorro had once saved Moonstalker from a lashing by Monasterio, the Indian expressed hostility toward the masked man instead of gratitude. McGregor boldly even took on sexual attitudes of the church as seen through Moonstalker's eyes. The writer included a tender lovemaking sequence between Moonstalker and a mission Indian named Arcadia. Their physical desire was seen as a blessing of life in contrast to the church's attitude that sex was a sin.

McCulley's Zorro fought for justice, but true to his contemporary vision, McGregor's Zorro often confronted moral dilemmas. He influenced them to the best of his ability. He might be able to rescue people from danger, but McGregor's fox was dealing with a range of human foibles. He understood that he couldn't save people from their own destructive instincts.

WARNER BROS. INTERNATIONAL ANIMATED SERIES

The Fox returned to the lineup of weekend cartoons on September 21, 1997, slashing across 91 percent of the country on 129 stations. Partnering with Warner Bros. International, Fred Wolf Films, which had previously created the successful *Teenage Mutant Ninja Turtles* show,

From the highly rated 1997 Warner Bros. animated series.

produced the new Zorro series. Following the successful European co-production model of the New World *Zorro* series in the early 1990s, Harvest Entertainment in Bristol, England, joined *Zorro* as the European production partner.

The new series is set in the traditional Los Angeles *pueblo* of Spanish California in 1820. The citizens are a mix of wealthy California land barons of Spanish descent, merchants, tradesmen, hard-working peasants, and local Indians. These residents are forced to abide by the harsh rules of a military garrison loyal to the king of Spain and administered by its cruel, ruthless commandant, Capitán Montecero. Zorro is accompanied by his traditional entourage, including his servant, Bernardo, who builds ingen-

Character models from the Warner Bros. series: Zorro, Isabela, Bernardo, Capitán Montecero, and Sergeant Garcia. (Courtesy of Warner Bros. International.)

ious mechanical devices; his father, Alejandro; and his steed, Tornado; along with the greedy commandant, Montecero. He is reluctantly aided by the bumbling Sergeant Garcia.

A female companion, Señorita Isabela, was added to the story line. She is not only a prominent part of the series, but Isabela knows that Diego is Zorro. She becomes his accomplice, along with Bernardo, in foiling the plots of evildoers. Grey Owl serves as Zorro's wise Indian mentor. While Diego again wears the guise of the scholar, Bernardo converts his inspired ideas into practical gadgetry. Zorro's lair contains the fantastic inventions that Diego envisions and Bernardo creates. Together with their arsenal of novel devices, Zorro and his friends combat the villains who want to deprive unsuspecting Californios of their freedom and prosperity.

Though the new series has a traditional setting, many of its stories

Zorro and his aide, Little Zorro (Bernardo), from the 1992 Mondo animated series.

venture into unimagined arenas. Zorro blows up a cache of explosives stolen by Montecero, saving just enough for his father to complete an irrigation project. The fox aids a Mayan priest in protecting his golden gods from Montecero's greedy clutches. The legendary Big Foot, or Sasquatch, even makes its way into a Zorro episode when an accomplice of Montecero masquerades as the hairy monster from the La Brea tar pits in order to steal cattle. A Samurai warrior, an iron man, a British admiral who makes Jules Verne–type gadgetry, pirates, conquistadors, and even an ice monster populate the series as unique villains.

The show's ratings have been very strong. While producers hope that a new series will make it to the top ten for its time slot, *Zorro* beat all expectations, ranking sixth for children two to five years old against thirty competitors. When six- to eleven-year-olds were included, Zorro ranked seventh overall. The *TV Guide* of October 25–31, 1997, had the following to say about the new series:

> There are some clever '90s twists: a feisty female character who shares Zorro's secret, and an array of gadgets Batman might envy, including grappling hooks, mechanical wings, even a steam-powered jet pack.

Outlandish? Of course; this is supposed to be the 1820s. But that's the fun part of this *nuevo Zorro*; it utilizes the animation medium in ways the live series couldn't to bring us larger-than-life bad guys (there's even a nineteenth-century Terminator) and slam-bang action. Still, the new Zorro respects some old traditions: Sergeant Garcia still needs to go to Weight Watchers.

MONDO TV

Italy's Mondo TV began selling its fifty-two episodes of a Zorro animated series in 1992. *The Legend of Zorro* featured a blond-haired, blue-eyed eighteen-year-old young man as the fox who rode a white horse named Tornado. Little Zorro, a nine-year-old orphan named Bernardo, served as Zorro's helper. A series of comics based on the Mondo series were produced in the Italian children's magazine, *Il Giornalino*. Mondo is currently developing an educational CD-ROM based on their Zorro series.

PLAYMATES TOYS

Playmates introduced its new Zorro toy line at New York's 1997 Toy Fair, where the convention halls were abuzz with talk of the sensational creations. One design had Zorro flip over the head of his horse, Tornado, and land perfectly on his feet, relying on a top-secret mechanism. Another Zorro tossed a knife, and the sword of a third Zorro made a perfect Z.

The toy line was designed for older boys, ages seven to ten, in the action figure category. As envisioned by Playmates, Zorro was a darker, more brooding character. Six different Zorro characters were initially released in guises representing the standard Zorro, along with Zorro and Tornado, plus such innovations as Barbed-Wire Zorro, Chain-Mail Zorro, and Cold-Steel Zorro. Diego even looked different from his traditional appearance. Sporting a ponytail, he wears no shirt, appearing heroic despite the bandages and cuts on his body. Zorro's disguises help him fight off the two villains in the line, Evil Ramon and Evil Machete.

Each of the designs has a unique action mechanism. A master of all blades, Cold-Steel Zorro forges steel daggers that he throws with precision

Zorro flips over the head of his horse, Tornado, and lands on his feet in this popular toy from the Playmates 1998 Zorro line.

from a special back carrier. Chain-Mail Zorro cracks his whip, encircling his opponents. Barbed-Wire Zorro displays rapid punching action. The traditional Zorro makes a Z with his sword. Don Diego's blade slashes with lightning speed. While Zorro may flip perfectly over Tornado's head, the Evil Ramon cannot make it over his horse, Bartola's, head. Ramon topples from his steed. Finally, the Evil Machete, branded with a Z in his forehead, shoots arrows from the stump of his arm.

The Playmates line also includes a deluxe Zorro role-playing set with a traditional hat, mask, cape, and sword. Concealed in the end of the sword is a secret spyglass.

ENDORSEMENTS

Capitalizing on his cross-cultural and intergenerational appeal, Zorro has been used to successfully endorse a wide range of products in television commercials. Heinz Foods introduced a new thick and chunky salsa with

Zorro breaking up a *bandido* gathering, carving a *Z* to chase them away. After tasting the salsa, Zorro altered his signature *Z* by adding the letters *H-E-I-N* in front of it. Duracell batteries created two battery-operated fencing dolls, "Dorro" and a soldier. Dorro sliced off one half of the soldier's mustache as the soldier's batteries ran down. Naturally, Dorro's batteries were still running strong. Manitoba Telephone Systems demonstrated the speed at which faxing artwork on its phone lines facilitated the creation of the Topps Zorro comics. EuroDisney shot a live-action commercial in which Zorro rode through the theme park outside Paris to promote its nighttime activities. Citroën used Zorro to introduce its ZX model car. Coca-Cola, Mission Foods, Listerine, Trivial Pursuit, Fujitsu, Coors, Premier Bank, Ford Mustang, and the California Lottery, among others, have all found Zorro an effective spokesman for their products at one time or another.

PUBLISHING

Pocket Books developed a series of Zorro books for readers of all ages. Jim Luceno wrote a novelization based on the movie *The Mask of Zorro*, geared to adults, and Frank Lauria adapted the film script into a novel for a younger audience. Chronicle Books published an illustrated novelization of the 1998 film in their Mighty Chronicle book series.

Tor Books created a series of original adult novels unrelated to the movie, written by Jerome Preisler. His books featured new villains such as Hidalgo el Cazador, a magician and adviser to Montezuma who went underground after the subjugation of the Aztecs by the Conquistadors. Cazador kept himself alive for more than three hundred years through sacrificial rituals, vowing bloody revenge against the Spaniards. He traveled the globe, gathering scientific and mystical knowledge to be used in the creation of a later-day Aztec empire with himself as the tyrannical leader. Zorro found an ally in Joachim, a hermetic Jesuit monk who was suspected of being a former Spanish soldier doing penance for his former reprehensible deeds. He had an arsenal of sophisticated weapons at his retreat. Tor also had the foresight to republish McCulley's *The Curse of Capistrano* (as *The Mark of Zorro*) in 1997.

Santillana is publishing a Zorro series in both English and Spanish for middle readers; the books are based on the New World series in the United States. Written by S. R. Curtis, the novels were previously published in Germany, Finland, Sweden, Holland, Russia, the Czech Republic, Poland, and Hungary.

Zorro also reached into cyberspace as the official Zorro Web site (http://www.zorro.com) premiered in November 1996. Designed by Ben Kaplan, the site featured a 3-D rotating horse and rider, courtesy of the graphic talents of Guy Williams's son, Steve Catalano.[6] History of the character, current business news, a collectors' corner, film news, links to other Zorro sites, and much more can be found at zorro.com. For Zorro trivia buffs, a "Teaser of the Week" appears, as do Zorro comics from contemporary illustrators. Zorro has become such an identifiable cultural icon that every major comic artist has done strips on the character. Displaying one per week on the Zorro web site, these comics have been featured in *Garfield, Heathcliff, The Far Side, Hi and Lois, Dilbert, B.C., Zippy*, and *Frank and Ernest*, among others.

Vintage Library is republishing some of the original Johnston McCulley Zorro stories via the Internet at http://www.vintagelibrary.com. Other electronic media is in development for personal computers and hand-held units.

Zorro has been appearing on stage for the past several years, with productions in children's theaters and small regional venues as well as historic London theaters.

The Birmingham Children's Theater produced *Zorro*, the play, by Michael Price Nelson, for a month in early 1997 targeting schoolchildren in the greater Birmingham, Alabama, area. The show also toured much of Alabama and her neighboring states through June.

According to Charlotte Lane Dominick, the theater's artistic director, over forty thousand students saw the *Zorro* show. "They were thrilled with the show, particularly the fight scenes." The theater hired a stage fencing master to choreograph the swashbuckling sword fights. It also prepared a teacher's guide with activities for children to take back to their classrooms. Journalist R. Charrey reported in the *Birmingham Post-Herald*:

"It was awesome," said Sidney, 8, his eyes lighting up. In preparation for the show, Sidney and his second-grade classmates learned about California under Spanish rule in the 1800s and mastered a few Spanish words such as *gracias, señor,* and *señorita.* . . . "The best part is that they can see the books really come to life," said second grade teacher Kelly McGough.

Zorro, El Musical ran in Mexico City from July 6 to December 15, 1996. Written and scored by Alvaro Cervino, the show opened at Teatro Aldama to enthusiastic reviews such as the following one by A. G. Danielly in the *Excelsior*: "A show that captivates the audience both by its perform- ances and above all by its magnificent musical numbers." Swordmasters Bob Anderson and Mark Ivie saw the show during the filming of *The Mask of Zorro* and were pleasantly surprised by the entertaining music, staging, sword fighting, and sets. Though developed for families with children, the show held their attention with ease.

The Burt Reynolds Theater in West Palm Beach, Florida, featured a Zorro play by David Richmond and Drew Frazier in December 1996. This play had previously been staged at Western Illinois University and had originally premiered at the Ensemble Theater of Cincinnati in 1993. *Cincinnati Post* reviewer Jerry Stein applauded Richmond's script for its comedy

> that gently satirizes the heroics. . . . This staged "Zorro" is great fun while capturing the high romance that has made the renowned masked hero so perennially popular.

Dale Doerman described Zorro in the *Cincinnati Enquirer* as

> great fun and much more than a romantic melodrama set in a tiled courtyard. It is a story of love and justice and a reminder of how closely the two are linked.

Richmond's and Frazier's *Zorro* is based on the traditional McCulley tale, with theatrical as well as expository enhancements. Working on a small stage, the playwrights effectively utilized shadow puppets to simulate the horse-and-rider chase scenes inherent in the Zorro legend. The transition of Diego into Zorro is induced by an Indian ritual in which a vision guides Diego to his calling as the fox. The padre, Fray Felipe, instructs Diego in an esoteric martial art of swordsmanship known as *secreto*.

The most impressive Zorro musical production was staged by London playwright Ken Hill, his final work before a tragic death from cancer. Ken Hill's *Zorro, the Musical* played at the Theatre Royal Stratford East in London from February 4 to March 25, 1995. Hill was a protégé of Joan Littlewood, the founding force behind much of the fresh and exciting postwar British theater with hits such as *Oh! What a Lovely War*. Her brand of drama became known as the Littlewood Academy of Irreverence.

Ken Hill's melodramatic treatment created a deliciously villainous pirate, a strutting Zorro, a fiery female rabble-rouser, and a comic mime. J. Tinker reported in London's *Daily Mail* that Hill's work blended "breezy high camp with low agit-prop, British pantomime with Hollywood silent film, and melodious operetta with a ripe raspberry blown in the face of propriety."

In the *Financial Times*, Sarah Hemming characterized the show as

> a delightful, self-parodying style peppered with pastiche—a pinch of Carmen here, a touch of Don Giovanni there—and reveling in theatrical and cinematic clichés. The spirit of the show is somewhere between *Monty Python* and Gilbert and Sullivan, but though it is all done tongue-in-cheek, it has just enough seriousness to retain the faint echoes of the great Spanish epics.

Hill gave a new twist to the Zorro legend. In his rendition, a Gypsy orphan, José, assumes the mantle of Don Diego after being banished to America for an inadvertent murder. On its way to America, the ship is attacked by pirates and the real Don Diego, another passenger, is killed. When José washes up on shore, he decides to become Diego in order to attain some status in the *pueblo* of Los Angeles. After seeing the people's oppression and hearing their myth of a man who will arrive as their defender, Diego becomes Zorro. Hill adapted Spanish zarzuela music for the score and wrote the lyrics.

Even though the play drew rave reviews, the tragic circumstances of its opening hampered the future of the project. Hill, who had successfully toured his adaptation of *Phantom of the Opera*, wrote the Zorro piece as he was experiencing a fatal reoccurrence of lung cancer. He had staged Act One and had roughed out Act Two by the third week of rehearsal, but his health was rapidly declining. Ken passed away two weeks before the show opened. On hearing of his death, the cast, which included his widow, Toni Palmer, took an hour off and then followed the age-old tradition of "the show must go on." Palmer told P. Hedley of *The Arts* that they got right back to work "because Ken would be furious [if] we stopped." Each performance became a tribute to Ken's life and his work.

The BBC, British Broadcasting Company, developed a five-part Zorro series that aired on Radio Four in July 1997 throughout the United Kingdom. The series of half-hour segments was based on McCulley's *Curse of Capistrano/The Mark of Zorro*. The series garnered praise from both the press and the public, labeling it great swashbuckling fun. The press reviews extolled the series, noting "stirring music and a cliffhanger in the best tradition of the old serials," as well as "fantastical adventure that you crave . . . an excellent comic-book style caper."

THE MASK OF ZORRO–GENE AUTRY WESTERN HERITAGE MUSEUM

The Gene Autry Western Heritage Museum in Los Angeles's Griffith Park devoted a major exhibit to Zorro. Using the fox as a means to explore stereotypes of Hispanics in the media, *The Mask of Zorro* ran through the summer of 1994, from June 18 to September 5, and drew record crowds. James Nottage, chief curator of the museum, explained to D. Knaff of *The Orange County Register* that the staff concentrates on multiethnic and multicultural aspects of life in the West.

> We are . . . continually challenging people with different perspectives of the region . . . We know that the West isn't all cowboys and Indians. It never was. And putting back in everything that's left out of that two-dimensional view of the West is what we try to do with every show, every catalog—and for each visitor that comes through our doors.

The Mask of Zorro examined the origins of negative Hispanic imagery from *bandidos*, cantina sluts, and lazy peons to heroic figures such as Zorro and the Cisco Kid. In the George Montgomery Gallery, the museum's main rotating exhibit area, the staff displayed Zorro memorabilia from the collections of Zorro Productions, the archive department of the Disney Studios, and other private contributors. A video presentation developed by John Langellier, director of publication and productions for the museum, accompanied the exhibit. "We hope that we've begun the process of making people reexamine decades-old images," said Chief Curator Nottage. "We've started to unmask Zorro."

Both Anglo and Hispanic stereotypes were challenged. Zorro was presented as a hero in the media, but other Mexican-Americans who challenged the existing power structure, like Tiburcio Vasquez, were portrayed as "outlaws." To Mexican-Americans, "outlaws" like Vasquez were seen as courageous freedom fighters. Those who grew up viewing revolutionaries as heroes were asked to reexamine whether the *bandido* image glorified violence.

Over half a million visitors visited the exhibit, which gave the museum ample opportunity to present its case.

A & E's Biography Series

On June 26, 1996, the Arts and Entertainment Network aired an hour-long feature, "The History of Zorro," as part of its Biography Series. Produced by Weller-Grossman Productions, the show captured highlights of the fox from his earliest days in the pulps through his legacy on the silver screen. Compiling footage from old Zorro films and television series, the producers presented California's defender of justice through the eyes and ears of those who knew him best. Individuals involved with the character were interviewed, including historians, actors, and Zorro collectors.

Actress Brenda Vaccaro reminisced about working on *Zorro, the Gay Blade*. Douglas Fairbanks Jr., recalled his father's magic tricks in the silent version of *The Mark of Zorro*. Britt Lomond related his staged duels at Disneyland with Guy Williams during the heyday of the Disney series, and Jan Williams recollected the excitement her husband experienced while working on the *Zorro* series. Duncan Regehr shared the image he sought to capture in portraying Zorro for the New World series. John Gertz, president of Zorro Productions, Inc., provided an overall perspective on the long-standing appeal of Zorro.

The compiled reflections, recollections, clips from old films, and legendary accounts of the past positioned the fox within a historical context for Zorro fans through the generations.

Zorro's legacy does not end here. It will continue to evolve, infusing the imaginations of children and adults alike, for the fox embodies a timeless heroism. He will fight injustice, cloaked by the dark of the night. With a jaunty toss of his head, a flash of his brilliant smile, a gentle touch of the hat, a rearing horse, and a flashing Z, Zorro will make his mark on future generations. The evolution of McCulley's character has been shaped by the actors who have played the fox; the writers who have given him voice, both on the screen and on the written page; as well as the contemporary period during which he was being presented. Zorro is an enduring legend who will remain with us as long as oppression stalks the globe and crusaders for justice infuse our most ardent dreams.

Zorro's signature farewell on Tornado. (Courtesy of New World International.)

A COMPLETE LIST OF JOHNSTON MCCULLEY'S ZORRO STORIES

1	*The Curse of Capistrano (I)*	*All-Story Weekly*	Aug. 9, 1919
	The Curse of Capistrano (II)	*All-Story Weekly*	Aug. 16, 1919
	The Curse of Capistrano (III)	*All-Story Weekly*	Aug. 23, 1919
	The Curse of Capistrano (IV)	*All-Story Weekly*	Aug. 30, 1919
	The Curse of Capistrano (V)	*All-Story Weekly*	Sept. 6, 1919
2	*The Further Adventures of Zorro (I)*	*Argosy*	May 6, 1922
	The Further Adventures of Zorro (II)	*Argosy*	May 13, 1922
	The Further Adventures of Zorro (III)	*Argosy*	May 20, 1922
	The Further Adventures of Zorro (IV)	*Argosy*	May 27, 1922
	The Further Adventures of Zorro (V)	*Argosy*	June 3, 1922
	The Further Adventures of Zorro (VI)	*Argosy*	June 10, 1922
3	*Zorro Rides Again (I)*	*Argosy*	Oct. 3, 1931
	Zorro Rides Again (II)	*Argosy*	Oct. 10, 1931
	Zorro Rides Again (III)	*Argosy*	Oct. 17, 1931
	Zorro Rides Again (IV)	*Argosy*	Oct. 24, 1931

No.	Title	Publication	Date
4	Zorro Saves a Friend	Argosy	Nov. 12, 1932
5	Zorro Hunts a Jackal	Argosy	April 22, 1933
6	Zorro Deals with Treason	Argosy	Aug. 18, 1934
	Reprinted	Cavalier Classics	July 1940
7	Mysterious Don Miguel (I)	Argosy	Sept. 21, 1935
	Mysterious Don Miguel (II)	Argosy	Sept. 28, 1935
8	Zorro Hunts by Night	Cavalier Classics	September 1940
9	The Sign of Zorro (I)	Argosy	Jan. 25, 1941
	The Sign of Zorro (II)	Argosy	Feb. 1, 1941
	The Sign of Zorro (III)	Argosy	Feb. 8, 1941
	The Sign of Zorro (IV)	Argosy	Feb. 15, 1941
	The Sign of Zorro (V)	Argosy	Feb. 22, 1941
10	Zorro Draws His Blade	West	July 1944
11	Zorro Upsets a Plot	West	September 1944
12	Zorro Strikes Again	West	November 1944
13	Zorro Saves a Herd	West	January 1945
14	Zorro Runs the Gauntlet	West	March 1945
15	Zorro Fights a Duel	West	May 1945
16	Zorro Opens a Cage	West	July 1945
17	Zorro Prevents a War	West	September 1945
18	Zorro Fights a Friend	West	October 1945
19	Zorro's Hour of Peril	West	November 1945
20	Zorro Slays a Ghost	West	December 1945
21	Zorro Frees Some Slaves	West	January 1946
22	Zorro's Double Danger	West	February 1946
23	Zorro's Masquerade	West	March 1946
24	Zorro Stops a Panic	West	April 1946
25	Zorro's Twin Perils	West	May 1946
26	Zorro Plucks a Pigeon	West	June 1946
27	Zorro Rides at Dawn	West	July 1946
28	Zorro Takes the Bait	West	August 1946
29	Zorro Raids a Caravan	West	October 1946
30	Zorro's Moment of Fear	West	January 1947
31	Zorro Saves His Honor	West	February 1947
32	Zorro and the Pirate	West	March 1947
33	Zorro Beats the Drum	West	April 1947

No.	Title	Publication	Date
34	*Zorro's Strange Duel*	*West*	May 1947
35	*A Task for Zorro*	*West*	June 1947
36	*Zorro's Masked Menace*	*West*	July 1947
37	*Zorro Aids an Invalid*	*West*	August 1947
38	*Zorro Saves an American*	*West*	September 1947
39	*Zorro Meets a Rogue*	*West*	October 1947
40	*Zorro Races with Death*	*West*	November 1947
41	*Zorro Fights for Peace*	*West*	December 1947
42	*Zorro Starts the New Year*	*West*	January 1948
43	*Zorro Serenades a Siren*	*West*	February 1948
44	*Zorro Meets a Wizard*	*West*	March 1948
45	*Zorro Fights with Fire*	*West*	April 1948
46	*Gold for a Tyrant*	*West*	May 1948
47	*The Hide Hunter*	*West*	July 1948
48	*Zorro Shears Some Wolves*	*West*	September 1948
49	*The Face Behind the Mask*	*West*	November 1948
50	*Hangnoose Reward*	*West*	March 1949
51	*Zorro's Hostile Friends*	*West*	May 1949
52	*Zorro's Hot Tortillas*	*West*	July 1949
53	*An Ambush for Zorro*	*West*	September 1949
54	*Zorro Gives Evidence*	*West*	November 1949
55	*Rancho Marauders*	*West*	January 1950
56	*Zorro's Stolen Steed*	*West*	March 1950
57	*Zorro Curbs a Riot*	*West*	September 1950
58	*The Three Strange Peons*	*West*	November 1950
59	*Zorro Nabs a Cutthroat*	*West*	January 1951
60	*Zorro Gathers Taxes*	*West*	March 1951
61	*Zorro's Fight for Life*	*West*	July 1951
62	*The Return of Zorro*		August 5, 1952
63	*Zorro Rides the Trail*	*May Brand Western*	May 1954
64	*The Mask of Zorro*	*Short Stories for Men*	April 1959

Year	Title	Star	Producer
1920	*The Mark of Zorro*	Douglas Fairbanks Sr.	United Artists
1925	*Don Q, Son of Zorro*	Douglas Fairbanks Sr.	United Artists
1936	*The Bold Caballero*	Robert Livingstone	Republic
1937	*Zorro Rides Again**	John Carroll	Republic
1939	*Zorro's Fighting Legion**	Reed Hadley	Republic
1940	*The Mark of Zorro*	Tyrone Power	Twentieth Century-Fox
1944	*Zorro's Black Whip**	Linda Stirling	Republic
1947	*Son of Zorro**	George Turner	Republic
1949	*Ghost of Zorro**	Clayton Moore	Republic
1958	*Zorro, the Avenger*	Guy Williams	Disney
1958	*The Sign of Zorro*	Guy Williams	Disney
1972	*The Erotic Adventures of Zorro*	Douglas Frey	RFA
1974	*The Mark of Zorro*	Frank Langella	Twentieth Century-Fox
1980	*Zorro, the Gay Blade*	George Hamilton	Mel Simon
1998	*The Mask of Zorro*	Antonio Banderas/ Anthony Hopkins	TriStar/Amblin

* Twelve-part serials.

ZORRO FILMS—FOREIGN

1952	*Il Segno di Zorro* (*Zorro's Dream*)	Italy	Mario Soldati	Walter Chiari
1958	*El Zorro Escarlata*	Mexico		
1961	*El Zorro Vengador* (*Zorro, the Avenger*)	Spain	Joaíquin Luis Romero	Luis Aguilar
1961	*Zorro Nella Valle dei Fantasmi*	Mexico		Jeff Stone
1961	*Espada del Zorro* (retitled *Zorro* for American release in 1963)	Spain/France		
1961	*Zorro Contro Maciste* (*Zorro versus Maciste*) (retitled *Samson and the Slave Queen* for American TV release in 1963)	Italy	Umberto Lenzi	Pierre Brice

Year	Title	Country	Director	Star
1961	*Zorro E l Tre Moschettiere* (*Zorro and the Three Mouseketeers*) (retitled *Mark of the Musketeers* for American TV release)	Italy	Luigi Capuano	Gordon Scott
1962	*Zorro Alla Corte di Spagna* (*Zorro at the Court of Spain*) (American release, 1977)	Italy/Spain	Luigi Capuano	Giorgio Ardisson
1962	*La Venganza del Zorro*	Spain/Mexico		Frank Latimore
1962	*Il Segno di Zorro* (retitled *Mark of Zorro* for American release in 1963)	France/Italy	Mario Caiano	Sean Flynn
1963	*La Tre Spade di Zorro*	Italy/Spain		Guy Stockwell
1963	*L'Ombra di Zorro* (*Oath of Zorro*)	Spain/Italy	Richard Blasco	Frank Latimore
1963	*Shade of Zorro*	Italy/Spain	Francesco de Masi	
1964	*Three Swords of Zorro*	Italy	Richard Blasco	
1964	*Behind the Mask of Zorro*	Italy	Richard Blasco	
1964	*Adventures of the Brothers X*	Mexico	Frederic Curiel	
1964	*The Lone Rider*	Mexico	Ralph Baledon	
1964	*The Valley of the Disappearing*	Mexico	Ralph Baledon	
1965	*Il Giuramente di Zorro*	Italy/Spain		Tony Russel
1965	*La Montana Sin Ley*	Spain		José Suarez
1966	*Zorro Il Ribelle* (*Zorro, the Rebel*)	Italy	Piero Pierotti	Howard Ross

Year	Title	Country	Director	Star
1968	*Nippotti di Zorro* (*Grandsons of Zorro*)	Italy	Franco Franchi and Ciccia Ingrassia	Dean Reed
1968	*Zorro il Cavaliere della Vendetta*	Italy/Spain		Charles Quiney
1968	*El Zorro la Volpe*	Italy		Georgio Ardisson
1969	*Zorro il Dominatore* (*Zorro, the Domineerer*)	Italy/Spain		Charles Quiney
1969	*Zorro, the Navarra Marquis* (*Zorro Marchese di Navarro*)	Italy	Francois Monty	Nadir Moretti
1969	*El Zorro*	Italy	Georgio Ardisson	
1969	*Zorro alla Corte D'Inghilterra* (*Zorro at the English Court*)	Italy	Franco Montemorro	Spyros Focas
1969	*El Zorro Justiciero*	Italy/Spain		Martin Moore
1970	*Zorro, the Knight of the Vengeance*	Spain	José Louis Merion	
1970	*Zorro la Maschera della Vendetta*	Italy/Spain		Charles Quiney
1972	*Les Aventures Galantes de Zorro*	Belgium		Jean-Michel Dhermay
1973	*El Hijo del Zorro*	Italy/Spain	Gian Franco Baldanelle	
1973	*El Figlio di Zorro*	Italy/Spain		Robert Wildmark
1974	*Zorro* (American release by United Artists in 1975)	Italy/France	Duccio Tessari	Alain Delon
1974	*El Zorro*	Mexico		Julio Aldama
1975	*Il Sogno di Zorro*	Italy		Franco Franchi

ZORRO TELEVISION SERIES

1957– 1959	Zorro	Walt Disney Studios	Live Action	78
1981	*The New Adventures of Zorro*	Filmation	Animated Series	13
1983	*Zorro and Son*	Walt Disney Studios	Live Action	5
1989	Zorro	New World Productions	Live Action	89
1992	*The Legend of Zorro*	Mondo TV	Animated Series	52
1997	*The New Adventures of Zorro*	Warner Bros. International	Animated Series	26

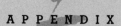

EPISODE TITLES—
WALT DISNEY'S ZORRO

1	"Presenting Señor Zorro"	21	"Zorro Springs a Trap"
2	"Zorro's Secret Passage"	22	"The Unmasking of Zorro"
3	"Zorro Rides to the Mission"	23	"The Secret of the Sierra"
4	"The Ghost of the Eagle"	24	"The New Commandments"
5	"Zorro's Romance"	25	"The Fox and the Coyote"
6	"Zorro Saves a Friend"	26	"Adios, Señor Magistrado"
7	"Zorro Sets a Trap"	27	"The Eagle's Brood"
8	"Zorro Rides into Terror"	28	"Zorro by Proxy"
9	"A Fair Trial"	29	"Quintana Makes a Choice"
10	"Garcia's Sweet Mission"	30	"Zorro Lights a Fuse"
11	"Double Trouble for Zorro"	31	"The Man with the Whip"
12	"The Luckiest Swordsman Alive"	32	"The Cross of the Andes"
		33	"The Deadly Bolas"
13	"The Fall of Monastario"	34	"The Well of Death"
14	"Shadow of Doubt"	35	"The Tightening Noose"
15	"Garcia Stands Accused"	36	"The Sergeant Regrets"
16	"Slaves of the Eagle"	37	"The Eagle Leaves the Nest"
17	"Sweet Face of Danger"	38	"Bernardo Faces Death"
18	"Zorro Fights His Father"	39	"Day of Decision"
19	"Death Stacks the Deck"		
20	"Agent of the Eagle"		

Season Two 1958–1959

One-Hour Specials 1960–1961

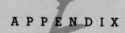

EPISODE TITLES—
NEW WORLD'S ZORRO

1989	1	*The Legend Begins, Part I*
1989	2	*The Legend Begins, Part II*
1989	3	*The Legend Begins, Part III*
1989	4	*The Legend Begins, Part IV*
1989	5	*Dead Men Tell No Tales*
1989	6	*Whereabouts*
1989	7	*The Bounty Hunters*
1989	8	*The Best Man*
1989	9	*All That Glitters*
1989	10	*Honor Thy Father*
1989	11	*A Wolf in Sheep's Clothing*
1989	12	*The Deceptive Heart*
1989	13	*Water*
1989	14	*The Magician*
1989	15	*Zorro's "Other Woman"*
1989	16	*Deal with the Devil*
1989	17	*Double Entendre*
1989	18	*Ghost Story*
1989	19	*An Explosive Situation*
1989	20	*The Unhappy Medium*

Year	Episode Number	Title
1989	21	*Palomarez Returns*
1989	22	*The Sure Thing*
1989	23	*Pride of the Pueblo*
1989	24	*Child's Play*
1989	25	*Family Business*
1990	26	*The White Sheep of the Family*
1990	27	*He Who Lives by the Sword . . .*
1990	28	*The Chase*
1990	29	*Freedom of the Press*
1990	30	*The Devil's Fortress, Part I*
1990	31	*The Devil's Fortress, Part II*
1990	32	*The Challenge*
1990	33	*The Wizard*
1990	34	*One Special Night*
1990	35	*The Don's Dilemma*
1990	36	*The Marked Man*
1990	37	*Master and Pupil*
1990	38	*The Tease*
1990	39	*Broken Heart, Broken Mask*
1990	40	*The Falcon*
1990	41	*The Old Flame*
1990	42	*Sanctuary*
1990	43	*Kidnapped*
1990	44	*Big Brother*
1990	45	*The Whistling Bandit*
1990	46	*To Be a Man*
1990	47	*Alejandro Rides Again*
1990	48	*It's a Wonderful Zorro*
1990	49	*The Newcomers*
1990	50	*Rites of Passage*
1991	51	*The Three Musketeers, Part I*
1991	52	*The Three Musketeers, Part II*
1991	53	*The Jeweled Sword*
1991	54	*Heir Apparent*
1991	55	*Armed and Dangerous*

Year	Episode Number	Title
1991	56	*A New Broom*
1991	57	*The Buccaneers, Part I*
1991	58	*The Buccaneers, Part II*
1991	59	*A New Lease on Love*
1991	60	*Turning the Tables*
1991	61	*A Love Remembered*
1991	62	*Mendoza the Malevolent*
1991	63	*Wicked, Wicked Zorro*
1991	64	*Rush to Judgment*
1991	65	*Test of Faith*
1991	66	*Dirty Tricks*
1991	67	*Silk Purses and Sows' Ears*
1991	68	*Miracle of the Pueblo*
1991	69	*A Woman Scorned*
1991	70	*They Call Her Annie*
1991	71	*The Word*
1991	72	*The Man Who Cried Wolf*
1991	73	*Balancing the Books*
1991	74	*Blind Man's Bluff*
1991	75	*Every Man a Hero*
1992	76	*As Ye Sow*
1992	77	*The Arrival*
1992	78	*Death and Taxes*
1992	79	*Conundrum*
1992	80	*The Discovery*
1992	81	*Love Potion #9*
1992	82	*Ultimate Justice*
1992	83	*Symbol of Hope*
1992	84	*Like Father, Like Son*
1992	85	*An Affair to Remember*
1992	86	*The Reward*
1992	87	*My World Is My Bond*
1992	88	*Stranger Than Fiction*
1992	89	*The Fox and the Rabbit*

1. Though difficult to trace, Louise may have been related to Frank Munsey, the owner of *All-Story Weekly*, the pulp magazine in which McCulley published his first Zorro story.

2. The first registered copyright for The Frank A. Munsey Co. as publisher of a pulp magazine was *The Golden Argosy*, September 8, 1883. Pulp publications merged and reemerged under a variety of titles, including: *The Argosy* ©1888, *Argosy Magazine* ©1906, *Argosy* ©1908, *Argosy Weekly* ©1917, *Argosy and Railroad Man's Magazine* ©1919, *Argosy All-Story Weekly* ©1920, *Argosy* ©1929, *All-Story Magazine* ©1905, *All-Story Weekly* ©1914, *All-Story Cavalier Weekly* ©1914, *All-Story Weekly* ©1915 (merged with *Argosy Weekly* ©1920), *All-Story* ©1929, *All-Story Combined with Munsey* ©1929, *All-Story—Munsey* ©1930.

3. Ian Wolfe, who played the Franciscan friar, dispensed blessings in the film without the correct Latin benedictions. (E. Connor, "The Genealogy of Zorro," *Films in Review*, Aug.–Sept. 1957)

4. The Yaqui Indians of Sonora, Mexico, were the only tribe to resist integration by the Spanish. They remained unacculturated, the only aboriginal tribe to conserve its original autonomy. To this day, they maintain their unique tribal rituals. (Publication of Ballet Folklorico De Mexico, April 1997)

5. This sexploitation feature made headlines when it appeared on Australian screens in place of the edited, R-rated, censor-approved prints, and again when a Minnesota council comprised of senior citizens sponsored showings to raise funds for a new center for the elderly. (T. Weaver, "Zorro," *Spectacular*, 1991)

6. Steve Catalano, Guy Williams's son, also designed the end credit for Zorro Productions, Inc. in the Warner Bros. animated series. Behind the word "Zorro," the caped figure rears on his horse against a full moon. The cape flutters in the breeze and the horse's tail moves.

SELECTED REFERENCES

BOOKS

Carey, G., *Doug & Mary: A Biography of Douglas Fairbanks & Mary Pickford*, New York: Dutton, 1977.

Chapman, C. E., *A History of California, the Spanish Period*, New York: The MacMillan Co., 1921.

Dooley, Gerry, *Out of the Night*, unpublished manuscript, 1992.

Fairbanks, D., Jr., *The Salad Days*, New York: Doubleday, 1988.

Fairbanks, D., Jr., *The Fairbanks Album*, Boston: New York Graphic Society, 1975.

Guiles, F., *Tyrone Power: The Last Idol*, New York: Doubleday, 1979.

Hayes, R. M., *The Republic Chapterplays: A Complete Filmography of the Serials Released by Republic Pictures Corporation 1934–1955*, Jefferson, N.C.: McFarland & Company, Inc., 1991.

Herndon, B., *Mary Pickford and Douglas Fairbanks: The Most Popular Couple the World Has Ever Known*, New York: W. W. Norton & Company, Inc., 1977.

Knill, H., *Early Los Angeles*, Santa Barbara, Calif.: Bellerophon Books, 1984.

MacLean, A., *Legends of the California Bandidos*, Arroyo Grande; Calif.: Bear Flag Books, 1989.

Margolin, M. *The Journals of Jean François de La Perouse*, Berkeley, Calif.: Heyday Books, 1989.

Mora, J., *Californios: The Saga of the Hard-Riding Vaqueros, America's First Cowboys*, Ketchum, Idaho: Dober Hill LTD, 1946.

Phillips, M. *Salomon Pico: History of Santa Barbara County, California*, Chicago: S. J. Clarke Pub. Co., 1927.

Pitt, L., *Decline of the Californios*, Berkeley, Calif.: University of California Press, 1966.

Ridge, J. R. *The Life and Adventures of Joaquin Murieta*, Norman and London: reprinted by University of Oklahoma Press, 1955.

Rolle, A. F., *California: A History*, New York: Thomas Y. Crowell Co., 1963.

Sanchez, N., *Spanish Arcadia*, Los Angeles: Powell Publishing Company, 1929.

Schickel, R., *His Picture in the Papers: A Speculation on Celebrity in America Based on the Life of Douglas Fairbanks, Sr.*, New York: Charterhouse, 1973.

Stedman, R., *The Serials: Suspense and Drama by Installment*, Norman: University of Oklahoma Press, 1971.

ARTICLES

Ailes, M., "Salomon Pico: The Angry Man Who was Zorro," *California Historical Courier*, April/May 1987.

Ansen, D., "A Neo-Latin Lover," *Newsweek*, September 4, 1995.

Archerd, A., "Just for Variety," *Daily Variety*, December 10, 1996.

Austin, Wade, "Johnston McCulley," in Sadler, Geoff (Ed.) *Twentieth-Century Western Writers*, Detroit, Gale Research, Inc., 1983.

Bianculli, D., "Series Fun in First Run," *The New York Post*, February 16, 1990.

Bowie, P., "From Spanish to Pioneer Banjo to Symphonic Strings: A Cultural Transformation in Southern California," *The Californians*, May/June 1983.

Brodie, J., "Desperado duo due to redo 'Zorro' " *Daily Variety*, September 14, 1995.

Burciago, J. A., "Tiburcio Vasquez: A Chicano Perspective," *The Californians*, May/June 1985.

Busch, A. M., "Hopkins takes a stab at 'Zorro'," *Daily Variety*, November 25, 1996.

Charry, R., "Ground Zorro: The Legendary Hero Finds His Mark with Local Children," *Birmingham Post-Herald*, January 31, 1997.

Clark, M., "Guy Williams: Relaxed, Retired & Lost in 'Space'," *Starlog*, January 1987.

Cook, D. A., "Z is for Zorro," *Collectibles*, Winter 1995.

Cox, D., "Wilson's taking up the sword for 'Zorro'," *Daily Variety*, December 14, 1996.

Danielly, A. G., "El Zorro," *Excelsior,* July 29, 1996.

Demarco, M., "The Everlasting Hero!" *Movie Collector's World*, April 24, 1992.

Doerman, D., " 'Zorro' more than melodrama," *The Cincinnati Enquirer*, May 20, 1993.

Dunkley, C., "Jones to hit her marks on 'Zorro'," *The Hollywood Reporter*, December 17, 1996.

Figueroa, A., "ZZZ," *San Francisco Chronicle*, January 15, 1990.

Fink, M., "The Insider," *People*, August 21, 1995.

Forsyth, H., "Santa Barbara's Blue-Blood Bandit," *The California Highway Patrolman*, February 1968.

Freemen, D., "Zorro Rides Back onto the Small Screen," *The San Diego Union*, December 31, 1989–January 6, 1990.

Galloway, S., "Rodriguez on 'All Hispanic Zorro'," *The Hollywood Reporter*, September 14, 1995.

Guinn, J. M., "The Old Pueblo Archives," *Los Angeles Times*, November 21, 1897.

"Hectic, Harassed, and Happy," *TV Guide*, March 16, 1957.

Hemming, S., "A Swashingbuckling 'Zorro'," *Financial Times*, February 16, 1995.

Hoffman, A., "Zorro: Generic Swashbuckler," *The Californians*, September/October 1985.

Hyem, J., "The Mark of Regehr," *Spectacular*, September 1991.

Jacobs, J., "Fairbanks' Dream House Comes True," *Los Angeles Times*, June 30, 1981.

Jefferson, D. J., "Another Hero of Yesteryear Tries a Comeback in 1990s," *The Wall Street Journal*, November 17, 1993.

Jones, R., "Swordplay on the Screen," *Flashback*, June 1972.

Kaye, E., "Anthony Hopkins, for Your Approval," *Premiere*, February 1994.

King, C., "Mary Pickford, Homemaker," *The Country Gentleman*, May 1928.

Knaff, D., "Challenging the Familiar Old West," *The Orange County Register*, August 12, 1994.

———"Shooting Down Stereotypes," *The Orange County Register*, August 12, 1994.

Macomber, F., "A Doug Fairbanks Dream Come True," *The San Diego Union*, December 5, 1982.

McGregor, D., "The Vengeance of Moonstalker," *Zorro*, April 1994.

Moline, E., "Alias Zorro," *TV Radio Mirror*, January 1958.

Price, B., "The Men Behind the Mask of Zorro," *Screen Thrills Illustrated*, August 1964.

Rubenstein, S., "Farewell, Zorro, You Old Fox," *San Francisco Chronicle*, May 10, 1989.

Samuels, A., and Giles, J., "Unchained Melody," *Newsweek*, April 7, 1997.

Schaefer, S., "Passion Play," *Marquee*, February 1996.

Stein, J., " 'Zorro' packs stage with innovation," *The Cincinnati Post*, May 20, 1993.

Sutton, L., "Zorro's New Logo: $ Original Caped-Crusader in Comeback," *Daily News*, November 18, 1993.

Tinker, J., "A Real-Life Heartache behind the Zorro Mask," *Daily Mail*, February 17, 1995.

Walker, M., "Banderas: Valentino for the 1990s?" *Los Angeles Times*, August 21, 1995.

Walter, T., "Cover," *The Commercial Appeal*, December 31, 1989.

Weaver, J. D., "El Pueblo Grande, Los Angeles from the Brush Huts of Yangna to the Skyscrapers of the Modern Megalopolis," privately printed, 1973.

Weaver, T., "Zorro," *Spectacular*, 1991.

"Zorro," *TV Guide*, October 25, 1997.

"Zorro Foiled His Rivals," *TV Guide*, April 26, 1958.

INTERVIEWS

The Mask of Zorro

Bob Anderson, Sword Master

Antonio Banderas, Alejandro/Zorro

Martin Campbell, Director

Doug Claybourne, Producer

David Foster, Producer

Celia Montiel, Production Designer

Alex Green, Whip Master, Stunt Double for Anthony Hopkins

Tad Griffith, Zorro's Stunt Rider

Anthony Hopkins, Diego/Zorro

Mark Ivie, Assistant Sword Master

L. Q. Jones, Three-Fingered Jack

Kim Marks, Director of Photography, Second Unit

Graciela Mazon, Costume Designer

From *The History of Zorro, arts and entertainment biography series*, Arts and
Entertainment Network, aired June 26, 1996
Marilyn Ailes, author
Henry Darrow, actor
Fairbanks, Douglas Jr., actor, author
Abraham Hoffman, historian
Patrice Martinez, actress
Duncan Regehr, actor
Jan Williams, wife of Guy Williams

Others
Jean Barnes, daughter, William Smart, manager of Fairbanks's Rancho Zorro
Steve Catalano, son of Guy Williams
Bill and Mary Culver, local historians on Fairbanks's Rancho Zorro
Charlotte Lane Dominick, Producer, Birmingham Children's Theater
John Gertz, President, Zorro Productions, Inc.
Nancy Larson, Writer
James Victor, actor

Sandy Curtis is the Vice President and Creative Director of Zorro Productions, Inc. Her extensive background in the development of books, software, toys, and screen and stage productions has been strongly influenced by her academic training, bringing a unique historical emphasis to the revival of the legendary fox. Among her other published works are seven Zorro novels for the juvenile market. She lives in Berkeley, California.